C000226101

INVASION

Forgotten Vengeance, Book One

M.R. FORBES

Published by Quirky Algorithms
Seattle, Washington

This novel is a work of fiction and a product of the author's
imagination.
Any resemblance to actual persons or events is purely coincidental.

Cover illustration by Tom Edwards
tomedwardsdesign.com

Isaac

United States Marine Corps Sergeant Isaac Pine lifted his head as the door slid open. He was still for a moment before his years of training kicked in, bringing him almost subconsciously from his chair to his feet, coming to attention.

His visitor was an older man. Twin streaks of white raced through the dark hair at his temples while wrinkles creased various points of his face and wise, confident eyes regarded Isaac with interest and curiosity. The full array of hardware on the man's chest was impressive, but Isaac had reacted to the five stars across his lapels.

"Sergeant Pine," the General said, his expression remaining professional. "At ease. Please, sit."

"Yes, sir." Isaac relaxed his posture, regaining his seat as the door closed. The General walked calmly to the plain steel table where Isaac was seated, taking a position in the chair on the other side. He held a narrow, translucent tablet of polymer in his hand, which he placed in front of him on the table, revealing the first screen of Isaac's military record.

Where had he gotten that?

"Sir, is this an interrogation?" Isaac asked.

The room was bare save for the table and two chairs, though Isaac had no question there was at least one camera hidden in the walls with multiple people watching the feeds. It would be stupid for them to trust him alone with the general. They hadn't bound his hands or feet. He could jump over the table and assault the man if that was his desire.

It wasn't. He had come here willingly, all the way from Earth.

The doctors of Proxima B had saved his life, removing a brain tumor the surgeon claimed would have killed him in weeks if it had gone untreated. An affliction that couldn't be cured back home. Had they saved him to question him? And why here, in a room straight out of a bad movie? Was he the enemy now?

That wasn't how this was supposed to work.

"I wouldn't call this an interrogation, Sergeant," the General replied.

"What would you call it then, sir?"

"A friendly introduction." The General stretched his hand toward Isaac. "I'm General Aeron Haeri of the Centurion Space Force."

Isaac stared at the hand. This wasn't protocol.

And it wasn't a friendly introduction. Something like that would have been held in the General's office. He would have been invited there, not escorted here under armed guard.

"It's okay, Sergeant Pine. You can shake my hand." Haeri smiled. "You aren't one of mine."

Isaac knew a little bit about the Centurion Space Force. He knew some of the history. Most of it wasn't all that good. But like it or not, the CSF had grown from the

United States Space Force, which itself had stemmed from a combination of the United States Marine Corps and the United States Air Force. Maybe they were on different planets, but they shared the same origins. They also shared the same enemy.

An enemy that was more of a threat than ever.

"No disrespect intended, sir," Isaac replied. He wasn't about to shake a four-star general's hand like he was somebody he met at a bar. "Technically, I am one of yours. Or you wouldn't have my military record."

General Haeri seemed to appreciate the response, his lips spreading ever so slightly into a smile. "All right, Sergeant. Let's get on with this then, shall we?" His eyes dropped to the polymer and Isaac's record.

"Sergeant Isaac Pine," he read. "MOS 5815, Special Reaction Team." He glanced up at Isaac again. "Military Police."

"Yes, sir," Isaac replied. "That was a long time ago."

"Not for you."

"No, sir."

General Haeri slid his finger across the slender tablet, flipping through the pages and reviewing the data. Isaac winced when the general navigated past a photo of his late wife. He closed his eyes and focused on his breathing to keep himself steady.

"High marks all around," Haeri said, glancing up at him again. "Your marksmanship scores are especially strong."

"I was always good with a rifle, sir." He paused while the general looked back at the data. "General Haeri, can I ask you something?"

"Please do, Sergeant. I prefer we keep things as informal as possible. We aren't enemies, after all."

Isaac wasn't entirely sure of that. On some level, they

were enemies. But that level paled in comparison to the shared threats waiting for them.

"You didn't need to come in here to read my file, sir."

General Haeri released his full smile. "That was a statement, not a question."

"The meaning is the same, sir," Isaac replied.

Haeri pushed the device aside and leaned forward on the table. He brought his hands together, locking his fingers. His eyes met Isaac's. There was no malice in them —only that same interested curiosity.

"I want to know more about Sheriff Hayden Duke."

"Sir? I'm not sure I follow."

"I've been in command of the Centurion Space Force for nearly twenty years. For eighteen of those years, things were calm. The CSF ran like clockwork. So did Proxima. The entire planet was in equilibrium. Stable. Quiet. My job was easy, and I went home to my wife and children every night believing they were safe. That their lives would be peaceful." He paused, his jaw clenching slightly. "And then Sheriff Hayden Duke happened."

"I don't think it's fair to blame Sheriff Duke for any of this, sir," Isaac said.

"No? Why not?"

"You have my file, sir. Are you familiar with my more recent history?"

"I've been briefed. You spent two hundred thirty-six years in stasis, intentionally placed there by an operative of the enemy to preserve your genetic potential. They forgot about you, the power ran out, and you woke up two months ago."

"That's an interesting way of framing it, sir."

"In what way?"

"Can I be blunt, General?"

"Please do."

"You're minimizing the threat. The operative wasn't some spy, and he didn't forget about me. He had his own people waiting there for me to wake up. The only reason I'm here and alive is because of Sheriff Duke."

"You say *he*. Do the Relyeh Ancients have genders?"

"That's not the point, is it, sir? I don't know if they have genitals or not. I never looked. But Shurrath seemed more like a he." Isaac stared at Haeri. He didn't seem like the kind of man that would waste a question. He was probing. But for what?

Haeri sat in silence, waiting for Isaac to decide where the conversation would go.

"General, the real point is that the Relyeh threat has been present since the trife arrived on Earth over two hundred years ago. If you believe things have been peaceful and your family is safe, I would argue that belief is pure ignorance."

Haeri leaned back slightly, an amused smirk sliding across his face. "Ignorance. I assure you, Sergeant, I've been anything but ignorant. When Rico brought you here, she promised me you would provide details about Sheriff Duke's activities on Earth. He claims to have had contact with the Others?"

"The Axon." Isaac corrected him, using the alien race's true name. "Yes, sir. But I think you already know about that. Gillick is one of yours."

"She's a Centurion officer, yes."

Isaac paused a moment, deciding whether to play one of his cards. Better to use it than lose it. "That's not what I mean, sir."

General Haeri's eyes shifted, revealing the location of one of the hidden cameras to Isaac. He lowered his voice. "Be careful about the allusions you make, Sergeant. Nothing is as simple as it may seem."

"Yes, sir. Gillick's team was infiltrated by Relyeh. They used her to advance their own agenda."

"That's not how she tells it."

Isaac fought to control his immediate response. He failed. "That's because she's a self-centered idiot. Sheriff Duke saved her life, and she didn't even realize—"

"That's enough, Sergeant," Haeri said, putting up his hand to silence him. "We aren't here to speak to Colonel Gillick's actions."

"Maybe we should be."

"We aren't. She's my responsibility, and she'll be handled as such. Tell me more about the Axon."

"Sir, Sheriff Duke made a deal with it. He's trying to negotiate an alliance."

"Against Proxima?"

"General, I think the fact that you even asked that question speaks volumes about Proxima's treatment of Earth. Could you even blame him if he were trying to form an alliance against you?"

"Perhaps not," Haeri admitted. "Relations between Proxima and Earth haven't been as positive as some of us might want. Mistakes have been made."

"Mistakes, General? You abandoned the people of Earth except for use in your experiments. You live up here in comfort and safety while the people down there suffer. And when someone down there finally tries to do something about it, you refuse to provide more than a minimum level of aid based on a ridiculous, ill-conceived, and outdated Zero Contact Protocol. I'm not surprised you don't sleep well at night."

"I may be in command of the CSF, but I don't run the planet, and I don't make the laws. I've done my best to handle Sheriff Duke within the constraints of my position.

I'm still not sure if he's a thorn in my side or a spear in my hand."

"Maybe you shouldn't be thinking of him in terms of how he can help or hurt you, sir. What about how you can help him help Earth? Sheriff Duke isn't seeking an alliance against Proxima. To be honest, General, after what I just experienced you're the last thing the people of Earth have to worry about. The trife were only the beginning. There's a new invasion coming. One that will tear up both our worlds if we don't start working together."

"The Relyeh?"

"There's a power vacuum, sir. A hole in their web of dominion. You can guess where the center of that hole is."

"Earth," Haeri replied. His smile was gone, his face stoic and tight as Isaac's words sank in.

"General, the Axon are losing ground," Isaac said. "Earth is already on the ropes. And you're sitting out here pretending this planet is safe, but it isn't. I promise you that. But there's still a chance to rally. A chance to save everything. But we have to seize the moment. The time for hiding is over."

Haeri stared at Isaac for a long moment. The tension between them was heavy. The pressure mounting. It was obvious to Isaac the General didn't like what he had to say.

But they had brought him here because they wanted him to talk. So he was talking.

"Why did you cure me, sir?" he continued. "Because you believed in my loyalty to the Corps, and by extension the Centurion Space Force? Because you believed I would help you? I can help you. Send me back to Earth. Send me with supplies. Ships. Armor. Guns and ammunition. Send me with the full weight of the CSF at my back. Or better yet, come back with me. Lead the fight yourself."

"The trife arrived over two hundred years ago," Haeri

said. "Since then, we've had no contact or interference from any other extraterrestrials. Why are you so convinced you need more aid than we're already providing?"

"You mean besides the fact that the trife are still in control of the planet?"

"We fought that war a long time ago, Sergeant. We lost."

"The people on Earth are ready for you to try again. In any case, the Hunger is like a hydra, General. Cut off one head and two more grow back. Sheriff Duke neutralized Shurrath. Something worse is bound to follow."

Haeri regarded him for a long moment, silent and thoughtful. Choosing his words carefully. Isaac understood. Like the General had said, things weren't as simple as they seemed. There were things he couldn't say in here. Things he couldn't do.

Even so, Haeri's next statement caught Isaac completely by surprise.

"I understand, Sergeant. I understand it was a mistake to bring you here. Whatever Sheriff Duke is planning on Earth, it's obvious he intends to sow dissent here on Proxima. He coached you to assist him in that goal. Fuel the fear of the people and watch how the planet burns. Payback for his misguided belief that the people who escaped Earth have abandoned it. The truth is hardly what you've presented here. What you've presented are lies and propaganda. The fact remains that Earth is a wasteland created by an accidental alien invasion over two centuries ago. The humans who survive there are tribal savages, and every effort we've made to redeem them have ended with the loss of Centurion lives."

Isaac stared at Haeri, stunned by the force of the rebuke. And the General wasn't finished.

"There are no other aliens out there except the trife.

We've spent over a hundred years searching as much of the galaxy as we can reach, and we've found nothing. The Axon and the Relyeh—the Others and the Hunger —they don't exist. They're code words Sheriff Duke and his followers use to manipulate the people. Words you've tried to use with me here, just as I expected you would. I'm not an Earther, Sergeant. I'm not an uneducated savage. You can't sway me with the same lies you use to convince scavengers and criminals to join the Sheriff's so-called posse."

Isaac opened his mouth to speak, to counter Haeri's unexpected tirade. He couldn't get a word in edgewise.

"Earth is over, Sergeant. It was lost a long time ago. Sheriff Hayden Duke is dangerous. Speaking to you, I realize how dangerous he's become. Why did I cure you? Information. Observation. And possibly conversion. I want to give you a chance to see the other side of the argument. You're a trained soldier. A valuable asset. We could use someone like you on the ground."

Isaac's heart pounded, his mouth suddenly dry. Haeri glanced over at the camera again. The General was playing games. Should he play along?

"You're a liar," Isaac said through gritted teeth. The sucker punch left him seething, but he didn't dare show it. "I don't know what your game is, but I'm not playing. Sheriff Hayden Duke is a good man. What he's trying to do on Earth is for the good of everyone there. And the Hunger is real, General. It's real, and it's coming. No amount of denial will change that."

"What you call denial, I call reality."

General Haeri tapped a small button on his collar. The door behind him slid open and a pair of guards entered the room. They were dressed in dark body armor, black helmets hiding their faces.

"Take the prisoner to the brig," General Haeri said. "Put him in isolation."

"What?" Isaac said. "You brought me here as a guest. You saved my life to throw me——."

"And I expected some level of gratitude," Haeri replied. "Not petulant posturing for a second-rate warlord." The General stood as the guards flanked Isaac. "If you won't help me deal with Sheriff Duke, my only other option is to remove both him and you from the equation. Take him away."

Isaac decided to try to get over the table after all, growling as he stood and lunged at Haeri. "You son of a bitch."

Haeri didn't even flinch as the guards grabbed Isaac's arms, the enhanced strength of their combat armor allowing them to easily hold him. He struggled in their grasp, but there was no way out of their iron grip. They pulled him toward the door.

"Wait," General Haeri said as the soldiers reached it. He turned to face Isaac. "I'll give you twenty-four hours to reconsider your decision."

"Go to hell," Isaac replied.

Haeri didn't speak as the guards dragged Isaac from the room.

2

Hayden

Sheriff Hayden Duke sat astride his horse, Zorro, at one end of a narrow street in the northern part of what was left of Tijuana, Mexico. Squinting against the sinking sun despite the protection of his wide-brimmed hat, he looked into the distance to where his deputies approached the rear door of an old warehouse.

"We're in position, Sheriff," Deputy Nick Solino said, his voice clear and crisp through the small silver badge resting on the collar of Hayden's uniform.

"Pozz," Hayden replied. "Breach on my mark."

Deputy Cortez moved to the door. He was one of Hayden's new recruits, an older man who had eagerly joined up when Hayden and a force of his United Western Territories deputies rode into Tijuana three days ago. The great-grandson of a United States Space Force Marine, he'd had his right arm severed at the shoulder to replace it with a mechanical augment, intentionally turning himself into what was essentially a cyborg.

Mongrel.

That's what they called people like that these days.

Some would say intentional dismemberment was insane, and Hayden couldn't quite disagree. But there was something to be said for the powerful prosthetics the United States military had developed in the wake of the trife invasion.

Hayden flexed the fingers of his hands. He would know. Neither of his arms were organic, both lost at different places and times and under different circumstances. He hadn't intentionally done the deed, but the outcome was the same. He didn't regret it. His options had been to save his limbs or save his wife.

One was replaceable. The other wasn't.

"Now," Hayden said.

Deputy Cortez threw the palm of his augment into the door, the force of his effort blowing it open and ripping it from its hinges. The door vanished into the darkness of the warehouse as Cortez moved out of the way, allowing a pair of deputies to move in from each side, leading with their rifles.

Hayden lifted his pair of sunglasses, hanging from a cord around his neck, and put them on. He tapped the side of the frame and the shaded glass immediately filled in with augmented input, giving him access to the same combat network his armored deputies shared.

He used his eye muscles to work the interface, shifting his left eye to a view through Deputy Solino's camera feed. His lead deputy was slowly moving into the warehouse with Deputy Kevitz beside him. Both the camera and Solino's helmet filtered out the dim light, creating a clear grayscale view for both watcher and wearer.

Visibility was limited by the volume of product inside the warehouse. The place was a mess, filled with pallets of building materials. Drywall, rebar, piping, tile. Most of it remained stacked, stored and forgotten for the last two hundred years, still in the same place where it had been abandoned. A few of the palettes had rotted beneath a leak in the roof, collapsing and spilling their contents across the floor.

Scavengers had done good work picking items of value out of the surrounding industrial park, and there was little value in the materials here, at least to the common survivor.

Solino moved deeper into the building, the deputies getting into formation behind him. They paired up against adjacent stacks of boxes.

"Solino, anything?" Hayden asked. He could see through the deputy's feed, but he didn't have the man's other senses to rely on.

"It's creepy as hell in here, Sheriff," Solino replied quietly. "There's a smell in the air. Musty and thick. It's making my spine tingle."

"No sign of the target?"

"Negative."

"Head south. I want to see down the aisles."

"Pozz."

Solino kept moving, reaching the corner of the boxes and swinging around them, leading with his rifle. Most of the rows were identical. Only the material on the palettes changed. Stacks of bagged cement mix stretched into the distance. The deputy went past them to the next row, freezing as he came out into the open.

The evidence of a small encampment was visible ahead. An old nylon tent rested against the wall, a number of sleeping bags splayed out in front, with a small mountain of refuse beside it. Garbage, mostly old food wrappers, was spread around the site, and a rusted old motorcycle still leaned on its kickstand.

And bodies. Hayden counted six right away. They were

a few steps away from the tent, the cause of death hard to see from the angle and distance. But Hayden didn't have to guess how they had died.

The killers were still there.

A warning flashed across Hayden's glasses. A sudden outline appeared in the distance, painted in front of the solid brick wall of the warehouse even though the target was on the inside. Judging by the position, it was crouched on one of the stacks of materials, ready to pounce.

"Kevitz!" Hayden snapped.

"On it," she replied.

She had already seen the target in her visor and was pivoting to defend herself. The enemy leaped down at her, the sound of gunfire reaching Hayden in his place outside the building. The threat vanished from his display.

"Target eliminated," Kevitz said, her voice calm.

Hayden switched to her feed. She was looking down at the dead alien. Slender and lithe, it was a meter and a half long and humanoid in shape with leathery, ink-black skin. It had three long fingers ending in sharp claws and an opposable thumb. While its feet were similar—large and clawed—the big toe was closer to the side of the foot to allow for better gripping. Its head was small, its elongated face possessing beady, dark eyes and a mouth filled with sharp teeth. The creature was naked and genderless, its pelvis and chest both flat.

A single xenotrife didn't look all that dangerous. And wasn't. Their hollow bones were brittle and weak, and their claws weren't sharp enough to penetrate the Space Marine combat armor the deputies wore. But then they had learned the armor was vulnerable at the joints—especially where the helmet met the body. A claw in any of those places could rip through the spidersteel mesh body-suit beneath the armor and into the flesh of the wearer.

And because of that, a trife slick was incredibly dangerous.

"Eyes up," Hayden said. "Where are the rest of the bastards?"

Kevitz began looking around, focusing on the top of the stacks. The other deputies did the same.

"We're clean, Sheriff," Deputy Solino said after a quick search. "No sign of any more."

"There are always more," Hayden replied. Trife didn't travel alone. Not ever. Where the hell were the rest of them hiding?

"We did a sweep, Sheriff. We'd see them on the grid if they were in here."

"Color me unconvinced. Stay sharp. I don't trust..."

The AR on Hayden's sunglasses lit up again, showing a pair of trife emerging from around the side of a stack of something that had managed to block the networked armor's sensors. Deputies Kevitz and Nan were on it in a flash, moving into position and catching the two trife in a crossfire.

"Told you so," Hayden said.

"Scouting party," Solino said. "There are probably a few more."

"Solino, check out the bodies. I'm on your feed."

"You sure you don't want to come in here with us, Sheriff?"

"Negative. You can't rely on me always being there to back you up. You're doing a fine job, Nick."

"Roger that."

Hayden switched his view back to Solino's camera feed. The deputy approached the small campsite, the bodies coming into view. Solino looked down at the closest corpse—a young man, probably still a teen.

"Sheriff, are you seeing this?"

Hayden's heart started to pound.

"Fall back," he said, fighting to keep his voice calm. "Now. Quick and quiet. I'm on my way."

"R...Roger," Solino replied as Hayden urged Zorro forward at a gallop.

Quick and quiet. The gunfire coming from inside the warehouse was anything but.

And the kid had been nearly torn in half.

A normal trife couldn't cause damage like that. But a Queen? A Queen could do that and worse. What was she doing down there?

He could see his deputies in the augmented reality overlay of his glasses. Their green outlines grew larger as they moved closer to him, both from his forward motion and their retreat. A red outline suddenly appeared from the northwest side of the warehouse, followed by another and another.

Nearly a dozen trife appeared in the area within seconds.

"Solino, you've got company," Hayden said, charging the building.

"Roger," Solino replied. "Targets acquired."

The sound of gunfire split the air, muffled inside the warehouse. Hayden approached the building, but things were going from bad to worse in a hurry. The first dozen trife weren't the end of it. More of the demons were pouring out of the area, multiplying and spreading. They had to be climbing up from a hole in the floor. If a Queen was down there, it meant there was a nest in that hole. And if there was a nest in the hole, it meant there was a power source down there too.

And the target they had come here to find, a murderer called Halsey, was already dead.

At least there was a silver lining.

The gunfire intensified as the trife charged the fleeing deputies, the entire scene playing out in color-coded outlines in front of Hayden's eyes. He could see how the red outlines approached the green ones and vanished. The constant report of gunfire got louder as he closed the distance. The trife were still coming, his system counting nearly a hundred already in the warehouse and more on the way.

"Sheriff, help!" Nan cried out.

Hayden switched to her feed in time to see trife jaws descending on the vulnerable neck joint. Nan screamed, and then the trife was thrown back by a sudden shower of bullets. By the time he pulled her vitals up on his HUD, they were flat.

Son of a bitch.

3

Hayden

Hayden pulled back on the reins, bringing Zorro to a quick stop at the entrance to the warehouse. The deputies were desperately trying to reach the door through the sudden onslaught of trife.

If he didn't do something, they weren't going to make it.

According to his HUD, nearly two hundred of the demons had appeared in the building, making their way toward the deputies by any means possible. They tried to flank them on the floor while also leaping from pallet to pallet. A few even clung to the warehouse rafters, hanging upside down to make their way forward.

It was nothing Hayden hadn't seen before. He had spent the last two years hunting trife, clearing out nests and trying to regain some of the land they had taken in the name of humankind. He had been successful too, turning hundreds of kilometers of land into a safe zone the trife had yet to penetrate.

At least, he had thought the trife hadn't gotten in. But the warehouse was fifty kilometers south of Sanisco—too close to home to contain a nest of the demons. How had they managed to stay hidden for so long?

He pulled his twin revolvers from their holsters as he slid off Zorro and charged through the permanently opened door. He immediately turned left, toward the sound of the fighting echoing through the building.

"Solino cut left," Hayden said, coming around the side of one of the stacks. "I'll cover your egress."

"Roger," Solino replied.

Hayden could see both Solino and Cortez on his HUD, just on the other side of a stack of shingles, their outlines running parallel across his lane. The trife followed close behind, hissing as they gave chase.

One of them lunged at Solino as he crossed the intersection. Hayden didn't hesitate, firing a round that caught the trife in the shoulder and knocked it away. It hit the floor and rolled, staying down when another round hit it in the chest.

Hayden kept shooting, cutting down seven trife while emptying the two revolvers. He swung back behind cover and quickly reloaded, using speedloaders to drop full cylinders of bullets into the guns.

The demons were still coming, closing on the defending deputies. The red outlines on the HUD left Hayden's immediate view a stained blur, the quantity of trife nearly overwhelming the system's ability to reflect their positions.

Hayden turned to follow one of the outlines, getting a glimpse of Cortez a few meters away. The recruit was using his augment to full advantage, throwing hard punches that crushed the bones of the delicate aliens, putting them out of the fight. Hayden's attention shifted to the rafters as a pair of trife dropped from overhead, reaching out to slash at Cortez with their claws. Hayden adjusted his aim and fired, rounds cutting through their skulls. Cortez stepped out of the way as they crashed into the floor.

"There's too many," Kevitz said, getting closer to Hayden.

"Pozz," Hayden agreed. "We're pulling out. Cortez, let's go!"

Cortez started toward Hayden, but then he turned to look down the aisle. And froze.

"*Mierda*," he said, eyes wide with fear.

Hayden's HUD picked up the threat an instant later. Shit was right.

The queen had emerged from the hole and was charging toward them.

"Move!" Hayden roared. But Cortez stood there, static. Terrified.

"Solino, Kevitz, get the hell out of here!" Hayden said, charging toward the motionless deputy.

"Sheriff, you can't make it," Solino replied.

"I'll make it, just go. Keep our escape route as clear as you can, and radio HQ for backup."

"Roger."

Trife tried to block Hayden's path, leaping at him from the top of the stacks. He shot them as they came, nearly point-blank, the rounds tearing through their flesh and blasting them away. His HUD went wild as a pair of demons tried to tackle him from behind. He spun around, coming down in a crouch and shooting the two trife. Revolvers empty, he holstered the guns with practiced ease and leaped up to race the queen to Cortez.

It looked like the queen was going to win.

"Cortez!" he shouted again, desperate to reach the man first.

The deputy finally snapped out of it, maybe because

his life was about to end. He leveled his gun at the queen and fired. Hayden couldn't see her yet, but the screaming hiss told him Cortez had only made her more angry.

A moment later, a claw the size of Hayden's head slashed out, catching Cortez in the face, cracking his visor, and turning his head aside so violently Hayden could hear the bones of the man's neck snap. Cortez's body was thrown into a pallet of boxes, the top three tumbling off into the next aisle over. The man's body came down on top of the boxes, his head twisted grotesquely to one side.

Hayden's momentum carried him toward the queen as she emerged from around the stack. Screaming almost directly into his face, he stood there, staring at a mouthful of long razor-like teeth.

He didn't hesitate, throwing a solid punch toward her face, needing to aim upward to reach it. The queen was nearly three times the size of the other trife, her skin tougher and body more muscular. She took the blow off her cheek, moving with it. Hayden felt the solid contact right before she returned the favor, catching him in the chest with her claws.

They dug deep into the hardened plates of the combat armor hidden beneath his shirt, catching on one of the seams and throwing him sideways. He hit a separate group of trife, knocking them over as they softened his fall.

They grabbed at him as he pulled himself up, their lesser strength preventing them from piercing his body armor.

"Get out of there, Sheriff!" Solino shouted over the comm. "Bronson's on the way in the chopper."

'On it!" Hayden cried out. He wrapped one metal hand around his vulnerable throat, threw the other one up to protect his face and charged almost blindly toward freedom

He didn't get far. The queen wasn't about to let him go.

Like all Relyeh, the trife communicated across an organic system called the Collective, which operated much like a computer network. A trife queen here could receive signals from another queen on the other side of the world, sharing information about threats and tactics, and helping one another mutate their genetics to better survive those threats. While the trife in the warehouse were hardly mutated from their original form, the reaction of the queen when she got a better look at him suggested she knew who he was.

She also knew how many of her kind he had killed.

She screamed and hissed, rushing Hayden. He would have run, but the trife had closed in around him, cornering him. They didn't attack. Not now. The queen wanted him for herself. But they weren't going to let him escape.

He braced himself, getting into a fighting stance. The queen swiped at him and he ducked below her claws then sidestepped her tail as it whipped around at his face. She screamed at him, teeth darting toward his neck. He didn't make the same mistake twice, backing away instead of retaliating. Her other claw slashed at him and he smacked it down.

"Solino, ETA?" he asked, the light on his badge still green. Still connected.

"Three minutes, Sheriff."

In the middle of a fight, three minutes was an impossibly long time.

Too long to try to stall.

The queen stood in front of him, rising to her full three-meter height. Her mouth opened wide, and she screamed in anger, ropes of yellow saliva stringing between her jagged teeth. She came at him again, claws slashing, tail whipping, mouth angling at him as she launched an all-out assault.

The queen's tail smacked Hayden and began wrapping around him. He didn't move. Her left hand sailed through the air to slash him in the side. He still didn't move. Her face dropped toward his, mouth open as if she intended to take his head off with one bite. And he still didn't move.

Instead, he threw his right arm up and into the queen's mouth, reaching to the back of her throat. She bit down on it, teeth pressing hard into metal at the same time he squeezed his hand into a closed fist. The motion activated the alien metal that coated his augment. It expanded out into a pair of blades that stretched through the back of the queen's mouth and up into her brain.

Momentum carried the queen's head down his arm until her face was only centimeters from Hayden's. Black eyes regarded him with shock, the sudden weight of her dying form pressing down on his arm.

He stared back at the queen. He didn't hate her. She was only doing what she had been created to do. He hated the ones who'd made her. The Relyeh Ancients. The Hunger. They had delivered the trife to prepare humankind. To subdue them and keep them weak.

Hayden refused to be weak.

He grabbed the queen's head with his other hand, holding it as he yanked his arm free. There were indents in it where her teeth had come down, but it was otherwise unharmed.

He opened his fist. The Axon liquid metal sank back onto his hand, coating it in a grayish-black sheen. The augment was unique. The only one of its kind. He had paid a high price to earn the prosthetic. Too high a price. The death of a friend was always a price he never wanted to pay.

The lesser trife reacted as expected. The loss of their queen confused them, and for the first dozen heartbeats they stood around him in shock. Then that shock turned to fear, and they hissed and began tripping over one another, fighting to get back to their nest and away from him.

"Sheriff, my ATCS is telling me the trife are running," Solino said.

"That's right," Hayden replied. "The queen is dead."

The deputy laughed. "You killed the queen?"

"It was her or me. It's nothing to celebrate. We lost two good deputies today."

"Pozz that," Solino replied, voice dropping as the excitement washed away.

Hayden reached up and tapped his badge. "Bronson, do you copy?"

"I copy, Sheriff," the chopper pilot replied. "I'm en route to your position for emergency evac. ETA two minutes."

"Copy that. Cancel the evac. The threat is neutralized."

"Sheriff?"

"Head back to HQ and pick up some explosives. We've got a nest to burn."

"Roger, Sheriff. I'm reversing course now. Updated ETA... fifteen minutes."

"Pozz that. Sheriff out."

Hayden tapped the badge to disconnect before glancing back at the fleeing trife. It didn't matter if they were running. If he let them maintain the nest, they would pick a new queen from among the group, form a mateball, and transfer the genetic material to the chosen one to make it bigger, stronger and able to reproduce.

In other words, the nest had to be destroyed.

The real question was, where had it come from? This

area had been clear for over a year and was well within the safe zone. Had the trife actually tunneled in from somewhere else?

He tapped his badge again. "Bronson, this is Sheriff Duke."

"I copy, Sheriff," Bronson replied.

"Bring the Rangers and three plasma rifles back with you."

"Roger. What are you thinking, Sheriff?"

"Something about this isn't sitting right. I want to dig a little deeper before we destroy the evidence."

"Roger. If you don't mind me saying, Sheriff—when you have a feeling, that usually means bad things are about to happen."

"I'm bound to be wrong sometime," Hayden replied. "Let's hope today's the day."

4

Caleb

Caleb descended the cracked and worn concrete ramp, following a line of evenly-spaced torches deeper into the underground parking garage. The guards at the base of the slope turned to watch him. Not because they were nervous about his presence. Their eyes were affixed to his body. In their perception he was a female in a worn and tattered dress with a long tear along the back that revealed half of her dirt-smeared backside.

Primitive savages. And you wonder why your kind lost the war.

Caleb glanced back at the guards, who didn't even pretend not to be staring.. Their eyes moved to his face, and one of them smiled and winked. "My shift ends in three hours. Should I come find you?"

Caleb faced forward without responding. Ishek's laughter resonated in his mind.

"It isn't funny," Caleb said.

On at least one level, it is. You chose to scan the beggar woman.

"I scanned her front. I didn't know her clothes were in such bad shape. And I didn't know she wasn't wearing underwear."

You've been back on Earth for two months. You've seen what this place has become.

Caleb sighed. It was a sad truth he was still struggling to accept, even though the outcome had always been known. His journey had brought him from Earth to the stars and back again. A journey that had taken over two hundred years to reach this point. When he had left, he was United States Space Force Marine Sergeant Caleb Card, leader of the Vultures, the most elite search and rescue team on the planet.

Now?

He wasn't sure.

Fate had brought him back to Earth through an Axon wormhole.

And he hadn't come back alone.

Ishek was a Relyeh Advocate—a cross between a slug and a worm—currently wrapped around his right bicep and connected to his mind through tendrites extending from the bottom of the alien's body all the way up to Caleb's cervical spine. The connection, the bond, allowed them to read one another's minds in what was supposed to be a symbiotic relationship beneficial to them both.

I don't appreciate being thought of as a worm or a slug.

"That's what you look like."

I'm more intelligent.

"Debatable."

Caleb felt a sudden pressure in his mind. Ishek's way of trying to pinch him for the statement. He deflected it easily. Time together had only strengthened their bond, changing them both.

For the better?

He wasn't sure of that either.

The Relyeh weren't friends of humankind. They weren't anyone's friend. They had spread across the galaxy, crossing thousands of light years and conquering any intelligent races they discovered. They subverted these races to their mission, either through enslavement, the adoption of their genetic material, or both. The Hunger was dependent on this constant conquest for survival, their entire evolutionary nature predicated on feeding off the universe's seemingly endless bounty.

Ishek was a Relyeh, and its bond to Caleb meant he also needed to feed like a Relyeh to survive. That meant access to the pheromones emitted by animals during periods of high stress. In other words—fear and pain. In that way, he had become like a mythical vampire, with a dark side that compelled him to ugly violence.

It was the reason he was in the garage. Ishek was hungry.

I hunger.

Ishek echoed the sentiment. In the beginning, the hunger was like a curse. He had tried to starve it out, only to find himself first wracked with pain and then unable to prevent Ishek from seizing control of his body. The Relyeh had no qualms about its need to cause stress. It had no morals, no conscience, and when it was that hungry, no control. Ishek had made him do something he didn't want to remember. Something he had pushed so deep into his mind he couldn't recall it now. All that remained was the vague memory that he had done something horrible. Something that had left him no longer able to consider himself a Space Force Marine. Marines were honorable and loyal. They weren't cold-blooded killers.

Like him.

Caleb reached the first level of the garage. Fires burned in metal trash bins spread across the floor, while groups of survivors huddled around them, talking and eating. A pungent odor wafted from a central firepit where slabs of meat hung on metal hooks over the flames. Trife meat.

I still can't believe you eat them.

"I don't eat them," Caleb replied.

But other humans did. Why wouldn't they? The trife were more plentiful than any other living thing on Earth, and the survivors had somehow developed an immunity to the poison they carried in their blood.

A tent city spread out beyond the cookfires. Dozens of various size tents in various states of decay rested across the garage floor surrounded by garbage. Mongrel dogs meandered among them, searching for trife bones with meat still attached or other morsels from discarded cans and previously packaged foods with an infinite shelf life.

People gathered around the tents. A man with an augmented leg stood beside a worn blanket with guns and knives laid out on display while a pair of thugs in thread-bare jeans and stained t-shirts looked them over. Caleb could almost sense them trying to decide if they could pay for any of the weapons and if they couldn't if they should try to take them. Their owner seemed to sense the same, because his hand shifted to rest on the handle of a sidearm, and he coughed to caution the thugs. They glanced up at him and walked away.

Further back, Caleb caught sight of a second man. He was more finely dressed in a woven cotton shirt and pants, his feet in sandles and his hair tied back. Freshly bathed women clothed only in old bathing suits or bra and panties lounged on blankets around him, smiling at the men who approached. Caleb watched as a handful of notes exchanged possession and one of the women stood and joined the man who had paid for her services. The pimp pointed at a nearby tent and the couple vanished inside.

Paying for reproduction. Primitive savages.

"Better to pay than to take."

That's a matter of perspective. Does the man own these women?

"Point made. I don't disagree."

I hunger.

"Me too. Are there any targets here?"

You tell me.

Caleb smirked. Ishek was testing him. He closed his eyes, opening himself up to the connection between himself and Ishek, and from Ishek to the Collective. He searched for nearby Relyeh, practicing the subtle feel of recognizing when another mind was close.

He remembered the one time he had searched the Collective and discovered the last thing he ever expected.

Another human.

The connection had lasted a second. Maybe two. He had called out, but there was no reply. That was nearly two months ago. He'd kept trying for weeks after that, hundreds of times, but he never found her again. Ishek told him he must have gotten mixed up and misread the connection, but Caleb was certain. He had gotten a glimpse of her memories.

He knew she was here on Earth, and her name was Natalia.

Natalia Duke.

He wanted to find her. A part of him needed to find her. But there was something he needed more. First, to feed. Second, to find out what had happened to the colony on Proxima, and if possible to get a message to them. He had crossed the galaxy with something of great value. Valuable research a lot of people had died to protect.

His mind held the secret to saving the planet, but he had nobody to share the secret with.

5

Caleb

Caleb walked past the men and women gathered around the cook fire, making his way toward the tents in the back. He could hear the men whisper as he passed, making quiet comments about this strange new woman in their village. He had copied her visage four hours earlier after finding her wandering the road leading into the area, hungry and disoriented. Ishek had wanted to feed on her. Caleb refused. She was in bad shape and had likely already been attacked. His real desire was to help her. To find her somewhere safe to rest and something to eat. There was nothing nearby, and he didn't have the time to stay with her. The hunger was real and growing, and he could only deny his symbiote for so long.

He had given her a few notes and a blanket. Maybe she was grateful. It was impossible to tell. She had looked him in the eye and offered a slight smile, but it was the best she could do. He helped her to the side of the road, sat her down in the shade of a tree, and continued ahead. The trife wouldn't touch her, not as long as she was unarmed and unthreatening. He couldn't vouch for anyone who traveled the road and happened to see her there.

That was life on the forgotten Earth.

He winced when he felt a hand grab at the holographic projection of the woman's nearly bare buttocks. His head whipped in the direction of the grabber, who offered a nearly toothless smile.

"You like that?" the man asked.

This one will do.

Caleb wasn't so sure. He had come here looking for other Relyeh.

You found none.

He couldn't argue that fact. Then again, some of the Relyeh were able to hide from the Collective. Servants of one of the Relyeh Ancients. He had already killed a few of them. He couldn't see them, but they could see him, and they didn't like him.

Probably because he wasn't on their side.

"Maybe I do," he replied to the man.

The others nearby laughed.

"Ooh, Rook, I think she likes you," one teased.

"You gonna get some of that, Rook?" another said.

"Do you have a tent?" Caleb asked.

The man kept smiling as he got to his feet. "We don't need a tent, darlin'. There's a dark corner right over there." He pointed to the corner of the garage, an area the survivors were using as a toilet.

How romantic.

Caleb tightened his lips to keep from reacting to Ishek's comment.

"What do you say, darlin'?" Rook asked.

I hunger, Caleb.

"Why not?" Caleb said. "Lead the way."

Rook beamed, reaching for Caleb's hand. Caleb let him take it.

They didn't get far. Someone tapped Caleb on the shoulder. He turned his head back to find the pimp standing behind him.

"Don't just give it away, my specimen," he said.

"What?" Rook said, pausing and getting in front of the pimp. "Why don't you butt the hell out?"

The pimp smiled calmly as he shoved a knife into Rook's stomach, pulling him close. The man's sudden pain and fear was thick in the air, and while Caleb hadn't caused it, he could still breathe it in.

Delicious.

Caleb hadn't caught on to the apparent flavor of the pheromones. He only understood that they either did or didn't satiate the hunger. Rook's grip on his hand loosened as he struggled to breathe. The pimp pulled the knife out, letting the man drop to his knees, clutching at his stomach to stem the flow of blood.

"There's nothing you can do," the pimp said. "Except die."

Rook gasped, his fear filling the air. Caleb was surprised by the sudden violence, but it was almost exactly what he had planned to do. He looked at the pimp, making eye contact. They searched one another for a moment.

He couldn't sense some Relyeh.

But they could sense him.

Caleb turned off the projection as his hand dropped to his sidearm, previously hidden by the projection. The people around him gasped and shouted in surprise, a nearly featureless black humanoid suddenly in their midst. The pimp was shocked for a moment too. Maybe the pimp expected Caleb was host to an Advocate, but he hadn't guessed he was wearing a Skin.

Don't kill him.

Ishek's request caught Caleb off-guard. He was slow to draw, giving the pimp the time he needed to leap toward him and stab with the knife. It hit the Skin in a flare of blue light, the blade deflected by the Skin's shields.

"Why not?" Caleb asked.

The pimp took a swing at him. He ducked below it, nearly tripping over someone as they tried to stand and run.

He might have information.

Ishek was right. Caleb deflected another punch and then rushed the pimp, tackling him. The dirty man tried to struggle until Caleb put a hand to his back, emitting just enough energy to signal the khoron inside him there was more than just its host's life at stake.

"Wait," the pimp said. "Don't." He stopped struggling.

"Who do you serve?" Caleb asked.

"What? I don't serve any—"

Caleb increased the energy output, burning the man's back. He gritted his teeth in pain.

"I said, who the hell do you serve?"

The pimp growled softly. "Nyarlath. The greatest of the gods."

Caleb nodded. Most of the khoron he had found served the same Relyeh Ancient. Even the ones who didn't said the same thing. Nyarlath was the most powerful leader of the Hunger. Not the strongest, but the oldest and most intelligent.

"Where is she?" Caleb asked.

The pimp started laughing. "Not here. But she's coming. Her brother is dead, and soon this world will know true fear."

He kept laughing, even as his hand started rising behind Caleb's back. Caleb didn't hesitate, sending a blast of energy into the khoron before the pimp could drive his knife into him. When the khoron died, the host died, the blade falling out of his hand and clattering on the cement.

We knew that was coming.

Caleb nodded slightly, turning to look at the weapon. It wasn't a knife after all. It was short and thin, with a violent, serrated edge. It was made of dark alloy. Alien metal. Axon origin. He had never seen anything like it before. Ishek filled in the blanks.

An Axon microspear. Originally designed as a torture device for use against my kind. It looks as though it's been weaponized.

"How many of you are on this planet that somebody made a weapon to kill you?"

Unknown. Enough. He said Nyarlath is coming.

Caleb picked up the microspear, looking up as the guards came running toward him, along with nearly a dozen armed scavengers.

He got to his feet, holstering his sidearm. He had nowhere to put the microspear, so he kept it in his hand as he raised them. "I don't want any more trouble," he said.

The guards leveled their shotguns at him. They couldn't hurt him if they wanted to, but there was no more reason to fight. He had gotten what he came for. He had satisfied the hunger.

The guards and scavengers stopped in front of him, unsure what to make of him. He knew how alien he looked. The Skin covered his entire body, including his head.

"Don't shoot," he said. "I'm leaving."

He started toward them, moving deliberately while they followed him with their guns. They didn't say anything as they parted to let him through. He could taste their fear. It would keep Ishek satisfied for a while.

He kept going, back across the garage to the ramp. The

guards followed him, making sure he left as though they had control over the decision.

He emerged back into the open air. The sun was setting—a bad time for most to be outside alone.

Not for him.

He didn't look back as he resumed heading north on the old highway, considering what the pimp had said. If Nyarlath were on his way, that was a problem. A big problem. But it was a problem he could help solve.

He just needed to get what he knew to Proxima.

It was more important now than ever.

6

Rico

Rico stood at the window of her apartment, looking down. The activity of evening traffic inside Dome Three left a field of color and light across the city below—a stream of life, safety and happiness that stood in stark contrast to the world she had recently left behind.

Earth.

Her eyes shifted skyward, toward the top of the dome. It was nighttime, which meant the atmospheric projectors were turned off and the sky, the real sky, was visible through the thick, transparent shield that protected them from the harsh elements of their home planet.

Once, not that long ago, the beauty of the sky and the billions of stars beyond brought her comfort. Now looking at them caused her to shiver.

"I still miss you, Sarge," she said out loud, thinking of her husband.

They had been in the Centurion Space Force together, assigned to Earth. They had spent years loving one another from afar, and when they had finally come together, fate had ripped them apart.

Earth had ripped them apart.

Austin was gone, killed by a madman who wanted the aliens to win. He had been dead for months now.

Rico still felt the loss. Every damn day.

She sighed heavily, refocusing her thoughts. As the liaison between Earth and Proxima, it was her responsibility to make sure whatever happened down there didn't affect anything that happened up here. Humankind's newer and better world had a tenuous relationship with their origins, and the latest developments had left her wondering where it was all going to lead.

As far as the population of Proxima was concerned, as far as the elected government was concerned, Earth was as it had always been. A civilized society of humankind that their ancestors had fled centuries earlier to escape oppression and form their independent society.

Rico shook her head. It was such bullshit, but after so many years the civilians bought it without question. So did the Centurion Spacers who didn't know any better. Who had never gained the clearance to be deployed there. It was Proxima's best kept secret and anyone who even hinted they might try to reveal it was dealt with quickly and violently.

She wasn't about to say anything to anyone who didn't already know. Rocking the ship wouldn't help Proxima, and it wouldn't help Earth. No, the only thing that could help them all was to keep the tenuous relationship going and try to navigate the dark water between fiction and reality where the Council, the military and the Trust—the planet's organized crime syndicate—operated.

The job to act as fulcrum had fallen to her when Austin died. She could only hope she was making him proud.

Rico turned away from the window, crossing her cube to the small countertop that served as a kitchen. There was no livestock on Proxima. The meats they had were all preserved in Petri dishes and grown in vats, processed and packaged to look like the real thing when it never could. Very few people even knew what the real thing looked like, but she did. There were cows and pigs and chickens on Earth, along with all kinds of other wildlife. The trife didn't kill them. They only killed humans.

She opened a small drawer and pulled out a package marked as turkey. She tore the wrapper off and threw it into the oven. She wasn't all that hungry, but she figured she should eat.

Her mind wandered to Sergeant Isaac Pine. She had brought him back from Earth with her under the protection of centuries-old settlement laws. Laws that allowed anyone born during the original trife invasion to become instant citizens of Proxima. Time should have made the laws irrelevant. Even today, regular humans didn't live much past a hundred years. But the original Council hadn't banked too hard on stasis, which was a new technology for them at the time. They had no way of knowing anyone on Earth had been asleep for all of those years.

But Isaac had.

Rico's finger hovered over the start button. Thinking of Isaac brought an empty feeling to her gut. He had come to Proxima because he was dying and their medicine was the only thing that could save him. And they *had* saved him. The tumor was gone. Isaac was healthy again. The last time she had seen him, he was still in the hospital while arrangements were being made to provide him with a permanent home and a new life.

And then he had disappeared.

She had gone to see him again, only to find his room at the hospital empty. She had recovered his discharge file, which claimed he had checked himself out. That was his right as a Proxima citizen, but why the hell would he do that?

She didn't think he had.

Her gut reaction was to confront General Haeri. She knew the general was a multi-headed snake. The commanding officer of the Centurion Space Force, and close to the top of the Trust's chain of command, if not its head. It meant he knew the truth about everything...and then some. He had access to secrets nobody else in the universe knew. Secrets one faction or another had been keeping for centuries.

It also meant he was dangerous.

Rico opened the oven door, considered repackaging the meal, and then slammed the door closed again.

"Damn it," she hissed under her breath.

Isaac vanished two days ago. She had searched for him through above-board channels, unsurprised to find he had fallen completely off the grid. He was a Proxima citizen, with all of the rights and privileges. But he was also a newcomer. A stranger. Someone nobody would miss except for her. He was easy to make disappear. She wanted to go to Haeri, but her mistrust gave her pause. She didn't ultimately know which side he was playing for, or what his end goals were. Did he want to sever all ties to Earth or improve relations? Was he for or against an alliance with the Axon? Or was he already under Relyeh control? It was impossible to guess. She imagined if Haeri wanted her to know where Isaac was, he would have already told her.

And that was enough to keep her in line.

Or it had been.

Two days had given her a lot of time to think. About the past, present and future. Hers, Proxima's and Earth's. Once, not that long ago, she was loyal to Proxima and only Proxima. But ignorance wasn't bliss. In the end, it hadn't saved Austin and it hadn't spared her any pain. The enemy was out there, and it wasn't only an enemy to Earth. It was an enemy to all of humankind.

She couldn't stand by while the Hunger prepared for their next invasion and General Haeri continued to play games. She couldn't afford to keep trying to balance one planet with another. They were all humans after all.

They all deserved to live free.

Rico turned on her heel, crossing the space to the comm terminal near her front door. She tapped on the screen to activate it. "General Haeri," she said. Her heart started pounding in anticipation.

"Special Officer Rodriguez," Haeri said a moment later. "It's about time you called."

Rico opened her mouth, but the words didn't come. Haeri's greeting took her completely off-guard. "You...you were waiting for me?"

"Of course. You want to know what happened to Sergeant Pine."

"That's right."

"I'm sending you a new file. Read it quickly."

The comm disconnected.

7

Rico

Rico hurried away from the comm terminal and into Austin's office. Her office, though she still struggled to think of it that way. There was another terminal inside connected to a secure military channel. She activated it, the interface projecting onto the top of the desk in three dimensions. She reached for her inbox, flipping it open. A new message appeared. She knew Haeri sent it, but his name wasn't on it. There was no name on it. No subject. Only a file.

She grabbed the file and opened it. She wasn't sure what to expect. Her conversation with General Haeri had been short and one-sided. She had no idea what the hell was going on.

The contents of the file spread out in front of her. A chart, two videos, a text document. She imagined they were listed in the order the general wanted her to consume them. She tapped on the map.

It expanded in front of her, the projection increasing in size until it filled her whole field of view. Now that it was larger, she could see it was a star chart. Proxima was outlined and labeled in blue. A second planet was outlined in green and marked as 'OBSERVATION ALPHA.'

Rico stared at it. "Ray, what's the distance between Proxima and Observation Alpha?" she asked, speaking to the terminal's AI assistant.

"Eight light years," it replied in a calm, neutral voice.

Eight? She studied the chart, rotating it with her hand. Proxima was the axis as it turned, showing her the mapped stars within a twenty light year radius of the planet. There were seven more of the green worlds marked as 'Observation,' each of them approximately eight light years distant.

A third planet was outlined in red. Earth.

Why had General Haeri sent her a map of explored space? And what were the Observation planets?

"I don't get it," she said, trying to make sense of the map.

"The chart contains an animation," the AI replied. "Would you like to play it?"

Rico sighed, feeling stupid. "Yes, please."

The chart rotated back to its original position. Then the first green planet, Observation Alpha pulsed a brighter green for a few seconds, attracting her attention. A moment later, a new mark appeared on the chart close to the observation planet, painted in yellow.

A timer appeared to the right of the yellow mark, displaying its velocity and heading as the continuing animation dragged it across the star map.

Rico stared at it, heart pounding more fiercely. She shifted her gaze to find Proxima and then drew an invisible line between the planet and the unidentified object.

It was coming right toward them.

She swallowed hard, her mouth suddenly dry. The animation ended with the yellow object already past Observation Alpha, the readings suggesting it was moving through the universe at over one hundred times the speed of light.

How was that even possible?

Centurion starships used folded space to travel the four light-years between Proxima and Earth, and even with that it took nearly two weeks to make the round trip. Real FTL travel like what she was watching couldn't happen.

At least that's what human science had taught her to believe.

She closed the chart and opened the first video. At first, she thought it was broken because it only displayed a blank, black screen. Then a single point of red appeared to the far left of the frame. By the next frame, it was a streak that crossed the entire screen. Then the display went black again. She was going to replay it when she noticed the video wasn't over. It started with the empty display and continued until the red light appeared. Then the recording seemed to slow down, the camera capturing the event at the highest rate it could manage.

It allowed her to see what was creating the light, which trailed out from the dark shape in a long line. It gave her a chance to be afraid.

She knew it had to be an alien ship before she saw it. Nothing could move that fast naturally. Even so, the sight of the vessel sent a shiver down her spine and raised a chill across her body, and she shook in place as she stared. The video had been edited, the image manipulated to invert the light and pull out the features of the object creating it. It was four kilometers long at least, and nearly half as high. It appeared to be made of stone or other hardened, non-metallic material. It was smooth and rounded at the bow and stern, with a center composed of interconnected bulbs that spread out to nearly double the diameter. Smaller streaks of light surrounded it, emitted from transparencies in the outer shell or external lighting along the hull.

To Rico, it looked less like a starship and more like a gigantic, barnacle-encrusted creature dredged up from the bottom of the sea and launched into space.

But it was a starship.

A Relyeh starship.

The Hunger had started their invasion centuries earlier when they had dropped the trife on the planet to begin their conquest.

It appeared they were coming to finish it.

The video ended, leaving her staring at the last frame, which was the closest shot the camera got of the starship as it passed. It was amazing to her that they had managed to capture such a clear view of the craft on its way by. It was almost as if Observation Alpha had been placed there for that very purpose.

Because it had, hadn't it? Whatever Observation Alpha was, she knew what it wasn't. It wasn't a Centurion installation. The Council hadn't sanctioned it. But General Haeri knew it existed. He had sent her the file.

To the regular civilian, the Trust was a whisper, a shadow organization that barely existed outside of vague conspiracy theories and unreported incidents. Rico had always known the Trust more for the problems they silenced than the problems they solved. A criminal organization that took advantage of the people of Proxima. But this was proof that maybe the Trust was something else. Something much more complex.

The Hunger was coming.

The Trust was waiting.

Rico closed the video. Her heart felt like it would explode from her chest, and she could barely breathe. So many blurry ideas had come into focus in the last few minutes, and Haeri wasn't done with his big reveal just yet.

She tapped on the next video in the file, finding herself looking down on Isaac from a camera mounted in the top corner of a what appeared to be a prison cell. She was right, Haeri had taken him. But why? And why show her this now?

Isaac looked to be in good health if a bit bored. He was lying on the cell's rack, staring up at the ceiling with a resigned expression on his face. At first, Rico thought she was watching a recording. Then she noticed the time-stamp. Haeri had sent her a real-time feed.

What was the general up to?

Rico watched the feed for a few more seconds. She left it open, pushing it aside to view the text document. It was a simple note.

Dome One, if you're Able.

That was it. It might have been cryptic to some.

She knew exactly what it meant.

8

Rico

Rico descended into the loop station closest to her apartment in Dome Three's A-District, a section of Praeton reserved for the wealthy and important.

Not that she was wealthy or important. But being the Special Officer responsible for relations between Proxima and Earth did afford her some small benefits, including the oversized cube in the fancy part of town. It didn't mean all that much to her. It never had, especially not after Austin died. The way the other residents stared at her when she left her cube was always a powerful display of snobbery that would have unnerved anyone who hadn't already stood toe-to-toe against a slick of xenotrife. It wasn't her style. It never would be.

She was glad to leave it behind.

And she *was* leaving it behind. She didn't need Haeri to spell it out for her. The clues were there, and she was smart enough to read them. The Relyeh were coming. Things were going to change. For her. For Proxima. For Earth. For better or for worse. At least she wouldn't be standing idly by while it did.

The loop station was quiet so late at night. Most of the residents were already in their home domes. When there were more people around, the advertisements that lined the walls and called out the products and services for sale faded easily into the background. Now they assaulted Rico's senses, each one vying for her attention as she swiped her wrist over the scanner to gain access to the platform. Only a handful of other people waited there with her, each doing their best to keep to themselves.

Rico patted her pants, feeling through them to the bodysuit she had put on beneath. It was light armor, a spider-steel weave that rested beneath the hardened plates of full combat armor. Tough enough to withstand a lighter caliber round or anything but a direct hit from a trife or knife. Light and thin enough to conceal. She knew she was going to need it.

She reached into her pocket. A hole in the back allowed her to continue through to the sidearm strapped to her hip. It was the latest Centurion tech, a miniaturized railgun that fired three-centimeter smart-darts at nearly a thousand meters per second. A standard size magazine held almost a hundred rounds, and she had an extra magazine tucked into a pouch resting against the small of her back.

The pod arrived within a minute, the bullet-shaped transport sliding to a stop on a soft hiss of air. The doors opened, the passengers making the exchange. Rico boarded near the rear, taking a seat by the doors and leaning back. The ride from Dome Three to Dome One would only take a minute, the pod rocketing just beneath the surface of the rocky planet. She felt the slight increase of momentum past the inertial dampening systems, and then again as the pod decelerated to a stop at Dome Two.

The process repeated, and she was standing when the doors opened.

She walked briskly through the station and up to the surface. The streets weren't crowded, the motorized traffic limited to a few scattered scooters and smaller vehicles. Rico hurried across the street, following one of the many narrow side streets that split the taller buildings. She needed to get across town, out of the more wealthy neighborhoods and into the Dregs.

That wasn't the official name for the oldest slums in Dome One, but that's what most of the residents called it. It was everything a slum was supposed to be. Dirty, crime-ridden,populated by addicts and thieves. The largest Reclamation Center in Praeton was located in the Dregs, offering temporary housing to nearly a thousand ex-convicts who had completed their sentences on off-world mining rigs and were hoping to make a new start.

But new starts were hard to come by on Proxima. Honest businesses didn't want to give cons another chance, and the Trust was ever-present, always on the lookout for the next desperate soul they could twist to their needs. A lot of the Center residents lost faith in the process and hope in their future, only adding to the already existing quality of life in their part of the dome.

Rico was alone and on foot, but she didn't hesitate to enter the Dregs, and she didn't worry about running into trouble. She was a former Centurion Marine. A clone with enough resemblance to her source material that any sober thugs would recognize her as someone to steer clear of. Any non-sober thugs wouldn't stand a chance anyway.

She made her way down the street, checking the time in a translucent overlay embedded in her eye. It had taken twenty minutes to reach the Dregs from her apartment in

Dome Three. Not bad. Even so, she was sure her contact was already waiting.

She could smell the Reclamation Center before she saw it, the scent of sweat getting thicker as she neared the building. Passing through one of the splits, it moved into her line of sight—a tall, wide building that nearly touched the top of the dome. It didn't look all that bad from the outside, save for the number of windows that had layers of gel patch over the cracks in them and the graffiti along the base. Then there were the ex-cons, sitting idly on the sidewalk outside the building in a group nearly one hundred strong.

"Hey Chica!" one of them yelled to her as she approached. "You looking for a man?"

Rico smiled. "Actually, I am. Is Able around?"

A group of six cons stood up, quickly surrounding her. "Who's asking?" one of them asked.

"Special Officer Rico Rodriguez," she replied.

"What generation are you?" a woman in the background asked. Rico looked over at her. She had a similar build and nearly identical hair, though her face was a little wider. She was a Rodriguez too.

"Sixth," Rico said.

"Damn," Rodriguez replied. "I wish I was sixth. I'm a fourth."

"You look good for your age."

"What good is that going to do me? No work for cons unless you want to join the Trust. I made a mistake, but I was a good soldier. No way I'm signing up with them."

"Copy that," Rico said.

"Special Officer," the man blocking her path said. "Centurion Spacer?"

"Adjunct. I told you, I'm looking for Able."

"What's your business with him?"

"That's my business."

"I'm making it my business."

"Are you his bodyguard?"

"No. Just a concerned friend. Able's a popular guy the last couple of days."

"Who else came to see him?"

"Some gort with silver-blonde hair."

Rico nearly bit her tongue. "Last name Bennett?" she asked.

"How'd you know?"

"Lucky guess." Her heart fluttered anew. "I need to see Able. Now."

The man rubbed at his chin. "How much is it worth to you?"

Rico was tired of the game. She lunged forward faster than the man could react, grabbing his neck and twisting him into a choke hold. "How much is your life worth to you? I'm a Special Officer. I can get away with it."

The man started coughing, his eyes dancing to his henchmen, expecting them to help. They weren't going to. Not against a Spacer clone.

"Ghost's Tavern," the man wheezed out. "Two strands east, and then—"

"I know where it is," Rico said, letting the man go. "Thanks for your cooperation."

She hurried away, not bothering to look back. The cons wouldn't harass her. Their lives were shit, but they still wanted to live them.

She was more confused than ever. What the hell was Haeri planning, and why had he sent a Bennett?

9

Rico

There was a time when Ghost's had been a popular place of business. Back when Praeton had first been founded and Dome One was the only dome in the city. It still wore the callbacks to that golden age proudly, it's stark metal interior a reminder of the days before the replicators were unpacked and the raw materials processed.

But the owner of the place kept the aluminum walls, table and bar polished. He kept the floor clean. The bathrooms cleaner. He provided live music, and his liquor was still made the same way it had been back then—cheap and hard.

It was early enough in the evening that there was still enough of a crowd in the old pub to fill the tables and most of the stools at the bar. The band was thankfully taking a break, keeping the volume down enough for Rico to hear herself think.

She approached the bar, knocking on the surface to get the bartender's attention. He was a burly man with a thick beard and enormous arms, his hair cut in a mohawk. He smiled when he saw her.

"Is that Rico Rodriguez?" he asked.

"It is," she replied. "It's been a long time, Jake."

"Hell yes it has," he replied. "I thought you were too good for Ghost's these days?"

"Not by choice. I've been on assignment."

"For six years?"

She nodded. "I'm still on assignment. I need to talk to Able."

Jake pointed up and to the left. Rico followed his finger to the second floor of the establishment, where a metal walkway provided access to private rooms.

"Thanks, Jake," Rico said.

Jake nodded in reply. He had been a Spacer once too. One of the few to get a job after Reclamation. Of course, it helped that the Trust had a substantial ownership stake in Ghost's. Jake knew better than to ask questions when it came to Centurion business.

Or Trust business.

Rico still wasn't sure which one she was working for at the moment.

She made her way across the bar, slipping between the other patrons and climbing the stairs. She headed to the room Jake had pointed out. The door was closed, the window beside it opaque. She knocked. "Able. It's Rico."

It took a couple of seconds before a muscular thug pulled the door open. Standing beside it, he glared at her. She ignored him, her eyes crossing to the aluminum table in the center of the room where half-downed drinks rested beside crumb covered plates. An elderly woman sat directly behind it. Rico's eyes tracked to the right where a muscular soldier with silver-blonde hair and two days' of scruff sat, looking back at her.

All of the air went out of her, and she balled her hands into fists to keep her reaction localized. Including a

Bennett was intentional. Designed to pull her deeper into whatever web Haeri was spinning. And she knew she was trapped the moment she saw him.

"Austin," she said lightly, still staring at the clone.

"Ryan," he replied, smiling. He knew why she reacted the way she did. Did he know this moment was the reason he had been grown?

The heavy beside her wanted to close the door. She stepped aside to let him, returning her attention to Able. Her contact was thin and stylish, with white hair and a semi-wrinkled face that had been rejuvenated at least twice. "What is this about?"

"You got the files, I assume?"

"I wouldn't be here otherwise." She knew Able as an informant for Centurion Intelligence. Was he a member of the Trust too? "I'm not going to get court-martialed for this, am I?"

"No guarantees. What we're looking at is way beyond politics or laws."

"The Hunger is coming," Rico said.

"With a vengeance," Bennett replied.

"I need more intel than that."

"No, you don't," General Haeri said as he opened the door and stepped into the room beside her. He had traded in his uniform for a pair of worn jeans and a synth leather jacket, and his clean-shaven face for a line of stubble. Rico would never have recognized him if he weren't standing right there, his face in full view.

"General Haeri," she said, coming to attention out of habit.

"Relax, Rico," he replied. "I'm not here as a general of the CSF."

"The Trust?" she asked.

"No. Not the Trust, either. Not exactly."

"What does that mean?"

"We had a three-day window for you to catch up on your own, so you're slightly ahead of schedule."

"I'm sorry, sir. I don't follow you."

"But you understand the danger we're in. An enemy starship is on its way here."

"Yes, sir. What I don't understand is why we're talking about it in secret here instead of sounding an alarm."

"Because the time for alarm hasn't arrived yet. The ship's position and velocity means it will be another week before it passes Proxima, and a week after that before it reaches Earth."

"Passes Proxima? It looked like it was headed right *for* Proxima."

"It'll go past by about three AU, assuming it maintains its current trajectory. We haven't figured out yet if the path is intentional and it's sending a message, or we just happen to be in its way, but we're pretty sure it's going to Earth first."

"Who's we?" Rico asked.

"The less you know about that, the better," Haeri replied. "Let's all have a seat."

The general walked past her, sliding in beside Able and leaving her no choice but to sit across from Bennett. She did, forcing herself to stay professional as she looked across at him. Clones were supposed to have their genetics modified just enough so that their physical appearance was unique. It was better for their mental health. But with Austin gone, his code was fair game, and Haeri hadn't wasted any time playing with it. Ryan Bennett was an identical copy of her late husband.

"Why him?" Rico asked, pointing at Bennett. She had never been one to mince words, and if Haeri said not to treat him like a general, then she was going for the jugular.

Haeri smiled. "I know what you're thinking, Rico. And on one level, you're correct. I want your loyalty in this. I need your loyalty in this. And if this is the best way to get it, then that's what I'm going to do."

"That's pretty twisted," Rico said.

"I don't care. This is bigger than morality. And it isn't the only reason. Bennett was one of the best soldiers we've had in the last fifty years. The Council jumped at the chance to bring him back."

"That isn't him."

"I know this is awkward," Bennett said. "But I am sitting right here."

Rico looked at him. "Sorry. This is a bit—"

"I understand," he said. "But we have a mission to worry about."

Rico had to remind herself he wasn't Austin. But that was exactly what he would have said.

"Let's stay focused," Haeri said. "Able, thanks for helping me arrange this."

"Of course, Aeron."

"Rico, I know you aren't sure about my motives, and that's fine. Suffice it to say, I've got the best interests of humankind at heart. Not only Proxima. All of humanity. I've had a long time to think about how to best ensure our survival in a universe that's a lot bigger and scarier than most people realize, and I recognize that we can't do it alone. In that sense, Isaac's arrival has been incredibly valuable, especially considering how it came about."

"We've only got two weeks," Rico replied. "Can you be a little more forthright?"

Haeri smiled. "That's why I chose you, Rico. You don't flinch. You get things done."

"I want to get things done right now."

"I'll keep it simple. We're preparing a counter-offensive

just in case the Relyeh ship does decide to stop here instead of continuing to Earth. But if it doesn't, we need to be able to attack the problem there."

"You mean Sheriff Duke?"

He nodded. "I mean Sheriff Duke. Like you, he's already proven he can get things done."

"So why all of this bullshit? Why not just send me back to Earth on a diplomatic mission?"

"Two reasons. One, I want Isaac to go with you, and the Council refuses to allow it, at least not before they pick his brain for everything he knows. He's the only survivor from the original trife invasion. You can imagine what that means to them."

"I can imagine it means they don't want him getting out into the open and countering the lies the entire planet's been living under for the last two hundred years."

"I'm impressed. You know how to play the game."

"It's not as hard as you want to think."

"I had to arrest him and put him in solitary. Council's orders."

"That's illegal."

"I know. So does the Council. But he's dangerous. And nobody will miss him."

"I missed him."

"Did you consider that put a target on your head too?"

Rico froze. She hadn't considered it.

"It might not be as easy as you want to think," Haeri said. "In any case, I need to get you and Isaac back to Earth to warn Sheriff Duke that things are going to get ugly in two weeks time."

"Don't you mean in a week's time? It'll take a week just to get there."

"We think we can get you there a little faster. How does two days sound?"

There was the anonymous 'we' again. If it wasn't the military or the Trust, who was Haeri referring to?

"How?"

"One of our scientists, Niobe Stacker, was working on an algorithm to improve space fold efficiencies," Haeri said. "Unfortunately, she didn't get to finish that work. But she got us far enough along that we were able to improve the calculations and upload the new algorithms into the fold computer of one of our ships. It'll drop you a lot closer to Earth than our current math."

"Is this a Centurion ship?"

"Not exactly."

"You're saying that a lot, Aeron."

"There are good people on Proxima who are doing dangerous things to make this happen. Things that will bring the wrong kind of attention from the Council, the military and the Trust. They all have their own agendas."

"And you don't?"

"I do. I told you, my motivation is to preserve humankind on both planets. I'm not the only one who feels that way."

"Sheriff Duke doesn't trust you."

"No, he doesn't. That's why I'm sending you and Isaac."

"Okay, so you have a ship for us. That sounds like the easy part."

"It is. I can't release Isaac to you without risking my cover. You'll need to break him out."

Rico smiled. "So, there it is."

"Yes."

She leaned back against the seat and sighed. "Can you get us equipment?"

"I'll take care of that," Able said.

"My fingerprints can't be anywhere on this or we're going to fail," Haeri said.

"And I can trust Bennett here?"

"Yes," Bennett replied. "I've got your back, Rico."

"He was coded to be loyal to me first and you second," Haeri said.

"That kind of coding is illegal," Rico replied.

"Everything you're about to do is illegal. But it just might save Earth. Hell, it just might save us all."

Rico picked up her head. Then she stood up, leaning over the table. "Then what are we waiting for?"

10

Rico

Rico had expected Isaac to be held in the brig on the Centurion Space Force base at the center of Praeton, and she was surprised when General Haeri told her she was wrong.

According to Haeri, while the brig in CSF Alpha was secure, it was also too high profile to make someone like Isaac disappear. Instead, the Council needed a place they could trust with certainty. A place that didn't carry the risk of someone saying too much to the wrong person.

A place outside the domes of Praeton.

They were sitting in a coffee shop, at a table near the window. Six hours had passed since their meeting with General Haeri, which had concluded with Able leading them from the private room to a hidden back door out of Ghost's and into a waiting transport. The transport had carried them to a warehouse the other side of the dome where Able had efficiently fulfilled each of Rico's requests, albeit with a personal twist on the meaning of some of her asks. With that done, they had been afforded a few hours to rest before boarding the transport again, taking it only a short distance before they were unloaded into the foot traffic to make their own way.

"What's our plan?" Bennett asked.

Rico glanced over at the clone, only maintaining eye contact for a moment before looking away. Bennett's eyes seemed to penetrate her soul without trying, digging too damn deep into her for her liking.

She looked out the window, raising her head to gaze up past the dome to the massive silhouette of the generation starship Dove at rest in the distance. Nineteen ships had landed on Proxima within a two-week span over two hundred years earlier, each of the ships having ferried between thirty and forty thousand settlers away from an alien-ravaged Earth to start a new life. The Dove was the first to arrive, the founding ship and cornerstone of Praeton. It was still in use today, home to a museum, a CSF starship hangar, and most importantly the Proxima Civilian Council and its adjunct political bureaus.

She had laughed when General Haeri told her Isaac was being held in the same apartments where dignitaries from Proxima's other cities would stay during sessions of the planet's Congress, finding it sadly amusing that it was the only place the Council felt it could trust. Then again, they intended to make a legal citizen of Proxima vanish without a trace.

The whole situation bordered on insanity.

She tapped on the small, flesh-colored patch Able had adhered to her wrist over her real identification chip. The fake would identify her as an employee of the Praeton History Museum, which was located in the smaller hangar near the back of the two-kilometer long ship. Bennett wore a matching patch that would claim he was an administrative assistant for the representative of Caesar, one of the smaller cities along the tropical hemisphere, about six hundred kilometers away.

"Chips get us in," she said quietly, reaching down to tug on the hem of her brown skirt, part of the uniform the museum guides wore. She hadn't been in a skirt since she was eight years old. "Uniforms get us close." She patted her large purse slightly, referencing the bodysuit and sidearm inside. "This gets us out."

"I don't think museum guide was the best choice," Bennett said. "A skirt? Don't you think you'll be recognized as a Rodriguez?"

He was in a navy blue guard uniform, a utility vest strapped over his shirt and a bodysuit resting beneath it. His sidearm was part of his suit.

Lucky bastard.

"Able apparently doesn't think so," she replied. "Either that or he has some personal vendetta against me that I would've rather settled with a death match."

Bennett laughed, and Rico's heart fell again. It had been months since she had heard that laugh. Damn, she missed her husband. "Maybe when this is over, you can get your wish."

She forced a smile. "Something to live for. I'll go first. Wait ten minutes and then follow behind me."

"Yes, ma'am."

"And don't call me ma'am. Not when we're about to break about a hundred laws. Rico will do."

"Copy that."

She stood up, straightened the skirt heading for the door. She was uncomfortable walking in high heels instead of combat boots. Maybe if she were going out to a fancy dinner or to a show, she could make do. But to break a non-fugitive out of a non-prison and steal a non-military starship? She didn't even know if she could run in the damn things.

She left the coffee shop, crossing to the closest loop station. She boarded the next pod. It stopped twice before coming back to the surface near the Centauri river, the lifeblood of the city. The clear water flowed through a crevice in the surface rock that was nearly twenty meters deep and ten meters wide.

The Dove had landed beside the river, and a short, transparent tunnel— offering access to both vehicles and pedestrians—had been built to connect the aged ship to the city. It was early morning now, and a flow of workers were already en route to their positions inside the vessel. Rico was careful to keep an eye out for other museum employees, certain they would know she was out of place. Able had already run the calculations and provided the excuse. The museum didn't open until nine, and she was arriving early to get a head start on the day.

Why not?

A Centurion checkpoint waited at the end of the tunnel, a guardhouse positioned between the two-lane road and the sidewalk. A pair of Centurion Marines stood on either side of the guardhouse, keeping watch while the pedestrians swiped their identification chips over a scanner. A Sentry bot hunched a few meters further back, waiting for trouble. It had been waiting a long time. There was zero history of violence within the Proxima Commons, the show of force more show than force.

That was possibly about to change.

Rico grabbed at her hair, ensuring her wig was secure. She hoped the Marines wouldn't recognize her as a Rodriguez. She had the facial features, but hopefully the wig, glasses and uniform would be enough to disguise her.

Why wouldn't it? She knew she was up to no good, but they had no reason to suspect her.

She forced herself to remain calm as she made it to the scanner. She slid her wrist over it, her face appearing on a display beside the machine under a different name. She didn't know how Able managed to create the false ID. Before today, she had thought the system was nearly unbeatable. Obviously, that wasn't the case.

She didn't make eye contact with the Marines as she went past, keeping her head down and trying to look confident. She glanced at the Sentry as she drew even with it. The robot didn't pay her any mind.

She was in.

A short walk brought her to an escalator, which carried her up from the ground level to the lowest airlock in the side of the starship. She went through the airlock and into an open corridor that arced gradually along the outer bulkhead. She turned left and continued walking.

The museum was in a straight line down the corridor, nearly a kilometer away from the entrance. Bennett wouldn't come this way. Instead, he would take another passage across the starship to the central bank of lifts. A small group was already waiting there for the lift to arrive, and she slipped into their midst when it did.

The lift ascended half a dozen decks, stopping at sixteen. The doors opened and the passengers all filed out. Rico lingered in the back, letting them all get ahead.

"Rico, do you copy?" Bennett said.

"I copy," Rico replied in a whisper. "What's your position?"

"Approaching the checkpoint."

"Roger. I'm on Deck Sixteen, headed for Metro. Ping me when you're in position."

"Copy. Bennett out."

Rico followed the group from the lift and down a trio of interconnected corridors to an open, double-wide hatch. A brass plaque hung over the hatch commemorating the city's establishment.

She stayed behind the others as they made their way from the hatch down another corridor which sloped gently down to the city proper. This part of the ship had once been home to the engineers who had been responsible for keeping the life support systems running. Most of those systems were offline now. Unneeded. Only the air scrubbers and water filtration units were still in use.

It was a long walk to get from the entrance of the ship to the city. There were shorter routes, but they were reserved for VIPs like politicians, high-ranking military and their entourages. In any case, the security through the express gate was even tighter than the civilian entrance.

It didn't matter.

They wouldn't be using either path to escape.

There was another way out.

A better way.

11

Isaac

Isaac paced across the living area of the small apartment, walking from the door to the bedroom to the window and back again. He was restless and frustrated, tired of waiting for something to happen.

When General Haeri had turned on him and summoned the guards, he thought he would wind up in a prison cell somewhere, in solitary confinement. And he did. For the first twenty-four hours, he'd been stuck in a cement box with nothing to do but stare at the ceiling. Haeri had come back after that and asked him a second time if he would join the Centurion Space Force as a spy.

He said no a second time.

He wasn't going to turn on Hayden or Earth. Sheriff Duke had given him somewhere to belong, and Earth was his home. It would always be his home. His wife and children had lived there.

And died there.

The trife invasion had changed the entire planet so quickly. First, the virus wiped out billions, and then the aliens went to work on the rest. That was only the first part of the story because the real war didn't start and end with the xenotrife.

The invasion had yet to truly begin.

The Relyeh had conquered hundreds of civilizations across thousands of light years. But they didn't eliminate their enemies. They absorbed them, using a portion of the population as food, a portion as soldiers and a portion to enhance their genetic library. They were powerful, numerous and maybe most importantly—patient. They were willing to bide their time to finish capturing a world. They were willing to sit in wait while their first line of attack did ninety percent of the damage.

Trife were the perfect weapon. They multiplied faster than the military could kill them, relying on radiation as their food. Most times, that meant power stations. Generators. The very thing advanced human civilization relied on to remain an advanced civilization. But it would never be enough to drop a massive EMP on the planet. The Earth's core produced enough heat to fuel the aliens—all they had to do was dig deep enough.

Isaac was there in the beginning, when the unexpected asteroid storm rained down on the planet and left a powder of debris across so much of the surface. The scientists called it a one-in-a-trillion event. A lot of them believed it was accidental. A random act of space. Even as the virus started killing millions and the world began to panic, nobody thought it was an act of aggression. Even when the first trife emerged from the dust and began their killing, only the conspiracy theorists thought of it as an act of war.

His survival was a matter of circumstance. Of luck, though he wasn't sure if it was good or bad. The brain tumor had made him accidentally valuable to the Relyeh because it also made him resistant to the best defense of the only race that had so far maintained a resistance against the Hunger. Solve the riddle of his resistance, break the stalemate. At least, that was the plan. Only the Relyeh never found out his protection was based on a fatal flaw, one that couldn't be reproduced without also being fatal. He was an anomaly. A disease. But he had been preserved because of it. Thrown in stasis to wait until the Hunger was ready to use him. Because they were patient above all.

That patience seemed to be at an end, and Isaac could guess why. The Axon were thousands of years more advanced than humankind. They had technology he could barely believe. And they were holding the Hunger back. Slowing their advance across the galaxy and fighting their domination. They were the fly in the ointment, the wrench in the gears of conquest. Their soldiers were machines. Self-replicating, artificially intelligent machines with a host of offensive and defensive tactics that made a single one of them more powerful than a million trife.

They shared a common enemy and should have been the perfect allies. But humans were like mice to the Axon. Primitive creatures that scurried back and forth with no real purpose save to reproduce. There was no benefit for them to align themselves with a race on the brink of destruction. There was nothing for them to gain. Earth sat in the middle of two warring factions, left to fend for itself and somehow find a way to keep going against impossible odds.

Odds that were going to get worse. It was only a matter of time.

Every resource counted. Every asset helped. Sheriff Duke had managed to convince a single Axon Intellect that maybe the two races could help one another. It was the best chance humankind would ever have to avoid the fate that had befallen hundreds of other intelligences.

And General Haeri had rejected it as bullshit.

Isaac threw a fist into the padded back of his couch in frustration. When Sheriff Duke had sent him to Proxima with Rico, it was with a mind that the general would be willing to listen to reason. It was with the understanding that Haeri was also part of the Trust and the belief that the Trust wasn't merely a crime syndicate but a secret line of defense against whichever enemy posed the most significant threat.

It turned out Hayden was wrong. Proxima's ongoing belief that Earth wasn't worth saving permeated deeper into their psyche than he'd expected. While Rico—a clone of all things—was on board with the notion that the survivors back home were worth saving, the general had made it clear he didn't agree.

And now Isaac was stuck here. Waiting…

For what?

He didn't know why Haeri hadn't left him in the brig in solitary confinement. Why had he been transferred here? He was still a prisoner. There were armed guards outside his door around the clock. So what was the point? To give him a soft couch to sit on? A comfortable bed to sleep in?

To what end?

He didn't need any of that. He was a Marine. Comfort was nice, but it was ultimately bullshit. He wanted action. Direction. If Haeri wouldn't accept the truth, if he wanted Sheriff Duke dead, then he didn't need Isaac. Why not just kill him already?

There had to be more to the story. Something happening in the background. A reason he was still alive. Did they want more information from him?

If that were true, why hadn't anyone come to question him? Why was he stuck here, endlessly pacing?

He couldn't believe they had saved his life for this.

Isaac gave up the line of thinking, moving to the front of the couch and collapsing on it. Maybe this was some kind of modern day torture.

He closed his eyes and thought of Amanda, piecing together his memories of the simple things that had made him love her. The way she laughed at his jokes. Her devotion to the kids. How beautiful she looked in sweatpants with her hair wildly bound up on top of her head. Her kindness and compassion for others.

He missed her.

He missed them all.

He started to doze off.

A loud thump against the door and his eyes snapped open. He heard another thump, and then a third, making the wall of his apartment shake.

What the hell?

He quickly scanned the room, looking for something to use as a weapon. There was nothing. He gave up the idea, crossing the room to the front door, which was kept locked from the outside.

"Myles?" he shouted. He had spent some time chatting with the guards through the door, because what else was there to do? "Paula?"

Something hit the door hard, causing him to jump back into a defensive crouch. Isaac moved laterally, getting in position to attack whoever came through.

Someone broke the door in, hitting it so hard it collapsed back onto the apartment floor. A woman in a black bodysuit rushed in, leading with some kind of pistol with a thick barrel. Isaac spotted three more similarly armed people behind her.

He lunged at her, slamming his hand down on her extended gun hand, trying to knock the weapon from her grip. She absorbed the blow, pivoting gracefully and grabbing his arm as he threw his weight against her. She kept turning with it, lifting him and throwing him over her shoulder, onto the floor.

The landing knocked the air out of him. How was she so strong? He didn't hesitate, rolling over to get back up. She kicked him in the stomach, straining his ribs and knocking him onto his side.

"Time to die," the woman said, pointing her pistol at him.

Isaac stared up at her. He had been waiting for something to happen.

This wasn't exactly what he'd had in mind.

12

Isaac

Isaac's eyes shifted to the barrel of the gun, waiting for the flash that would signal the end of his life.

It didn't come.

Gunshots cracked from outside the room and the woman looked back toward the door. Isaac didn't waste the opportunity. Pushing his attacker off him, he stumbled to his feet and dived behind the couch. Moments later, silent rounds tore through the couch stuffing millimeters above his head, burying themselves in the wall behind him.

He heard a grunt and then a thump, and the woman was suddenly grappling with another woman in a brown skirt-suit. They hit the floor next to the couch, the skirted woman straddling his attacker and trying to get control of her gun.

She looked over at Isaac. "A little help?"

Isaac finally recognized her, and he scrambled over, grabbing the assassin's arm and helping Rico pin it to the ground. The assist allowed Rico to throw a series of hard punches into the other woman's temples, the force of the blows sufficient to overcome the protection of her helmet and knock her out.

"Rico, what the…," he started to say, going silent when he caught sight of another threat coming through the door. He grabbed the pistol from the unconscious woman's hand, rose and took aim at the man pointing a gun at him.

The man collapsed before he pulled the trigger, revealing a security guard behind him, gun pointed in his direction.

Isaac shifted his aim to what he perceived to be a second new threat. This man however lowered his weapon.

"He's with me," Rico said, getting to her feet.

"With you?" Isaac parroted. "Rico, what the hell is going on? And who is *he*?" he asked, waving the pistol at the only other man still on his feet.

"That's Bennett. We're getting you out of here," she replied.

"How did you know where to find me?" he asked.

"I have my ways. Bennett, grab my bag. I dropped it in the hall."

She started to undress, quickly pulling off the brown jacket and going to work on her blouse buttons.

Isaac turned back around to see her shimmy out of her skirt and kick off her shoes. She was down to her bra and panties when Bennett came back into the room holding a large purse.

"These idiots screwed up the plan," he said, kicking the dead man in his boot before tossing the bag onto the couch.

"We'll make a new plan," Rico replied, unzipping the bag. She lifted a black bodysuit from it, quickly stepping into the light armor. "Who do you think sent them?"

"Haeri?" Isaac offered.

"No," she said. "It wasn't Haeri."

"How do you know?"

Rico closed her bodysuit and reached into the bag again, removing a sidearm. She snapped it to the hip of her armor before glancing over at the downed soldier.

"Isaac, his helmet's got a hole in the back but the body-suit will stretch to fit you. Hurry up and put it on."

Isaac rounded the couch, grabbing the dead man and turning him over. "How do I open the suit?"

"I've got it," Bennett said, crouching across from Isaac and grabbing at the straps across the front of the armor. He had the assassin stripped in seconds.

"How do you know it wasn't Haeri?" Isaac asked again. "That asshole didn't listen to a word I had to say. He called me a liar and stuffed me in here."

"And then sent Dark Ops to kill you?" Rico asked. "What would be the point of that? If he wanted you dead he could have gotten rid of you three days ago."

"You're saying someone put him up to it?"

"I'm saying it isn't that cut and dried. Suit up. Move it, Marine."

Isaac pulled on the bodysuit. Bennett helped him seal it and then handed him the dead woman's gun.

"That's a CGS-20," he said. "Coilgun. The sound suppressor is built into the design. Silent and deadly at close range."

"Tell me about it," Isaac said, taking the weapon and attaching it to the magnetic mount on his hip. "Damn near killed me with it."

"Here," Rico said, handing him a small earpiece.

Isaac accepted it and slipped it into his ear.

"Can you hear me?" she asked.

"Pozz," Isaac replied, her voice loud and clear over the comm. "I copy."

"Good. We were trying to get in and out of here

without causing a scene, but since somebody sent this kill team in ahead of us, we'll have to play things by ear. I'm not too happy about that, but it is what it is. We've got a ride waiting in the main hangar. We just need to get there. I imagine the alternate ops teams and your guards, once they wake up, will try to stop us. They're just doing their jobs, so make sure you only kill the bad guys. "

"How do I make the distinction?"

"Bad guys," Bennett said, pointing at the two dead assassins. Then he pointed at himself. "Good guys."

"Roger that," Isaac said. "Why are we still standing here?"

Rico smiled. "Bennett, you have point."

"Roger," Bennett replied, moving out into the corridor. He waved them ahead, and they stepped over the bodies of the dead assassins and ran for the end of the hallway.

"Where are we?" Isaac asked as they reached a lift.

"You don't know?" Rico replied.

"They blindfolded me on the way in."

"Try not to let the irony kill you on the way down. Bennett, we'll take the stairs."

Bennett redirected to the right, moving around the side of the lift to an emergency staircase. He went down first, sweeping the area with his gun. "Clear."

"Irony? What does that mean?" Isaac said.

"This is temporary housing for the Proxima Civilian Council," Rico said. "You're as close to the planetary government as anyone gets. But apparently none of the freedoms apply to you despite your legal right to citizenship." She rolled her eyes.

"And they say clones get the short end of the stick," Bennett said.

"The Council brought you here to make you disappear," Rico added. "And somebody wants you dead."

The stairwell echoed as one of the doors opened beneath them. Bennett pulled up, stopping them and retreating as bullets began hitting the wall ahead of him.

"Somebody *really* wants you dead," he said. "We need another way out."

13

Isaac

"Rooftop," Rico said. "I'll take point."

She reversed course, leading Isaac and Bennett back up the steps. They didn't re-emerge onto the same floor as Isaac's apartment—the thirtieth—instead continuing to climb. Isaac heard the footsteps behind them as they charged up the stairs, fighting to stay ahead of the soldiers.

"Rico, this is Haeri," the General said, his voice cutting into their comm connection. "We've been compromised."

"I'm aware of that, sir," Rico replied. "How?"

"Unknown. Sitrep."

"We've got the package in our possession, but evacuation is proving challenging. We're headed for the rooftop."

"I'll arrange assistance."

"Sir, do they know you're involved?"

"Also unknown. I'm monitoring the situation. Your mission is the priority."

"Roger."

They continued climbing, reaching the fortieth floor.

"How many floors does this building have?" Isaac asked. He was starting to get a little winded, while Rico and Bennett seemed completely unfazed.

"Forty-two," Rico replied. "We're almost there."

They reached the forty-second floor, ascending the last row of steps to the door leading out onto the rooftop. Rico pushed it open and fell back. She grabbed Isaac's arm, pulling him with her as a barrage of gunfire erupted into the doorway. The bullets tore into the walls and door, nearly shredding it to pieces as they rolled down the steps together, coming to a stop at Bennett's feet.

Bennett crouched over them, ready to shoot at the first person to step through the splintered door.

"Isaac, are you okay?" Rico asked.

"Pozz," Isaac replied. "You?"

"Nothing serious." Rico pulled herself up. Isaac noticed blood running down her bodysuit from her arm.

Nothing serious?

"They're going to wait for the team on the stairs to catch up," Bennett said. "We can't stay here."

"We can't go up there," Isaac said. "It's suicide."

"We try to lose them on this floor," Bennet said. "Circle back to the stairs and go down."

"No time," Rico replied. "We have to go up and out. I'll get their attention."

She took a step toward the roof. Bennett grabbed her arm. "No. I'll do it," he said. "Sheriff Duke trusts you."

"We're going back to Earth?" Isaac said.

Rico nodded. "That's the plan. If we can get to the hangar."

She stared at Bennett. There was something in her eyes Isaac didn't expect. A strange mix of sadness and relief. Who was this soldier to her?

"You're up," she said to Bennett.

"Roger that." He started up the steps, staying close to the side. "Get ready."

A sudden whine sounded from outside, followed by the rapid-fire thumping of a machine gun. Isaac expected to see Bennett get thrown backward by the sudden massive attack. Instead, he started waving them up.

They rushed to the top of the steps and out onto the rooftop. The enemy soldiers were all down, a small, armed drone floating in the space between the roof and what looked like another ceiling. Smoke was pouring from the cannon mounted to its snubbed nose.

"You're clear," a new voice said through their comm.

"Thanks, Able," Rico replied.

"You don't have a lot of time. Security drones are on the way."

"Roger. So are the other soldiers." Rico glanced at Bennett and then Isaac. Her face was tight with pain, her arm still bleeding. She pointed toward another nearby rooftop. It seemed to Isaac that the buildings were all identical in height. "Over two blocks and down. Able, can you keep them from closing the seals?"

"Working on it," Able said.

"Let's go."

Rico guided them across the rooftop at a sprint. She didn't slow as she neared the edge of the building, gathering herself and jumping. She landed smoothly a few meters away, tucking her shoulder and rolling back to her feet.

"Don't look down," Bennett said.

Isaac could tell there was a gap between the rooftops. He didn't love the idea of jumping, but he knew they didn't have a choice. He leaped, glancing down as he passed over the gap. He came down feet-first, stumbling. Rico caught him.

"You should have rolled," she said.

"Next time," he replied.

Bennett joined them. They charged across the rooftop toward another building.

A buzzing noise quickly intensified in volume. They were halfway across the rooftop when a trio of blue and white drones with flashing lights mounted to the tops cleared the edge of the building ahead.

"Stop. Put your hands up."

The voice was deep and tinny through the drones' loudspeakers.

Isaac began to slow.

Rico and Bennett didn't.

They raised their pistols and started to shoot. The drones reacted immediately to the threat, firing back and taking evasive action. Too slow. The rounds ripped into the machines, shredding through delicate parts and sending them crashing downward, trailing smoke as they vanished from sight.

Rico made the edge of the building first, leaping the gap to the next. Isaac picked up the pace again. He hit the edge of the rooftop and pushed off, launching through the air. He was halfway across when he realized he didn't have enough speed and wasn't going to make it.

A rapid heartbeat later, a strong arm wrapped around him, grabbing him in mid-air. Bennett flew easily over the gap holding Isaac, and they landed roughly on the other side, tumbling to a stop.

Isaac clenched his teeth, his ribs twinging from the landing.

Bennett hopped back up, holding out his hand. "Come on."

Isaac took it, and Bennett pulled him back up.

"You're hit," Isaac said, noticing the three small darts implanted in Bennett's shoulder and chest.

"Stun rounds," Bennett replied. "Put a charge in me." Isaac could see his smile through his helmet visor. "Civilian law enforcement isn't equipped to handle clones."

"Less chatter, more running," Rico said. "Ike, you okay?"

"Pozz," Isaac replied. "It's only my pride that's hurt."

"Don't compare yourself to us. You did great."

"For a normal human, right?"

"You did great," Rico repeated. "Come on."

They made it to the building's emergency stairs. Rico swiped her wrist over the control pad. A red LED flashed.

"Shit," Rico said. "Able, do you copy? My chip's dead."

There was no response.

"I've got it," Bennett said, swiping his wrist over the panel. The LED flashed green. "They haven't figured out yet whose ID I'm using."

"They will now," Rico replied.

"Too late." He pushed open the door. "Ladies first."

Rico smirked and headed into the stairwell. Isaac went in behind her, with Bennett taking the rear. They bounded down the steps two and three at a time, rushing to the fortieth floor. Rico led them out of the stairs and across to the lift, tapping on the control pad. It left them static in the hallway while they waited for the cab to arrive.

"What is this place?" Isaac asked.

"The main hold of the Dove," Rico replied.

Isaac recognized the name. "The Dove? You mean the generation ship?"

"That's the one."

"This is Metro?"

"That's right."

Isaac couldn't believe it. He had heard people talking about the ships while he was stationed in Dugway. He knew they were putting cities inside them. He hadn't realized he was in one of them now.

The lift arrived, the doors sliding open. They piled in and started to descend.

"The settlers who landed here used the blocks to build out Dome One," Rico explained. "Everything in here now is a reproduction. There are nineteen blocks arranged in a square around the main congress. One for each of the ships that landed here." She glanced at Bennett. "I expect opposition when we hit the ground. Good news is, we caused enough mayhem it'll make it hard for any more assassins to come at us."

"What's the bad news?" Isaac asked.

"They're going to send in the CSF," Bennett replied. "We've got about four minutes to get clear of the hold before the cavalry arrives."

Isaac had a vague idea of the size of the space from the renderings he'd seen. "Is that possible?"

"We'll make it happen," Rico said. "Bennett, stun rounds."

"Roger," Bennett said. He cycled the round from the chamber and then slipped the magazine from his gun, replacing it with another one, this one marked with a square of green at the bottom.

"Ike, don't shoot anyone," Rico said, swapping out her pistol's magazine too.

"Roger," Isaac replied. "Don't let me get shot."

"They'll be firing stunners too. It'll hurt, but you'll live."

Isaac glanced at the counter for the lift. They were almost to the bottom.

"Stay behind us," Bennett said.

The two clones moved in front of Isaac, guns raised and ready. The lift cab slowed to a stop as the counter hit zero.

And the doors slid open...

14

Rico

Rico's eyes flashed over the lobby. The civilians had already cleared out, leaving two squads of law enforcement officers spread behind limited cover. Three behind the registration desk. Two behind a couch. Four more in a pair of doorways on either side of the room, and one standing front and center, ready to order them to stand down.

Like that was going to happen.

She felt terrible about shooting the law officers, but the stun rounds would only knock them down and keep them frozen for a few minutes, which would be enough time for them to make their escape.

If they were able to escape.

The whole mission had gone sideways. Someone else on the outside was playing games of their own and had nearly gotten to Isaac first. Able was unresponsive, Haeri had gone silent, and the Centurion Space Force was no doubt on its way. Would their special starship be there when they arrived?

If they arrived.

There was no time to question. No time to doubt. The lift doors finished sliding open. Bennett was already shooting. She didn't need to communicate the objectives with him. She had worked with Bennett, her Bennett, long enough to know how he would approach the situation. She filled in the gaps, focusing on the two behind the couch. The lone officer in the center of the lobby was already falling to the floor, his body paralyzed by Bennett's stun round.

"Ike, stay behind Bennett!" she snapped, breaking to the left and firing at the officers behind the sofa. The good thing about the stunners was that they didn't need to hit any specific part of a person to be effective. A hit to the shoulder was the same as a hit to the chest or even a toe.

The officers saw her coming, and they redirected their attack toward her. She sprinted parallel to them, staying just ahead of their fire. She shot at them, the volume of her rounds ensuring she hit them. Both officers dropped from sight, temporarily frozen.

Rico dropped the empty magazine from her pistol, quickly swapping it for her other stunner mag. She dived forward, sliding across the floor to get behind a table. Shots hit the table and ricocheted harmlessly away as she shifted to her knees, pivoting ninety degrees to wind up in a direct line with one of the officers. They stared at one another for a split-second. He tried to bring his gun to bear. Too slow. Rico squeezed the trigger; the officer shuddered and collapsed.

"Clear," Bennett announced through the comm.

"Clear," she repeated, getting back to her feet.

A quick survey of the room showed all ten officers down. The last one she had shot was looking up at her, able to move his eyes but nothing else.

"Sorry about this," she said to him as she stepped over his prone body. "You'll be okay."

They hurried out of the building and into the street. A rumble in the distance signaled the approach of a large vehicle. The CSF was closing in.

"There," she said, pointing to a pair of police scooters resting along the curb.

"Rico!" Isaac cried. "Heads up."

Rico looked up. A pair of military drones zoomed overhead, slowing and banking to come back around.

"Get on!"

She hopped onto one of the scooters. Isaac mounted it behind her, wrapping his arms around her waist. She squeezed the throttle and the small transport shot forward, nearly causing Isaac to fall off.

They raced along the main street, quickly clearing the square of buildings that boxed in the Proxima government, breaking into a large park. Walking paths crossed manicured lawns, fields of flowers and sections of trees, each a different species or group of species brought from Earth. Dirt had been brought into the hold to add gently sloping hills and create basins for freshwater ponds where ducks were preening themselves and ignoring the chaos to come.

"Move!" Rico shouted, waving her arm at the civilians ahead of her. "Get out of the way!"

They scattered as she drove the scooter onto one of the paths. A steady flow of people—the crowd was a mixed blessing—came from the stern end of the ship, back toward the checkpoint where she had entered an hour earlier. They would force the defenders to be more stingy with their shots.

But it was also slowing them down.

"We've got company," Bennett said through the comm.

Rico risked a glance back over her shoulder. The open space behind them had allowed the drones to descend into prime firing position. The CSF transport was visible further back, approaching from a divergent direction.

"I can take them out," Bennett said.

"Negative. They might hit civilians on the way down." Rico turned her eyes forward again, breaking off the trail and taking to the grass to better avoid the pedestrians. Moving further from the civilians would give the drones a clearer shot, but she didn't want any of them getting hurt because of her.

She sped up, pushing the throttle nearly to its limit. They couldn't outrun the drones, but maybe they could outmaneuver them. She aimed the scooter toward a line of trees, zipping across the grass, Bennett hot on her tail. She started swerving left and right like she was in a slalom, avoiding a straight path to keep the drones from getting a lock.

"Almost there," she said, eying the trees ahead.

The scooter hit an incline, rocketing up it and launching into the air, coming down hard enough to slip out from under she and Isaac. Rico barely managed to maintain control, planting her foot to keep them upright as they went down the other side and into the waiting trees.

She glanced back. Bennett was right behind her. So was one of the drones. It entered the small patch of forest still on their tail. She weaved around the trunks, watching for raised roots as she threaded her way through the foliage.

The drone behind them opened fire, the rattle of its guns echoing around them as bullets tore into the trees.

"Shit!" Isaac cursed behind her.

Rico guided the scooter hard to the left, getting it

around a tree, which absorbed the rounds that would have otherwise chewed through them. She cut to the right, slamming on the brakes behind another large trunk. She could hear the shift in the drone's thrusters as it slowed to circle in on her. She grabbed her pistol and leveled it where she believed the machine would emerge.

The drone banked sideways around the the trunk, the wing becoming visible before the cannon could come to bear on them. Rico was ready for it. She emptied her magazine into the drone, the stunner rounds sending an overload of electricity through it. It sparked and hissed before dropping from the air.

"Nice," Isaac said.

Rico smirked as she snapped the gun back to her hip. Grabbing the handlebars, she spun the scooter back toward the exit to the city. Bennett slowed to come even with her, and they burst from the treeline together, racing across the grass toward the large, open hatch leading into the corridors of the Dove. The path ahead was clear, the transport falling further behind.

They were going to make it.

A sharp scream sounded from somewhere above. Then the ground exploded in front of Rico, pummeling her with a sudden shower of debris and causing her to lose control of the scooter. She dropped it as gracefully as she could, the bodysuit and grass absorbing the impact as both she and Isaac slid to a stop.

She pushed herself to her knees, finding Bennett on the ground a few meters away, also getting back to his feet. "Ike, are you okay?"

"I'm getting a little tired of falling down," he replied. "What the hell was that?"

"I can't believe they fired a rocket in here."

She stood up as the drone slowly descended in front of her, stopping at eye level.

"Special Officer Rodriguez," General Haeri said. "Put your hands over your head and wait for collection. You're under arrest."

15

Rico

Rico looked back at Isaac. She could see the anger and betrayal in his eyes. She was tempted to feel the same. But she couldn't believe Haeri would sell them out like this. Not after everything he had said at Ghost's. But what if the third-party had compromised his position? What if he were under duress?

Two more drones approached, settling into a guard position.

"Able, do you copy?" Rico said softly. "Able, are you there?"

There was still no reply.

"General? Are you on the comm?"

Nothing. Damn it.

"Special Officer Rodriguez, I repeat," General Haeri said again. "Put your hands over your head and wait for collection. Don't make me utilize additional force."

Rico put her hands up, folding them on top of her head. Bennett and Isaac did the same. The drones continued to hover around them as the transport—a standard APC, wide and low-slung, with large wheels and a heavily armored shell—neared, stopping along one of the nearby paths. It had likely come from the CSF barracks beneath the city, carried up from below on a large industrial lift. It was an odd response to the emergency. The APC was slow and not especially maneuverable.

A squad of soldiers climbed out. They were all dressed in combat armor and carrying plasma rifles, the dark visors of their helmets hiding their faces.

"A little overdressed?" Rico said as they approached.

They didn't speak as they grabbed her hands, pulling them down behind her back and binding them. They did the same to Bennett and Isaac.

"Sergeant, take them back to the barracks, and then transport them to CSF HQ," General Haeri ordered.

"Yes, sir," the sergeant replied. He put his hand on Rico's back. "Let's go."

Rico didn't resist. Not that she could have if she wanted to. Her hands were literally tied. She glanced over at Isaac, her eyes apologetic.

"This isn't your fault," Isaac said. "You did your best."

"It wasn't good enough," she replied softly.

The Centurion Marines led them to the ramp at the back of the APC. Another squad was already waiting inside. They stood up as Rico, Bennett and Isaac ascended the ramp into the vehicle.

"Take a seat," the sergeant said. Rico sat with Isaac beside her and Bennett across from them. The Marines boarded the APC, and the sergeant hit the control for the ramp. It slammed closed with a sharp clang.

The sergeant grabbed his helmet, lifting it off his head. Rico smiled as his face became visible.

"I know you," she said.

He smiled back. "I know you too." He raised his hand

to his neck, rubbing at it. "It's still sore." He looked up toward the cockpit. "Able, get us the hell out of here."

Rico turned her head in time to see Able lean out past the driver's seat, her face appearing through the open door to the APC's cockpit.

"On it. Good to see you again, Rico."

"Good to see you too," Rico replied. The other Marines were taking off their helmets. She recognized the other Rodriguez and a few of the others who had been sitting outside the Reclamation Center. "Damn good to see all of you." She shifted in her seat, showing her bound hands. "I don't suppose you can get these off us?"

"Absolutely," the sergeant replied. "My name's Drake, by the way. Former Centurion Space Force Captain Isaiah Drake. That's Jorge, Spot, Lucius, and of course you already know Jesse."

The other Rodriguez clone smiled. "Hiya, sis."

Jorge crossed the APC, kneeling in front of her. He was probably the youngest of the group. Dark hair, dark skin and a bright smile. He was a clone too, but she didn't know what model. He tapped on the bracelets, entering the code to unlock them. They fell off her wrists into his waiting hand.

"Thanks," Rico said.

"De nada," he replied, repeating the process for Bennett and Isaac.

"You're all former Marines?" Isaac asked.

"Not Lucius there," Drake said, pointing to another fresh-faced soldier. "He's still in the Academy. Or was until this morning."

"I don't understand."

"I do," Rico said. "Part of it, at least. Haeri had you in position in case something went wrong."

"That's right," Drake replied.

"When the assassins showed up and then the drones, you were already in position in the barracks with Able. You used the drones to take out the enemy combatants, and then you took over for the real APC crew. Able didn't answer my hail because she was otherwise occupied."

"Guilty as charged," Able said, listening in to the conversation from the front. "Haeri was worried there was another mole in the organization."

"Which organization? CSF? PCC? The Trust?"

"None of the above. Just the Organization."

"I'm totally confused," Isaac said. "Why was I being held like a prisoner? Why the complicated escape?"

"Because it's complicated," Able said.

It *was* complicated, but Rico was starting to understand. "The Organization predates Proxima, doesn't it?"

"It does. It predates the trife invasion completely, by a long time."

"Rico," Isaac said. "Can you start over and explain it as dumbed-down as possible?"

"I've got a name you might recognize," Able said. "Doctor Riley Valentine. Does that name mean anything to you?"

Isaac's face paled as he nodded. "She worked at the lab where I was stationed. Where I was put into hibernation. She was studying the Relyeh. And the Axon."

"She was a member of the Organization. We stepped up our recruitment efforts when the trife arrived."

"And Haeri is a member too, then?" Rico asked.

"Correct. So are you, now, like it or not. The Organization is committed to protecting humankind. Beyond politics, beyond laws, beyond morals, if it comes to that. No holds barred. No bullshit. It's a creed we hold sacred. You can't have a division in something as important as defending our species against alien threats."

"So this mole," Rico said. "Any idea who or what it is?"

"It could be a khoron," Isaac said. "Or an Axon."

"Or just a human who doesn't get it," Rico added.

"We don't know. This was an Organization operation, which means they infiltrated our ranks. As soon as we figure out who it is, they're dead space. No questions asked. But right now, we've got bigger problems."

"What kind of problems?" Isaac asked.

Rico turned to face him. "There's a Relyeh warship headed for Earth. We think it intends to finish the invasion."

"One starship?" Isaac said. "You have ships. Can't you stop it? Shoot it down or something?"

"No. For one thing, it's moving over a hundred times the speed of light. Even if it slows down as it approaches, that's still way faster than anything our weapons can target."

"How can anything move that fast?" Isaac asked. "Wouldn't it crash into a star or something? The impact at that speed…"

"You've got some science in you," Able said. "They must have some kind of tech to keep them from colliding with anything."

"They'd have to, wouldn't they?" Spot said. She was a small woman of Asian descent, with short black hair and a delicate face. "To cross thousands of light years."

"For another thing," Rico continued, "it's big."

"How big?" Isaac asked.

"Big enough not to be able to blast it out of space even if we could hit it."

"So we're going back to Earth to do what? Warn them about a ship the more advanced human civilization can't stop?"

"Essentially."

"How is that going to help?"

Rico opened her mouth to answer. Nothing came out. She closed it again, shaking her head. "I'm not sure, but Hayden's always managed to come through, and the situation is pretty desperate."

"How long until the Relyeh ship arrives?"

"Two weeks."

"It took a week to get from Earth to Proxima. I imagine the round trip is the same?"

"Normally it would be, but Haeri outfitted our ship's computer with an experimental algorithm that will hopefully help jump us in closer to Earth."

"I don't like the words experimental and hopefully," Isaac replied.

"There's a lot not to like about the situation," Rico agreed. "But it is what it is. Complaining won't help. If you'll excuse me." She stood and went to the APC's cockpit. Looking through the forward viewshield, she could see they were out of Metro and passing through the large vehicle access corridor that led directly to the main hangar.

Able glanced over at her. "Not what you were expecting, is it?" she asked.

"I never expect things to go according to plan," Rico replied. "But this is a little more outside the norm than usual. What about Haeri?"

"He can take care of himself. And if he can't, the Organization will pick him up."

"Haeri said it was better to stay ignorant, but I want to know more about the Organization. "

"It doesn't matter now. Once we leave Proxima, we can't come back. You, me, the group back there. We've got a new role to play."

"Where did you pick them up? Drake and his team?"

"The Reclamation Center. Good Centurions who

made bad choices, either during or after their tours. We didn't pick any of them quickly, except maybe Lucius. He's Drake's brother, in case you didn't realize. Anyway, the Organization's been waiting for this for years."

"What? You knew the Relyeh were coming?"

"We knew they would come. We've been preparing."

"How do you know it will be enough?"

"We don't. Not at all. Heck, if I were putting money on it, I wouldn't bet on us."

Rico shook her head. "That's some vote of confidence."

"We've been behind since day one. Survival means beating the odds."

"Well, if anyone has a knack for beating the odds, it's Sheriff Duke."

"That's what I've heard."

Able reached forward to tap on one of the control screens. Rico looked out the viewshield again. The APC was rolling into the main hangar. So far, everything was normal. Techs moved around the expansive deck, bringing supplies and tools to the dozen or so starships still kept in the Dove. They were all older models, more boxy and rough than the newer craft. Thirty meters long and nearly ten meters tall, with stubbed wings for atmospheric flight control and an assortment of plasma cannons mounted both beneath the wings and over the fuselage. There was no visible cockpit. It was embedded deep inside the craft behind the armor plating, the pilot able to use both advanced sensors and dozens of external cameras to fly by. Centurions called the model Buses because these days they were used solely for transporting VIPs from one city to another.

It was strange to Rico to observe the complete non-reaction to the chaos she had been in the middle of only minutes earlier. The entire ship should have been on lock-down while Centurion forces ensured there was no threat to the government. They had fired a rocket inside Metro!

But there was nothing. It was business as usual. Would the incident even make it to the evening news?

She had a feeling it wouldn't. Powerful players wanted to keep the whole thing quiet. How deep did the veins of secrecy, loyalty and history run?

She knew where they originated. Before the trife came. Before Earth was lost. Before the generation ships landed here and founded a new human civilization.

"We can talk more about the Organization once we're off the planet," Able said.

The APC crossed the hangar, heading for one of the Buses. The back ramp of the ship was already open and extended, waiting to receive the vehicle into its hold.

"So that's it? They're just going to let us leave?"

"I don't know if let is the right word," Able replied. "But we are leaving. We glitched the system. We've got about forty-five seconds left before the fun starts again."

"Glitched the system?"

Able smiled. "A ghost APC is headed back to a barracks full of sleeping Centurions. I told you, we've been preparing for a long time. And we're just getting started."

16

Rico

"Rico, you're flying," Able said as the APC stopped inside the dropship. The side hatch opened and she headed for it. "You better get this thing off the deck and out of CSF targeting range in the next forty-five seconds or we're toast."

Rico was right behind her. "They're going to try to shoot us down?" she asked, realizing she should have expected as much.

"We've already broken about fifty laws."

Rico jumped out of the vehicle behind Able, turning left and sprinting toward the stairs at the front of the hold. Able went the other direction, hitting the controls to close the rear ramp.

Rico glanced back when she reached the steps. Isaac was out of the APC and following her closely. She scaled the stairs to the main deck, hurrying past the seats there to the bridge at the center of the ship. She tapped the control pad to open the hatch and dropped into the pilot's seat, quickly activating the controls. Her primary training was as a pilot, and she had served with her Bennett on Earth as his squad's drone operator. In truth, flying the smaller recon drones in gravity with a pair of joysticks and a low-res screen was much more challenging than steering a big spacecraft through the black.

The Bus began to hum slightly as the reactor came online.

Thirty-five seconds.

The door to the bridge slid aside. Isaac entered, followed by Able.

"You sit there," Able said, guiding him to the station to the back and left of Rico. The older woman took the command station, sitting down and strapping in. "Rico, whenever you're ready."

"Do we need to call it in?" Rico asked.

"Only if you want them to try to stop us sooner."

Rico smirked. "The outer blast doors are closed."

"Already handled."

The klaxons around them started flashing, and a loud clang sounded as the doors began to part, Proxima's outer atmosphere pouring in. It was breathable but harsh, and a stiff wind immediately started blowing through the hangar. The techs below scrambled, unaccustomed to the doors opening without advanced notice.

Twenty-five seconds.

"Capricorn, this is Flight Control. We're registering unauthorized power up. Power down immediately. I repeat, power down immediately."

Rico glanced back at Able, who smiled mischievously. "Like that's going to happen."

The blast doors continued to part. Rico started increasing the throttle, preparing the ship for takeoff.

"Capricorn, you will comply immediately," Control said.

"Sorry, Control," Rico replied. "I've got a date, and I'm already late."

"Time's running out," Isaac said, pointing up at the displays.

Fifteen seconds.

Rico glanced over to their left. Another military APC rolled into the hangar, and armored Centurions began jumping out, raising their rifles toward the Bus.

"C'mon Rico, time to go!" Able shouted.

Rico looked at the blast doors. They weren't open all the way.

But they were open far enough.

"Hold on."

She engaged the main thrusters at full throttle, sending the ship lurching forward, its skids still on the deck. They scraped along the floor as the Centurions started shooting, sending plasma bolts into the armor. Rico adjusted the vectoring thrusters, pushing the craft off the deck as it neared the blast doors.

"We're going to hit!" Isaac shouted.

"Negative," Rico replied. She adjusted the vectoring again, and the left wing tipped up higher than the right. Not too much. Not too little. They squeezed through the gap between the doors with centimeters to spare, rocketing out and up.

"Nice flying," Able said, her voice finally calm.

"I'm not done yet," Rico replied. She was a former Centurion. She understood how planetary defense worked.

Five seconds.

Not enough time to get clear of the atmosphere. That was okay.

They weren't going to outfly her.

The Capricorn continued to ascend, shooting toward the dark purple sky. Marks appeared on the primary display, a warning that a targeting system was searching for a lock. Green shapes appeared on the grid displayed directly behind the starship's controls, the computer picking up incoming friendlies approaching from the CSF base to the north.

Except they wouldn't be so friendly when they arrived.

Rico banked south, still climbing. The edges of the primary display turned red, and then the screen split, showing the view from the rear camera. Two flashes triggered from the planet's surface behind the domes of Praeton—projectiles fired from ground-based launchers. They shot toward the Capricorn in a hurry, giving Rico only seconds to react.

It was more than enough.

She cut the throttle and rolled the dropship over, pushing heavy Gs as the starship soared back toward the surface. The missiles zipped past, missing their target by less than a meter. They detonated an instant later when the ground control knew they had missed.

Rico hit the thrusters again, swooping down and picking up speed. The Centurion fighters closed in, prepared to fire projectiles of their own. The targeting warning resumed, the tracking systems attempting to lock on them once more.

"We're going in the wrong direction," Isaac said.

"We're going exactly where I want to go," Rico replied.

The Bus banked and started climbing, turning into the oncoming fighters. Rico's eyes narrowed as she activated the weapons systems, bringing plasma cannons online.

"Rico, you aren't authorized to use force," Able said.

"I don't need your permission," she replied.

The displays showed the Centurion starfighters achieving lock. They loosed their payloads, sending four missiles arcing toward the Capricorn.

Rico didn't flinch. She stayed on target, firing the plasma cannons directly ahead of the Bus. The steady stream captured three of the missiles on their way in, detonating them just ahead. The fourth made it through, angling for their bow.

She snapped the ship sideways, the projectile flashing past as she continued the roll, coming out level and rapidly closing on the fighters. Her finger rested on the trigger, the reticle slipping over one of the Centurions. If she squeezed the trigger, odds were good she would make the kill.

But she didn't want to kill. They were on the same side, even if they didn't all know it.

She opened the throttle instead, cutting the ship between the starfighters and launching toward space. The Centurions blurred past and tried to turn around while the ground-based rockets continued to track. The edges of the display turned red again, but this time the screen didn't split. The warnings vanished instead, the defense system suddenly giving up on their escape.

"Haeri shut them down," Able said before Rico had a chance to ask. "We're free and clear."

"Roger that," Rico replied. "Shall we set a course for Earth?"

17

Hayden

It took almost two hours for Hayden to get everything organized. There was a lot to do, starting with removing the bodies of Cortez and Nan from the warehouse. It was a somber affair, one he always oversaw personally whenever he could. He hated losing people. Even after two years and hundreds of casualties, he still felt it when someone died. He still took it personally.

It was his failure that had led to their deaths. Whether it was in the planning or execution, he always believed there was something he could have done differently or better. He should have sounded the retreat as soon as the first trife appeared. His assumption that it was a scout group had cost his deputies their lives.

Some people wallowed in the blame. Hayden wasn't one of them. Self-pity didn't work. It might soothe his guilt, but it would also leave him a weak mess, and the world already had enough of those. Too many people counted on him to be strong, to stand up for justice and keep the peace. The best way to honor the lives that were lost was to do the best job he could do...every single day.

Without fail.

Without complaint.

Without hesitation.

He helped carry Cortez out on a stretcher, holding up the front end while Solino and Kevitz took the rear. Hayden wasn't a muscled behemoth, but his augments did offer him more strength and stamina than an average human possessed. But he did feel the strain in his legs, especially in his knees. And he felt it in his right arm where the augment's control ring connected to the organic tissue, muscles and nerves. His career was a dangerous one and had led him to replace that arm multiple times. Too many times. The entire system was damaged, leaving him in near-constant pain. He lived with it, again without complaint. It was a reminder of his mission.

And what he had lost.

They brought Cortez to a helicopter—a Bell Iroquois his wife Natalia and her team of mechanics and engineers had brought back to life with the help of a network of scavengers. The chopper was rusty and dirty, but it was functional and valuable, carrying personnel and supplies across the the United Western Territories, connecting the cities of Sanisco, Sanose, Tijuana, Lavega, Haven and Dego.

Except the last three weren't really cities anymore. A run-in with the Hunger had cost him almost half the population of the UWT and left those areas in ruin. They would rebuild in time, but for now the survivors had been coming north to Sanisco, the capital, huddling up for safety in the wake of the destruction.

That was only part of the fallout. The reduced control of the cities had brought the rats out of hiding with the belief there was an opening to seize back some of what Hayden had taken. Would-be warlords and gangs had moved into the abandoned areas, along with scavengers, thieves and traffickers—all looking for whatever scraps they could find. The warehouse had been home to one of those gangs, the intervention here intended to be a signal to the others that law still existed in the UWT, and nobody could ignore it without bringing the Sheriff down on them. Maybe the message was still intact, but at what cost?

Two deputies. Killed by trife that didn't belong.

"I'll make sure you didn't die for nothing," Hayden said as he helped place the stretcher inside the helicopter. The pilot, Bronson, strapped it in.

"Sorry about Cortez and Nan, Sheriff," he said. "They were good people."

"Pozz," Hayden agreed. "Bring them home and then circle back."

"Roger," Bronson replied. "Try not to die in the meantime."

"You know me."

Bronson nodded and moved to the cockpit of the chopper. Hayden, Solino and Kevitz backed away, joining the deputies the pilot had delivered earlier.

The Rangers were Hayden's most skilled team of deputies, Special Forces who had gone through Centurion Space Force training with Rico, and with Bennett before her. Except most of Bennett's trainees were gone now too. More fallout from his fight against the Hunger.

The Rangers standing in front of him were a mostly-new group and weren't as experienced as he would have liked. Hicks was the squad leader and the longest-tenured deputy on Hayden's staff. The man was his former Chief Deputy who had begged to be part of the Rangers to help get them back into fighting shape following their losses. While there had been a time when Hayden and Hicks were enemies, but that time was long past.

"Rangers," Hayden said, acknowledging them.

They snapped to attention, arms down at their sides. "Sheriff Duke, sir!"

"Chief Ranger Hicks, are we ready to go?" Hayden asked. The helicopter's engines raised in pitch behind him as Bronson prepared for takeoff.

"Yes, Sheriff," Hicks replied. "Ready and eager."

"Then let's do this. Solino, Kevitz, you have the door."

"Roger, Sheriff," the two deputies replied.

Hayden knew they both wanted to go back into the warehouse to make amends for the deaths of Cortez and Nan. But the Rangers were better trained and better armed, and they needed someone outside the building, keeping watch for both returning trife scouts and possible human intervention.

"Solino," Hayden said. "Helmet, please."

He handed Solino his hat and glasses, accepting a helmet in return. He pulled it over his head, the base clicking when it latched to the connector in the combat armor. A HUD popped up in his visor, and then the armor indicated it was networked with the rest of the Rangers. Five designations appeared across the top of the visor, each outlined in green to show they were healthy.

"This is Sheriff Duke. Comm check."

"Ranger One online," Hicks said.

"Ranger Two online," a woman's voice announced. Hayden glanced at her designation on the HUD. Her surname was Jackson.

"Ranger Three online," another man said. Bahk.

"Ranger Four online," a third man announced. Rollins.

"Ranger Five online," a second woman said. Ivanov.

"All units online," Hicks said. "We're ready to roll, Sheriff."

"Pozz that," Hayden replied, leading the group back into the warehouse.

He grabbed his plasma rifle from his back and turned it on, keeping it level in front of him. With the queen dead, the trife would be less inclined to fight until they were threatened.

He had every intention of threatening them.

He crossed the warehouse to the corner, the night vision in the helmet keeping the quality of his vision stable even as the amount of light decreased. He came to a stop in front of the hole the trife had climbed from. Their claw marks were easily visible in the rock beneath the building's floor, which had cracked, crumbled and collapsed into an underground excavation. There was no obvious sign of trife below, either visually or on the Advanced Tactical Combat System's sensors, meaning the hole continued beyond the immediate area.

"Do trife dig tunnels?" Hicks asked, coming up beside Hayden and looking into the hole.

"Not that I've ever heard of or seen," Hayden replied. "But they evolve quickly."

"Do you think it's a response to the goliaths?"

Hayden glanced at the Ranger Chief. The goliaths were the only reason the UWT was able to remain as trife-free as it did. "We can't rule it out."

He looked back at the hole. If the trife were tunneling below the surface to get around the goliaths, the people of the UWT might be in for a new deadly threat before they recovered from the last one.

But not if he could help it.

18

Hayden

Hayden and his Rangers descended into the hole on a pair of ropes, landing on hard earth nearly ten meters below the warehouse floor.

"I don't get the impression that hole was supposed to be there," Hicks said, looking up at the breach.

"It probably collapsed during the fighting," Hayden replied, referring to the Relyeh attack on the city.

He turned in a circle. The bad news was that the excavation was a tunnel after all, and it stretched into the darkness headed both north and south. The good news was that it appeared to be human-made, not trife-made. There was no evidence of claw marks on any of the walls, though there were more than a few scrapes and scratches in the floor and leading up to the warehouse.

"Wrong place, wrong time?" Hicks asked.

"It seems that way. The trife were probably passing through and saw the hole. We just happened to be there when they did. The thing about that is, queens don't normally migrate."

"You think something stole her food source?"

108

"Or it died. Some of the reactors are nearing their end of life."

"That makes more sense. What do you think, Sheriff? Do we split up?"

"No. Strength in numbers." Hayden followed the marks on the floor. "It looks like they're heading north."

"Then I take it we're heading north?"

"Pozz. Standby." Hayden switched channels on the comm. "Solino, do you copy?"

"I copy, Sheriff," Solino replied. "What's up?"

"We found a tunnel beneath the warehouse. We're going to follow it north. Do you have my comm position?"

"How do I get your position, Sheriff?"

"The glasses. Put them on and tap the side to activate the ATCS. It'll link to the nearest sister signal if it finds one."

"Roger."

Hayden waited for Solino to do as he instructed. The glasses were a scaled-back version of the same combination of system-on-a-chip computer brain and visor-mounted heads-up-display in the combat armor. It would allow the deputy to link into their network. He would have had Solino do it earlier, but the battery in the glasses wouldn't last nearly as long as the power supply embedded in the back of Hayden's armor.

Hayden knew when Solino had joined because the designation came up in the HUD. He switched back to the team comm channel. "Welcome to the party, Solino."

"Thank you, Sheriff," Solino replied.

Hayden glanced at Hicks. "You and I have point. Vee formation."

"Roger."

"Solino, follow us from above."

"Roger, Sheriff."

Hayden moved out ahead of the other Rangers with Hicks, and they started walking along the tunnel.

"How far do we take it?" Hicks asked.

"Until we find the trife or lose contact with Solino," Hayden replied. "We can't let them make another queen, especially this deep inside UWT territory."

"Roger that."

They kept walking. The tunnel started to curve after a while, the heading changing from north to northeast, and then to the east as they reached the one hour mark. The depth remained the same, the passage sitting a short distance beneath the ground, passing uninterrupted beneath the city and past its outer perimeter. Deputy Solino remained dutifully above, following the signal as best he could. Hayden lost contact with him a few times as they passed beneath the wreckage of a building or through a particularly dense portion of rock, but they always reconnected before they had to turn back.

Another hour went by. Hayden passed a message to Bronson through Solino to ground the helicopter somewhere safe and wait for instruction. There was no sense burning limited fuel for no reason. The tunnel continued, straightening out on an eastern route and spreading far enough ahead to vanish into darkness.

Hayden and the Rangers spent two more hours traveling the tunnel, at which point Hayden started to become concerned. He had thought there might be another exit somewhere along the route. A sealed hatch or something. That didn't seem to be the case. They were four hours deep into the passage with no clear way back to the surface and no idea how much further they would have to go. Did it make sense to follow the trife if the tunnel didn't end anytime soon?

Hayden decided he would give it another hour. If they

didn't discover anything worthwhile by then, they could mark the spot and head back to the warehouse. With the right equipment, they could make a new hole and rejoin the search from there.

"Is Hallia talking yet?" Hicks asked, trying to make conversation to help pass the time.

"A little," Hayden replied. "She's got momma down cold."

Hicks laughed. "What about da-da?"

"I think she'll get Ginny before she gets da-da. Her big sister spends more time with her than Nat and me combined."

"How is that going? Ginny, I mean?"

Hayden smiled behind his helmet. Ginny was a stray, an orphan who had latched onto Hayden after he saved her life in Dego. She was a good kid, a strong kid. She had become part of the family almost by default.

"It's a shame her parents didn't live to see what she's growing into," he replied. "She's going to have an impact somewhere."

"Sheriff or engineer?"

"Maybe both. She's fearless and curious. And I think that's rubbing off on Hal a little bit too."

"You're a lucky man, Sheriff. I don't know how you do it."

"I sure am. What about you?"

"What about me? I don't get enough time off to get into any relationships."

"That's not what I heard."

"What did you hear?"

Hayden laughed again. "That a certain Chief Ranger has been seen spending a lot of time hovering around Medical. But that has nothing to do with Nurse Tia."

"I will neither confirm or deny that statement. In fact, I—"

Hick's voice cut off as he identified the sudden appearance of a red mark on his HUD. Hayden saw it too, and he immediately brought the squad to a stop, aiming his rifle forward.

It appeared a moment later. A single trife bounding toward them through the passage.

"I've got this one," Hicks said, taking aim.

"Hicks, wait," Hayden said.

The trife kept coming, in long strides on all fours, racing at them like they weren't even there. Hayden moved aside to let it pass, and it continued through the Rangers without slowing, vanishing a few seconds later.

"What the hell?" Jackson said.

A tense silence enveloped them. Hayden turned back to the passage, sharing the Ranger's sentiment. The behavior was strange. Trife always traveled in groups. This one seemed like it was running away.

But from what?

Hayden looked forward again. He started walking cautiously ahead, a single step at a time, rifle raised and ready to fire. The Rangers did the same.

Another red mark appeared on the HUD. Hayden didn't stop moving this time. The trife ran between him and Hicks, ignoring them in its desperate effort to escape.

"Are you sure we should be going forward?" Bahk asked.

Another red mark appeared, and then two more. The trife raced past them.

"Solino," Hayden said. "What's the situation topside?"

"Sheriff," Solino replied. "Everything's clear up here."

"What's my relative position?"

"You're under the street. There's a building straight

ahead. A big one. It's got some lettering still on it, hold on. Dep. Department. Department of H-E-A and U-M-A-N Services. I don't know, Sheriff. Some of the letters are missing."

Hayden wished Isaac was with him. The Marine would probably know what the building was. Not that it mattered. Whatever was sending the trife running, it was down here, not up there.

"Sheriff," Hicks said, getting Hayden's attention. The Chief Ranger was pointing his rifle toward the side of the tunnel.

A dead trife was there, it's arm missing. The wound to the shoulder was jagged and deep.

"It looks like something took a bite out of it," Jackson said.

"Sure does," Hayden agreed. That would explain why so few of the trife were returning. "And I want to know what."

He broke into a run. The other Rangers howled and followed behind him, encouraged by his lack of fear.

The sound of hissing and groaning became increasingly loud as Hayden charged, along with a noise like a wet towel slapping the ground. A few more trife ran the other direction as he approached, his HUD lighting up with a few more red marks, and then finally a larger one.

The tunnel was dark, and the edge of the night vision's range left everything shrouded in silhouette and shadow. Even with his limited sight, Hayden could make out the scene of chaos and violence approaching. There were already dozens of dead trife on the ground, their blood making the floor of the tunnel slick, their smell making Hayden nauseous. They littered the area, each of them with a bite taken from somewhere on their bodies.In some cases multiple bites. Movement in the shadows, combined with the ATCS sensors, revealed about twenty trife still fighting back against a much larger target. One with multiple limbs, each of them independently trying to grab a trife.

"How did we get to hell without a road sign?" Rollins said, his voice deep and scratchy.

The creature seemed to notice them. It lurched forward, its large shape slipping from the shadows and revealing a grotesque alien form.

19

Hayden

The alien was nearly the height of the tunnel, its full form challenging to discern in the darkness. It seemed as though it was composed of tentacles, dozens of which spread out from a central mass, forcing it to remain bent in the confines of the passage. Its flesh was slimy and moist, mottled and peeling. The end of each appendage featured an individual wide mouth of sharp teeth beneath a series of multi-faceted eyes. There were more eyes on the central mass as well, along with a primary maw that could easily swallow any of them whole.

Hayden wasn't easy to frighten. This thing terrified him.

"Oh, hell no," Rollins said, pulling to a stop. He didn't wait for the order to start shooting, immediately unleashing bolt after bolt from his plasma rifle at the creature.

The bolts lit up the tunnel, the sudden flashes disrupting everyone's night vision. Hayden cursed as his eyes tried to adjust, his visor bathed in pure white and hiding the monster from view. He could hear its groaning increase in volume as the plasma struck it, but he couldn't see if the attack was having any effect.

"Hold your fire until you can see!" he shouted through the comm. He could still see the red outline of the creature on his HUD, the sensors trying to keep up with the movement of its tentacles.

Rollins screamed, and Hayden watched his designation turn orange, indicating he was wounded. Impatient, Hayden grabbed his helmet and ripped it from his head, tossing it aside and spinning toward the stricken Ranger. One of the tentacles had reached out and grabbed Rollins, wrapping around him while the mouth at the end was clamped down on his arm, his combat armor keeping it from shearing the limb off.

Hayden fired plasma into the tentacle, satisfied when the flesh melted away beneath the gas and the appendage relaxed. His victory was short lived. He caught movement from the corner of his eye, just barely dropping beneath one of the tentacles as it tried to scoop him up.

"Fire at will!" he heard Hicks shout, the helmets finally adjusting. The Chief Ranger started shooting, targeting the creature's central mass.

It reacted immediately, wrapping a pair of tentacles around its face and blocking the bolts. The weapon was able to hurt it, digging deep gouges in the limbs that began to leak bodily fluids, but how much damage could each tentacle absorb?

The creature heaved itself toward them, using some tentacles for locomotion and sending half a dozen forward at the Rangers. They shifted their fire to match, pounding the limbs with plasma as they tried to back away.

It still had Rollins and was pulling it back toward its gaping primary mouth. Hayden charged forward, continuing to fire at the appendage, each bolt taking another piece out of the wet flesh.

Two more tentacles came at Hayden, dropping from over his head. He dove aside as they hit the ground with a familiar wet slap, He rolled back to his feet, switching his plasma rifle from bolt mode to stream. He held down the trigger, a blast of superheated gas spreading three meters out ahead of him and into the tentacles.

The alien gurgled loudly in response, nearly every tentacle on the thing suddenly reaching for Hayden. He swung the rifle across his body, keeping them back while the Rangers blasted the creature with enough firepower to take out a tank.

The monster's limbs began to fall away, detaching as they became too damaged and before they could nega-tively impact the rest of the creature. Four of them fell dead in a matter of seconds.

It wasn't enough.

Rollins screamed again, the tentacle holding him nearing the monster's primary mouth. Hayden didn't give up. He kept charging, switching to a single-handed grip on his rifle and pulling one of his revolvers. He aimed and fired, sending bullets into the tentacle clutching Rollins.

"Let go, you son of a bitch," he hissed.

His plasma rifle ran out of fuel, sputtering out.

The creature didn't hesitate, its tentacles closing in on him again. He punched the first one that reached for him, knocking it aside. Then he tossed his revolver from his right hand to his left, closing his right fist. The Axon blade extended from his augment, and he slashed it through the next tentacle to get too close, cutting the head of it completely off.

Rollins screamed one last time as the creature dropped his body into its mouth and he disappeared.

"Noooo!" Hayden cried, slashing another tentacle off. A second grabbed his ankle and pulled, yanking him off his feet. It lifted him into the air, where two more reached for him with gaping mouths.

Plasma bolts hit the limbs, forcing them off course while Hayden curled up and slashed the one that had grabbed him. He fell back to the ground, the crash absorbed by his armor. He rolled sideways as another limb tried to smash him, and then stood up in front of the creature. It reared up in front of him, pressing against the top of the tunnel and filling the entire thing. More tentacles reached for him, and he noticed it had left its central mass unprotected.

"Hit the center!" he shouted, firing at its mouth. His bullets vanished into its throat, and it began screaming much louder, clearly in pain.

The Rangers reacted instantly, shifting their aim from the tentacles to its head. Dozens of bolts dug into it before it could defend itself. Blood and ichor poured from its mouth.

A number of appendages reached for Hayden in a last ditch effort to grab him. He punched and clawed them away, their speed diminished, the monster finally dying.

The Rangers advanced toward it with renewed hope, pounding it with plasma.

It howled one final time and died.

20

Hayden

Hayden wrinkled his face. The smell from the fresh carcass was nearly unbearable, made more so because he knew where it was coming from.

He turned back to Hicks, who was in the process of changing the cell on his plasma rifle.

"Is everyone else okay?" he asked.

Hicks nodded. "I think I'm going to have nightmares for weeks, but I'm good otherwise."

"Sheriff," Jackson said, holding his helmet out to him.

Hayden took it and slid it back on. The network reconnected a few seconds later. He felt like someone punched him in the gut when he saw Rollins' red designation.

Another dead deputy. Damn it.

"Where did that thing come from?" Ivanov said. It was the first time she had spoken since the Rangers had arrived.

"It's Relyeh," Hayden said. "Part of the Hunger."

"How do you know?" Hicks asked.

"Because it isn't from Earth, and it isn't an Intellect."

"What is it doing underground?"

"Good question. We need to find out."

"Sheriff," Ivanov said. She had his plasma rifle.

He accepted it too, dropping the spent cell out of it and replacing it with a fresh one. "Thanks."

He approached the central mass of the creature. He didn't want to look into its mouth, but he needed to know if there was enough left of Rollins to bury.

There wasn't.

"Rollins?" Hicks asked.

Hayden shook his head. "I'm sorry."

"You did your best to save him. More than any of us could have done. We're lucky to only lose one against that thing."

Hayden nodded, though it wasn't much comfort. He climbed over the prone tentacles, getting past the carcass to continue along the tunnel, the Rangers following behind him. The trife were all gone, having fled during the fighting. The path ahead was clear.

"Solino, what's our relative position?" Hayden asked.

"You're almost directly under the front of that building," Solino replied. "The door is gone, but it has a reinforced metal seal still intact behind it."

Interesting. What kind of building was this that it was armored against intrusion? "Do you see any windows?"

"Now that you mention it, not until about eight meters up. And they're all still intact. No sign of squatters or scavengers getting inside."

Very interesting. "Bahk, I want you to stay in position here to maintain the network link to Deputy Solino."

"Roger, Sheriff," Bahk replied.

Hayden led the rest of the Rangers forward at a quick walk, eager to figure out what this was all about.

He didn't have to go far. The tunnel ended fifty meters later, at a metal blast door that had been torn open by the tentacled Relyeh as though it were made of paper.

"Jailbreak?" Jackson ventured, eying the damage.

"Seems like it," Hayden replied. "But unless Proxima scientists are hiding inside, why would that thing have waited two hundred years to break out?"

He approached the ravaged metal. The hole was a lot smaller than the creature, which must have compressed itself to slide through. He stepped inside and found himself standing in what looked like an airlock. The room was filthy from the passage of time. Dozens of small nozzles lined the walls and ceiling, and there was a drain in the center of the floor. A second seal sat directly in front of him, also punctured.

"What do you think?" Hicks asked, stepping through the hole into the room.

"Looks like it was intended to sanitize people on their way through this door."

"To keep something from getting out or to keep something from getting in?"

"Good question. " Let's go find out," Hayden said, waiting for the others to step through the seal.

Hayden was impressed by the way they were handling the situation, staying focused despite what they had just seen and despite the death of their squadmate. Hicks and Rico had trained them well.

"Stay tight. Stay alert," he said, leading them through the second door. It fed out into a cement corridor lined with overhead LED bulbs. A trail of slime was visible on the floor, though it seemed too small to be from the creature they had just killed. Even so, it gave them a starting point.

Hayden followed the trail down the corridor to an intersection, where it turned right. He did the same. The next hallway had a few doors along the sides, all of them made of rounded iron hatches as if they were on a naval ship instead of in a building. The Rangers tested the doors as they passed, pushing them open to reveal individual offices, most of which were completely bare save for a simple desk and chair. No computer, no paperwork, no personal effects.

"Seems like the place was abandoned," Hicks said.

"Probably during the war," Hayden replied. "Maybe when the ships left Earth?"

"A reasonable assumption."

The marks from the Relyeh went to the right again, down another corridor, and then turned right a third time at a stairwell. The door to the steps had been ripped off its hinges, and it was resting on the floor below.

Hayden started down. He drew his revolvers when he reached the halfway point, slowing to approach the lower level more cautiously.

He made it to the bottom of the stairs, guns out and ready to shoot. He was in a large, tiled room. A laboratory of some kind. Computer terminals and scientific machinery filled most of the open room, their specific purpose unclear. Marked containers filled a pair of shelves in the corner, while what looked like a freezer door rested against the far wall.

Hayden looked down, finding the trail of ichor again and tracing it across the room to a hole in the wall, about the same size as the punctures in the seals further out.

"This is like a horror movie," Hicks said.

There was a collection of old movies and players in Sanisco that the residents were free to come and use. Hayden rarely had time to participate, but Ginny had told him about a few. It did remind him of one of the films she had described.

The room beyond the wall was cool, as though it had been insulated and frozen at one point, but the loss of power had given it time to thaw. How recent was the loss of power? Had the trife come this way because they could still feel the residual radiation? This wouldn't be the first location to house its own micro-reactor. The devices were common enough, especially in the wake of the trife invasion.

The darkness of the facility made it difficult to see into the space. The night vision was doing its best, but it still required a minimum of light to enhance. Hayden could only see about a meter into the room, to the edge of something resting on the floor.

"Time to switch to lamps, I think," he said.

"Roger that," Hicks replied. It was important to keep the switch synced so that no one blinded anyone else with the sudden light. "On three. Two. One. Now."

Hayden squinted his eyes a few times to activate the light built into his helmet. The system handled the changeover with minimal interruption, the visor gradually filtering the new light until he had a clear, color view of the room ahead.

And the creature crawling toward them.

21

Hayden

Hayden took a step back as the creature lunged at the hole. It was a match to the one they had downed in the tunnel outside, though it was only about one-tenth the size. A baby? Or had the one in the tunnel grown that fast? By feeding?

Either way, it was in the air and launching toward his chest. He squeezed his right hand closed, getting it up in front of him. Half a dozen tentacles latched onto his arm with their teeth, causing a blue glow from the energy shield beneath. Immediately sensing it couldn't bite into his arm, the creature used it to pull itself forward to his helmet, wrapping itself around and trying to yank it off.

"Damn it," Hayden cursed, grabbing the monster and trying to pull it away. Its body was slick, making it hard to keep a grip on it.

"Hold still," Hicks said. He put his plasma rifle against the side of the creature's central mass and pulled the trigger. The bolt went clear through it, and it fell limp.

Jackson helped Hayden quickly remove it from his helmet. "Shit, Sheriff," she said. "It cracked the material."

"Another few seconds, it would have cracked my skull," Hayden replied. "Thanks for the save."

"Anytime," Hicks said.

Jackson tossed the creature aside. Hayden crouched to get a better look in the hole. His stomach churned when he saw the web of hardened slime that lined the walls, ceiling and floor. There were bulging pockets throughout the wet mess, two of which had been cracked, spilling slime and aliens to the ground.

"Disgusting," Hicks said, looking past him.

"We need to burn it," Hayden replied. "Jackson, Bahk, you're up."

"Roger, Sheriff."

The two Rangers moved to the hole, setting their plasma rifles to stream mode. Hayden and Hicks retreated a couple of steps.

"I wouldn't do that if I were you."

The woman's voice came from behind Hayden. He spun around, hand grabbing a revolver, drawing it and aiming it at the speaker's head, all in one fluid motion. She was middle-aged, a little heavy, wrinkled and gray. She wore thick horned-rimmed glasses, a black skirt, white blouse, low-heeled pumps and a gray lab coat. She looked like a scientist, but there was something off about her.

"Who are you?" Hayden asked. And why had the ATCS allowed her to sneak up on them?

"I'm their mother," she replied, smiling. "They are my Children."

"Congratulations," Hicks deadpanned, his rifle trained on her.

"If you kill them, you'll make me very angry," she continued. "Do you want to make me angry?"

"Undecided," Hayden said. "Which Relyeh Ancient do you serve?"

The woman seemed surprised by the question, raising her eyebrows as her smile diminished. "So you know. Interesting."

"Answer the question."

"The one I serve has been waiting. We have all been waiting. The path is clear. The pieces in place. The Children prepared." Her eyes narrowed. "You've already killed one of mine."

"It was trying to kill me."

"The Children will test humankind. The worthy will survive. The remainder will become fodder to our hunger. You have proven yourself worthy."

"Good on me," Hayden said. "This is my planet. You, your Children, and your Master aren't welcome here."

"Is it war you seek, then? It is war you cannot win."

Hayden held back his emotion. He didn't know what this was all about. This was the last thing he expected his day to turn into. Know your enemy. The only thing he knew about these creatures was that they were Relyeh, and that meant they had to die. Could he tell Jackson and Bahk to go ahead without bringing hell down on the UWT and his family...again?

On the other hand, could he walk away from this and leave them to emerge? The first one had grown ten times its size in a matter of hours.

"I don't seek war," he replied. "I'd be happy to negotiate a peace settlement."

The woman's smile returned. "We are the Hunger. We do not negotiate. You are worthy. You will await the coming of the Master, and then you will submit. There is glory in serving the Master. Accolades without end."

"What about my wife?" Hayden asked. "My children?"

"The worthy will survive. The remainder will become fodder to our hunger."

"Sheriff?" Bahk asked. "What do you want to do?"

Hayden stared at the woman. There was still something about her that didn't seem right. He glanced at Hicks, spotting his eyes through his helmet. He saw it too.

"It sounds to me like you've already got your intentions," Hayden said. "And they aren't going to change whether I burn your Children or not."

"But you will survive as a servant of the Master."

"No thanks. Bahk, Jackson, do it."

They responded by triggering their rifles, sending twin gouts of superheated plasma into the room and washing it over the cocoons.

The woman didn't show any emotion. Her voice remained cold. "You will regret this decision."

"Maybe. Maybe not. You want war? War it is."

Hayden pulled the trigger, sending a round through the woman's skull. Only it didn't do any damage, passing harmlessly through and hitting the wall behind her.

"The Master is coming," she said, nonplussed by his attempted murder. "The end of human freedom is at hand. Soon, this world will join hundreds of others under our dominion."

Hayden squinted his eyes and looked up at the ceiling. He found the holographic projector a moment later, little more than a pinprick of light on a sliver of dark alloy connected to the ceiling. Had the hologram been programmed to intercede in the event of outsiders entering the room? That couldn't be. It had known they had killed one of the Relyeh in the tunnel.

Was the enemy watching them right now?

That was only the first of his questions. The next few to slip into his head concerned him much, much more.

True-to-life holograms were Axon tech. The dark alloy was Axon metal. How long ago had it been placed here?

By who?

Did its presence suggest this Relyeh had conquered one or more of the Axon worlds?

If that was the case, whoever was speaking to him through the hologram was right. He was probably going to regret this decision.

He was still glad he had made it.

He smiled at the hologram, aimed at the projector, and fired. The device popped free of the ceiling, sending the woman into a wild spin across the room before it struck the floor and went dark.

Bahk and Jackson's rifles went dark too. They stood and backed away, leaving the room awash in burning alien material.

"Sheriff, the target is destroyed," Jackson said.

"Pozz that," Hayden replied. "Rangers, let's see if we can find our way topside through this place. We need to haul ass back to Sanisco."

"Roger," Hicks said.

"Solino, we're on our way up. I'm not sure where we'll come out, but I want Bronson here when we do."

"Roger, Sheriff," Solino replied.

"I don't like any of this," Ivanov said.

"Me neither," Hayden said. "But we don't have to like it. We just have to deal with it."

He walked over to the damaged projector and picked it up, shoving it in his pocket. Natalia would be pissed if he left without it.

He had known for a while now that the Relyeh invasion wasn't over and that this day would come. The timing was shit, but was there ever a good time for something like this? Wishing, complaining, worrying. None of that would help.

Fighting? The odds were ridiculously stacked against them.

But even the Hunger couldn't keep a good Sheriff down.

22

Caleb

Caleb crouched beside a tree. It was early morning. Still dark. A slick of trife spread out across a field in front of him, nearly a thousand strong. It was a large group, out of place in the middle of the open field.

He was more interested in the farm than the trife. The property was fertile and active, with bands of wheat and corn visible well into the distance. A windowless stone and steel structure sat beside the fields of grain, with a pair of large granaries on either side. Caleb used his Skin to zoom in on the granaries, spotting the guards standing at the top of the towers facing the trife. They had no doubt seen the creatures, but so far hadn't taken any action against them.

The whole scene was curious. Clearly, the farm had been designed to withstand the demons. Trife however had no interest in burning crops and starving humans, only slaughtering them wholesale. So the existence of the farm and the hardened construction was intriguing. It wasn't newly made, that much was evident by the natural staining on the concrete. It also wasn't the original build. It had gone up after the trife invasion, which meant there was someone out here who was not only surviving the demons but thriving in spite of them, and that someone needed enough wheat and corn to feed hundreds, if not thousands of people.

After spending the last few months passing through towns and villages sparsely populated by ragged, struggling survivors and joining nomadic groups—continually trying to stay one step ahead of the next trife slick and quietly ending small bands of roving bandits and gunslingers, it was an incredibly welcome change.

And it was about to come under attack.

Leave it alone. The uluth cannot penetrate the stone, and the sentries know they are present.

"We can take a bite out of them and lead some of them away. It'll make the whole group easier to handle."

For all you know, this farm belongs to another random would-be warlord.

"What does that matter? Humans help humans fight trife. That's the way it should be."

That doesn't mean it's always the way things are. From what we have seen, humans are more likely to take advantage of one another than join together to fight the common enemy. It's not surprising. Many worlds have fallen to the Hunger, and most have reacted the same way.

"Well, this human is still a Marine. I took an oath to protect the people here. Just because that was two hundred years ago doesn't make it any less valid today."

Even if they don't appreciate it? Even if they would just as soon kill you as thank you?

"Yes. I came back here to help humankind fight against the Hunger."

You can't do that if you die before you deliver your message.

"We aren't so easy to kill."

We also aren't invulnerable, and that is a great number of uluth.

I understand our symbiosis has merged some of my arrogance into you, but now I warn you against giving in to it.

"That's your part of me talking."

Likely so. Let us remain cautious, Caleb.

Caleb sighed silently. Ishek was right. He wanted to help, but his mission was bigger than a single slick of trife. It would be different if they were about to launch an assault on an unprotected group of travelers. But they were gathering to attack a defensible position.

Which also made little sense.

"What do you think they're doing here?" he asked. "I don't feel like this is a raid on the farm. That's a lot of trife for as few people as may be hiding in that bunker."

Unknown. We can look into the Collective, but it's risky.

Caleb understood the risks. He tried not to tap into the Hunger's mindshare more than was necessary. While he had learned to block some of the probes against Ishek's link to the network, he wasn't skilled enough to prevent a more powerful Relyeh from accessing the Advocate's mind, and by extension his own. It was especially dangerous because of the package he was carrying—as Valentine had put it, a means to destroy every trife on Earth.

That wouldn't solve the Nyarlath problem completely, but if they could end the trife threat before the Relyeh Ancient made her appearance it would begin to put them on much more stable footing.

But did they have enough time?

"Reach out as quickly as you can," Caleb said. "Don't linger. I want to know what else is nearby."

A pressure built in Caleb's mind as Ishek entered the Collective. The Advocate was only gone a few seconds.

Multiple slicks are organizing nearby. You are correct. This isn't about the farm. I only took a moment, but I believe there is a city close at hand, which is the target of their attack. They intend to move in on it as one group.

"A single queen?" Caleb asked.

No. Multiple queens are working together.

"That's unusual."

Agreed.

"Did you get a count?"

No. But the other slicks are more substantial than this one.

"Best guess?"

Forty-thousand. Maybe more.

Caleb breathed in sharply. Forty-thousand trife all pointed at the same target? He had been on Earth during the worst of the original fighting, a member of the Marine Raiders. New York had fallen against fewer demons, and it was one of the most heavily defended cities in the world at the time.

What the hell were they preparing to attack?

"We need to warn them."

We don't know who they are.

"We still need to warn them. For that many trife to gather indicates the settlement's population must be large."

And well defended. They might not need our help. We are only one.

Caleb watched the trife. They had been static since he arrived, but now they started moving, a ragged line advancing north toward the bunker.

We're too late anyway.

"We can still get ahead of them."

Caleb activated the Skin and scanned the back of one of the trife. Millions of nano-emitters embedded in the fabric cast out perfectly formed light, enveloping him in a holographic projection that perfectly mimicked the scanned trife.

The advanced technology was created by the Axon to

allow their artificial intelligences to infiltrate other civilizations. It allowed them to become duplicates of almost anything as long as it was a roughly similar size and shape. The Skin had been exceedingly useful to Caleb during his exploration of present-day Earth.

Caleb ran forward, stooping a little to better match the trife's gait. He came up on the back of the line, drawing a hiss from one of the demons that was more greeting than challenge. He hissed back, the Skin adjusting the sound through the cowl that covered his face so that it more closely matched the trife's vocalization.

He advanced with the creatures, marching a little faster to get further up the line. Once he was out in front, he could pull away and make a run for it. Between his conditioning and Ishek's ability to flood him with chemicals to enhance his speed and strength, he would arrive at the human city ahead of the trife.

He looked up at the sentries as the slick drew closer to the granaries. He used the Skin to zoom his optics in on them. Two armed guards stood on the top of each silo, looking down at the trife but not revealing any intent to attack. Their rifles sat on straps at their hips while their eyes remained fixed on the mass.

They aren't afraid.

Caleb hadn't realized it yet, but Ishek was right. The sentries weren't afraid of the slick in the slightest. Did they know how many of the aliens were heading for their home? He had only been back on Earth for a short time, but he had never experienced such a complete lack of concern for the enemy before. What did they know that he didn't?

It was an unexpected and valuable discovery. Valentine had learned through the Relyeh Collective that humankind was still fighting this war. Still losing this war. Everything he had seen since had confirmed her report.

Until now.

Somebody was succeeding against the creatures.

But who?

And how?

The Skin's heads up display changed suddenly, outlining the shape of something approaching in the distance. Something airborne and mechanical, and coming in fast. Caleb turned his head toward its position in the sky. The craft was in range of the Skin's sensors, but still outside his line of sight. But only for a moment.

He located the UFO when two bright flashes lit up the sky ahead, giving him the briefest glimpse of the ship as it rocketed toward his position. The flashes descended even faster, dropping toward the front line of trife. The single bright light broke apart as it reached three hundred meters, splitting into nearly two dozen smaller lights that spread across the field.

Incoming.

Caleb's heart started pounding and he crouched into a ball, pulling himself as tight as he could and activating the Skin's shields. The missiles hit a split-second later, detonating across the slick. One of them struck only a few meters away, the sound of the explosion deafening, the force enough to lift Caleb off his feet and throw him sideways. The Skin's shields flared, absorbing the otherwise killing impact. He landed hard, rolling to a stop amidst the remains of dozens of trife.

Pulling himself to his knees, Caleb's eyes swept across the suddenly decimated alien line. Hundreds of trife were already gone, leaving the slick a ragged mess of confused survivors.

Gunshots crackled, and one of the surviving trife near

Caleb screamed as it was taken out by a hail of bullets fired from the sentries on the nearby silos. The Skin's HUD captured more activity from the bunker. The doors had opened and a squad of soldiers rushed out, shooting into the remaining demons.

I told you not to get involved.

"Shut up," Caleb said. He got to his feet. The Skin had dropped the projection to activate the shields, revealing him as a dark humanoid shape in the middle of the battlefield.

Would the humans see him as friend or foe?

Bullets tore at the ground, quickly tracking toward him. He rolled aside as they cut the dirt where he had been standing, redirecting to keep him targeted.

Foe.

Caleb started reaching for the cowl of the Skin. Maybe they would stop shooting at him once he pulled it off and showed them he was human.

Maybe they won't. You were embedded with the uluth.

Caleb gritted his teeth, realizing Ishek was right. Whoever these people were, he had severely underestimated their ability to handle the threat. Then again, why wouldn't he? Whoever these people were, their capabilities didn't line up with anything Valentine had led him to believe about the survivors on Earth.

Of course, it wouldn't be the first time Valentine had lied or withheld information, either.

He needed to get out of there. Let the action calm down and then continue north in search of the city.

He turned to run; at the same time he noticed the aircraft was coming back across the field, much lower than before. He looked up, surprised by the size and shape. It reminded him of the dropships on the Deliverance, only sleeker and more advanced—an iterative evolution of the centuries-old design.

It screamed overhead, thrusters casting the entire field in a blue-orange hue as a large shape dropped out the back, its jets slowing its forward momentum and dropping it almost smoothly to the surface.

Directly in front of him.

The object straightened up. Nearly two and a half-meters in height, it was humanoid in shape, a large, powerful mass of heavy armor with an oversized head. A series of tubes ran from the base of the head to its back, toward the business end of a massive rifle mounted within easy reach.

Caleb wasn't sure if it was a robot or if there was a human inside. An opaque slit crossed its face, which could be either part of a visor or the protective covering for a series of sensors and cameras. The uncertainty left him unsure. The thing was blocking his escape.

Fight or flight?

He didn't get to make the choice.

23

Caleb

The armor lunged at Caleb, deceptively fast for its size. Even with Ishek's ability to enhance his reflexes, he barely avoided the giant hand that tried to grab his shoulder, ducking aside as he activated the Skin's weapons system. Energy flowed through the Skin, pooling at his fist as he threw a hard jab into the armor's chest plate. The strike hit the armor, a flash of energy adding to the force of the punch, managing to knock it back a step. Off balance, it stumbled and then regained its footing, again coming at him.

A flurry of jabs and hooks followed, the armor choosing a melee of punches when it had a rifle on its back. The intensity of the assault drove Caleb backward, ducking and dodging the blows. He tried to block one with his forearm, the Skin's shields taking the hit, the force still throwing him back. At least whatever energy was absorbed was returned to the suit's energy stores, regenerating its supply.

Caleb rolled across the field and popped back to his feet. The armor didn't hesitate, continuing after him.

Caleb raised his hand and fired a blast of energy at his attacker, who reacted a split-second ahead of the shot, sidestepping before leaping at him, the thrusters on its back carrying it into the air.

It landed directly in front of him, swinging interlocked hands like a giant club. Caleb tried to get out of the way, but he wasn't fast enough. The attack caught his shoulder, spinning him around and sending him sprawling on the ground.

It fights well.

"Thanks for the feedback." Caleb grunted, scrambling back to his feet as the armor approached again. "This would be easier if I could destroy it."

So destroy it.

He couldn't. He didn't know if there was a person inside the armor or if it was a robot. Either way, it was still a weapon against the trife. He didn't want to do too much damage to it.

"We need to get out of here."

He set himself in a defensive posture, hands up and ready for the next attack. He wasn't sure, but he thought the armor flinched, hesitating for a moment.

A sharp hiss drew the armor's attention. It turned as a group of trife rushed it, the demons leaping at it to bring it down. It caught the first demon in one large hand, crushing its neck and tossing it away. It kicked a second one and punched a third. The rest of the group managed to climb on the armor, hissing and scratching at the metal to rip it apart.

Caleb backed away as more trife began to regroup on the armor, recognizing it as their biggest threat. Out of the original thousand, only a couple hundred remained.

The armor continued fighting back, grabbing trife and tossing them off it, crushing their bones and breaking them in half. Caleb continued watching for a few more seconds while he decided whether to use the distraction to run or to stay and help clear the field.

If it's a machine, it won't identify you as a friendly regardless of your actions.

If it was a machine, it was one of the most advanced human machines Caleb had ever seen. But he had been gone for a long time, sent halfway across the universe on a generation ship that had fled the planet two centuries ago. While most of what he had seen of his homeworld so far was the miserable acceptance of becoming the second most dominant race on the planet, he had no conception of humankind's current military capabilities, at least not here on Earth.

Whoever ran the farm had advanced technology. Did that mean they had a connection to Proxima?

He was static for a few more seconds as the armor continued to pummel the trife. He was forced to make a decision when it started reaching for its rifle. If it were a robot, it would shoot him the same as it would shoot the trife. Without hesitation. Without question.

He didn't want to be here when it finished with them.

He turned and ran, sprinting back toward the trees where he had originally emerged. It wasn't enough to find cover behind them. He needed to get clear of the area, at least far enough away that the aircraft wouldn't be able to track him. He had passed a small abandoned town a few klicks back. He could wait there while the smoke cleared and then continue north to the settlement.

He heard the gunfire behind him, the armor's weapon piercing the night sky with crackling thumps as it poured out its ordnance. The Skin's HUD showed the trife dying behind him, the entire mass attacking the armor dead in a matter of seconds. He glanced over his shoulder in time to see it turning toward him.

Run faster.

He almost laughed at Ishek's suggestion as he leaped into the trees and dove behind the nearest trunk. Large caliber slugs pounded the wood, chipping out the sides and digging through it, the rounds punching through and over his head. He crawled laterally away from the tree, getting up and sprinting away again as the large oak began to drop behind him, crashing at his back and offering a little more screen for his escape.

He didn't slow until he reached the town ten minutes later. The Skin showed the area was clear—it surprised him the armor hadn't given chase—and it stayed that way for the next ten minutes.

Caleb ducked into an old pharmacy and sat on the floor behind the counter. "That was too close," he said, his heart pounding though his breathing had remained steady the entire time, thanks to Ishek.

It means some of you humans have some capacity to fight back. That can't be a bad thing.

"No, it can't. I just need them to stop fighting me."

Despite the dropship's efforts, there was still a massive group of trife ready to descend on the human city. Assuming the same scene that had played out at the farm was being duplicated across all of the assembled slicks, he needed to get there to help.

But could he even get close without being shot at again?

He had to try.

24

Nathan

General Nathan Stacker, eased off on the trigger, ending the onslaught of shells that had torn the old oak tree apart at the trunk and sent it toppling into the tree line. The Other was gone, having escaped capture thanks to the trife attack.

They *were* working together—the trife and the Other—weren't they? He hadn't expected to find one of the artificially intelligent humanoids amidst the trife when he ordered Pyro to fire the clusters into the slick, but when he'd seen it he'd wanted to catch the bastard.

That mission was a failure. The AI was a better hand-to-hand fighter than he imagined. Hell, it had dropped into a Marine defensive stance while it waited for him to come. But it made sense that the alien would be loaded with human fighting styles to use when fighting humans. It had been designed to appear as a human for the same reason.

Nathan scanned the field. A few scattered trife had survived the combination of cluster rockets, sniper fire and fire support from the Marines stationed inside the bunker..

They were wandering back and forth in an odd display of confusion. Nathan didn't blame them; the attack had come hard and fast and had likely left them trying to resist their queen's orders to continue the attack. A handful of trife against the group that had cut them to nearly nothing in a matter of minutes? The creatures weren't known for their self-preservation instinct, but that was pushing the limits of sanity.

"General," Pyro said, her voice tight through the comm. "We're getting reports from the outer markers. There are more trife moving toward the city."

"Roger," Nathan replied. "From what direction?"

"Uh. Every direction, sir."

Nathan's chest tightened in response. What the hell was going on out here? "I need pickup."

"Already on my way."

Nathan turned, leaning back to look up through the large helmet. It was an updated version of the powered combat armor his late father had invented for his also late brother John, based on the original design but improved with stronger synthetic musculature and a mixture of titanium and alien alloy Pyro's team had concocted.

Some of his officers thought it was a bad idea to risk his best engineer as a pilot, but among everyone he had tested, she'd had the strongest aptitude at the controls of a Centurion dropship.

He found the ship descending quickly toward the surface, the rear ramp already open to collect him. He moved into position as it continued its sharp drop, landing thrusters roaring for the last few seconds to stop the high-velocity pickup. The landers flexed as the craft landed. Nathan climbed back inside.

He hit the controls to close the rear ramp at the same

time the ship began to rise again, holding tight as g-forces tried to pull him into the bulkhead.

"Get us over the action," Nathan said, moving across the ship's hold.

"Roger that, General," Pyro replied. "How are your levels?"

Nathan checked the suit's HUD. "Eighty percent."

"Not terrible, but I feel like there's still something off with the superconductors. You weren't out there that long."

"I'm sure you'll figure it out."

Nathan stopped near the middle of the hold. Pulling his rifle from his back, he rested it beside a stack of ammunition boxes and pulled the ammo box from his back, disconnecting the feeder from it. He put it in a new stack of boxes and opened a fresh box of the large rounds. He snapped the end of the new feed into the side of the rifle. Finished with the reloading, he walked over to a sizable contraption against the side of the cargo area and backed into it.

Mechanical arms descended on the armor, unscrewing the bolts holding him inside, lifting the helmet from his head and cracking the protective shell open. The activity revealed his large, powerful cyborg body, the result of battle-inflicted wounds that had left most of the right side of his body ravaged and replaced.

He stepped out of the armor, rubbing the sweat from his bald head as he crossed the hold in his underwear.

Heading up the steps to the main deck, he continued to the bridge door at the midpoint of the craft, the door opening as he approached.

The bridge was small and round, equipped with a central pilot station flanked by two other control stations and a central command chair near the back. Control surfaces rested in front of each station, while displays

covered the overhead, providing a full view of the outside
world through a selection of externally mounted cameras.

"General," Pyro said, flicking her head around to greet
him from the pilot's station. Her red hair was cut to her
shoulders, framing her round, porcelain face, which was
slightly flushed at the cheeks. "Where the hell did that
Other come from?" she asked, her green eyes burning into
him, waiting for an answer.

"I don't know," he replied. "It got away."

"You don't want to chase it?" she asked, returning her
attention to the displays.

"Not if Edenrise is about to come under attack. This
was supposed to be an isolated slick."

"They won't get through the shields."

"That may be true, but I should be there when they
try."

"You might not get another chance at it, General."

Nathan dropped into the command seat. He was
slightly annoyed by Pyro's pushing, but he knew why she
was so persistent. An Other had nearly killed her. She
wanted a chance for vengeance.

"Understood," he replied. "Just follow the order."

"Yes, General."

The ship continued to climb, gaining velocity as it shot
north back toward Edenrise.

"General Stacker," a voice said through the comm.
"This is Lieutenant Burke."

"Burke," Nathan replied. "I've heard we're going to
have guests for breakfast. What's our status?"

"Sir, I'm collecting sensor reports from the outer markers. Estimates put the enemy forces at close to sixty-
thousand."

Nathan's mouth opened, but he didn't speak right
away.

"Sir?" Burke said.

"Did you say sixty-thousand?" Nathan asked.

"Yes, General."

Edenrise had been standing for over a hundred years. He had never seen or heard of a force of trife that large attacking the city before. Not since the shield tower had been erected and activated.

"Send out the alert. I want all available units both active and reserve to report for immediate deployment to the outer walls."

"Yes, General."

"Try to contact the scout teams as well. Tell them to stay clear of the incoming slicks and keep hidden."

"Yes, General."

"Thank you, Lieutenant. Stacker out." He closed the comm link. "Pyro, I want a flyby of the outer markers. I need to see them for myself."

"Roger, General."

The dropship banked as Pyro updated the vector. Nathan looked up at the ground-facing displays, vacant for the moment.

"If they try to attack, the shields will hold," Pyro said.

Was she trying to convince him or soothe her own fear and worry?

Sixty-thousand. It was a staggering number.

Why Edenrise?

Why today?

"Let's hope so," he replied.

25

Nathan

Nathan watched the displays as the dropship swung across the first of the outer markers— large, scaffold-like radio towers covered in custom-made sensors extending from the metal like branches.

A small cement outbuilding sat near the tower, but right now it was impossible to locate beneath the thousands of trife moving through the area. A large group of them had stopped at the tower and were eagerly attacking its four legs, slashing at the metal with their hard, sharp claws. It would take time for them to cut their way through, but they would get there eventually. Not that there was any benefit to the destruction. The markers were an early warning system, and the warning had already been sent.

"I was hoping the reports were wrong," Pyro said.

"They weren't," Nathan said flatly in reply. His jaw was tight, his chest tighter. There had to be close to ten-thousand trife below, a line of them like an oil slick spreading back to the west. Where had they all come from? He had done his best to keep the nests away from Edenrise. There were no reactors, no strong radiation sources anywhere near the city to attract them.

How far had these creatures traveled?

It was possible they had covered hundreds of kilometers. Maybe even thousands. It was possible the groups were working together in perfect unison. They knew the queens could communicate with one another, and each trife from the same nest formed a network of sorts, able to silently receive orders and react. But the ability for different groups to work together wasn't the same as the practice of one group working together. In his experience, nests of trife often attacked one another when they came in contact, even if there were humans to kill. They were territorial creatures.

This was so far out of the ordinary, he had no ability to guess at what was causing it. Humans had come to rely on that territorial nature to survive. If something had changed, if the trife decided to all work as one...

Humankind would be extinct on Earth within weeks.

"Stay on course for the next marker," Nathan said.

"Roger, General," Pyro replied, banking the craft to head to the next marker.

Nathan tapped on the control surface near his metal right hand, activating the comm. "Lieutenant Burke."

"General Stacker," Burke replied. "All units are activated and preparing for deployment to the wall."

"ETA?"

"Fifteen minutes, sir."

Nathan looked at the display again. The head of the slick was a kilometer away, within ten klicks of the city. The edge of Edenrise was visible near the horizon, the shields tinting the air a slight blue.

"Tell them they have ten," he replied. "No excuses."

"Yes, General," Burke said.

Nathan was silent for a moment. His next order sat at the edge of his lips, but he was hesitant to give it. Capitulation to anything wasn't his strong suit.

"Raise the alert level," he said at last. "And begin evacuating the city. Get them on the vessels." The words were sour through his mouth, but they had to be said.

"General?" Burke replied. Pyro whipped her head to look at him in surprise.

"There are sixty-thousand trife bearing down on the city. We have historical records of the shields holding against ten-thousand, but this is significantly more. I'm not willing to risk thousands of innocent lives on an outcome we can't be assured of. Put them on the ships and keep them ready to sail. If everything goes well, we'll neutralize the threat and everyone can go home."

"Yes, General," Burke said. "Understood. It will be done."

"Stacker out."

Nathan cut the comm link. Pyro was still looking at him. "What?"

"Be careful, Nathan," she replied.

"I'm not going to let innocent people die to keep a secret," he said. "Besides, where the hell is the Trust when we really need them? Or Centurion Space Force, for that matter? We should have the firepower to turn back an assault like this, but we don't. We're on our own out here. Just like we've always been."

Pyro offered a reassuring smile. "We'll get through it." She turned her head back around. "Approaching outer marker Epsilon."

Nathan's eyes were fixed on the displays. The scene at the second marker was almost identical to the first. A massive number of trife were marching on Edenrise, some of them stopping to attack the radio tower.

"I've seen enough," Nathan said. "Head back to the city. We'll load up on all the clusters we have and head back out. We can thin the ranks by a few thousand at least."

"Roger, General."

The ship banked again, streaking toward the city.

Edenrise had existed under another name long before the shield had gone up, one of many population centers spread across the former United States of America. It was composed of a collection of buildings of different shapes and sizes and densities, some untouched by the ravages of the first trife war, others broken, crumbling and long abandoned, and the majority in one phase of reconstruction or another that would take another century or more to complete.

The sea abutted the east end of the city, the north side an inlet that had once provided a home to the warships of the United States Navy. A few of the ships still rested there, floating calmly against reinforced piers, acting as both supply storage, housing, and in this moment an emergency escape plan for the many residents.

And there were a lot of residents. Nearly fifty-thousand. Edenrise was the largest city on the planet. It was also the safest city, thanks to the energy shield that radiated out from the spire in the center, offering a level of protection that couldn't be found anywhere else. Not even Proxima had a shield like it, because they didn't have a power source like it.

The shields meant the residents of Edenrise had lived in relative safety for nearly fifty years now, save for a single incident where the shield had failed and some trife had made it inside. They had little concept of the world before the invasion, little concept of the lives of other humans outside the shields. They didn't know the constant danger.

They didn't know the constant fear. They went about their daily business without concern for the outside world, able to walk the streets at all hours, spend their free time at the beaches or parks, and otherwise live a somewhat normal life.

It was as much a paradise as its new name suggested. A paradise the enemy was on the verge of shattering, for reasons still unknown to Nathan.

Pyro guided the dropship over the top of the city, vectoring toward the towering, needle-like spire that stood sentry over the settlement. It was one of the few structures that wasn't already in place when the trife invasion began, and it dwarfed everything around it.

"Edenrise Control, this is General Stacker," Nathan said. "Set a five-second break for oh-three-forty-five and synchronize."

"Copy that, General," one of the controllers in the room at the base of the spire replied. "Standby for entry."

A signal was passed to synchronize the countdown. Pyro set the ship to circle above the spire while they waited. The shields would shut down for five seconds, offering a brief window for them to slip below.

Nathan's eyes fixed on the down-facing camera. The external sound feed was currently shut off, but he didn't need it to imagine the blare of the emergency alert system and a calm voice from Control urging the residents to make for the old naval ships. Most of them were following instructions, acting calm while they retreated to their homes to grab a few meager belongings and head for the ships. Most, but not all. Some of the civilians didn't understand the need to be ready. They might even refuse to leave their homes. It was the price of security when that security became threatened.

Nathan knew the countdown had completed when the

dropship banked and dropped more rapidly than before, the inertia pulling him back into his seat. They swooped in beside the spire, circling it on the descent. Five seconds later, the shields went back on, casting the city in a web of protection once more.

They continued to drop, reaching a hundred meters before leveling off and easing over to the airfield near the ships. Ranks of soldiers were already organized on the grounds beside the airfield, uniformed, armed, and ready to head for the western wall just inside the energy barrier. The walls had been built long before the shields, the geography of the city and the surrounding water leaving only one side vulnerable to the trife. Twenty meters high and composed mostly of crushed vehicles, it had seen its share of fighting over the years and had remained intact throughout.

The soldiers waved at the dropship as it passed over them. They landed on the tarmac near one of the large hangars where the Liberator vehicles and equipment were kept. A pair of armed and armored officers were already waiting for him there, along with a car to take him wherever he asked to go.

Nathan stood as the ship touched down. Pyro started to stand too.

"Stay here," Nathan said. "I'm going to get those clusters loaded ASAP, and I want you airborne again. We might have enough time to do two runs if we can move fast enough."

"I can deliver them fast enough," Pyro said, regaining her seat.

"I know you can. You have the bridge." Nathan squeezed her shoulder before hurrying from the bridge and down into the cargo hold. He stepped back into his powered armor, waiting while robotic arms closed it around him. He moved out to the back and opened the rear ramp.

"General Stacker," Major Bushi said. Short and thin, he didn't have the look of a soldier, but he had the spirit of one. He was standing with Colonel Daw, an older, grizzled former scavenger with thin white hair and a stubbly, wrinkled face. and only half his original teeth.

Nathan activated the suit's external speakers. His voice came out deeper and more synthetic through them. "Bushi, find Captain Jonas. I want the dropship loaded with cluster rockets ten minutes ago."

"Yes, sir," Major Bushi said, sprinting toward the hangar.

"Colonel, I want you leading the defense of the wall."

"That's why I'm here, sir," Daw replied. "Burke says we're looking at sixty-thousand of the bugs."

"We're hoping to drop those numbers a bit, but yes. They'll be at the wall within the hour."

"We'll be at the wall within twenty minutes, General."

"Follow me."

Nathan headed away from the dropship. He could hear Captain Jonas' harsh shouting behind him, screaming at her techs—"Get the damn cluster rockets loaded already! What the hell is taking so long?" He appreciated her enthusiasm.

He made his way to the head of the assembled soldiers. An entire company was already assembled, another getting into position further afield. He increased the volume on his speakers as he came to a stop in front of them.

"AT-TEHN-SHUN!" he snapped, the word reverberating through the speakers.

A thunderclap sounded as a thousand men and women straightened and clicked their booted heels together.

"Every last one of you came to Edenrise searching for

the same things. Security, freedom, family, community," Nathan said. "Every last one of you volunteered to become part of the USSF, and to carry on the traditions of our ancestors as defenders of our way of life, but here in the city and out there beyond the shield—you're warriors. Fearless and brave." He paused for a moment, walking down the front line. He could see the fear in some of the soldier's eyes. He could see resolved fury in others. "I don't know why the trife decided today was a good day to pick a fight. I don't know why they're teaming up against us. What I do know is that we're the USSF, this is our home and shield or no, those bastards aren't getting in!"

"Hoorah!" the soldiers shouted in reply, their cry loud enough to echo across the entire city.

Nathan couldn't hear Colonel Daw's orders as he passed them to each of the leaders through his comm, and a moment later the platoons began to move out. They would cut through the city along cordoned streets back to the wall, where they would ascend to the top and wait for the hell to come.

The plans for defending the city had been drawn up a long time ago and practiced every year on John Stacker Day, in honor of the first General Stacker, who had kept the war against the trife on Earth going long after the generation ships had fled and who had founded the original Edenrise. Nathan was a clone of the general, a spitting image of the famous war hero.

That practice was paying off now, keeping the troops organized as they deployed to their defensive positions. Nathan went across the field to Second Company and repeated his short speech, sending them out with boosted morale before crossing the fields to the Third. Edenrise had five companies in total, each boasting between one thousand and twelve hundred soldiers. Fifty-six hundred humans against sixty-thousand trife.

He was glad they had the shield.

He turned when he heard the dropship rising behind him, and he watched as it circled the spire, ascending away and past the shields. The trife were getting close, enough so that he was able to use the zoom on his armor's visor to keep the ship in view as Pyro dropped the clusters across one of the slicks. He heard the explosions in the distance, though not as far in the distance as he would have liked. Then the ship circled back, re-entering the energy field within ten minutes from launch and repeating the process one more time.

Nathan didn't have time to linger and watch the second run. He joined the Fifth on their march west to the wall.

"Major Bushi," he said through his comm as he walked.

"Yes, General," Bushi replied.

"Have a transport loaded with rounds for my rifle and have it positioned near the center of the wall."

"Yes, sir."

Nathan checked his levels. The suit had recharged some while it was plugged into the dropship, returning the battery to ninety percent. Extended heavy use would drain the supply in about four hours, after which the powerful armor would become a useless iron prison.

There was no way the battle was going to last four hours. He expected to either be celebrating or dead within two.

26

Nathan

Nathan stood at the top of the outer wall along with every last one of the fifty-eight hundred soldiers in his military. They spread from one end of the curved barrier to the other—men and women in various degrees of protection and uniform, their equipment reflecting their rank and skill. The people waiting on either side of Nathan wore full Centurion combat armor, the rarest equipment they had on hand. Others wore lesser Edenrise-produced uniforms, reinforced across the arms, chest and legs, with simple steel helmets to protect their heads. Still others wore basic utilities—dark green, slightly faded and threadbare. The newest recruits on the wall didn't have official uniforms, having to settle for their already worn clothes and a hand-me-down rifle from the general stores.

The defensive plans called for spreading the capacity evenly across the wall, leaving the view across the barrier identical from either direction. The soldiers intermingled to provide maximum protection to all sections of the secondary defense.

Nathan was at the center of the force, standing directly

over the main gate into the city. Normally, a special hood was extended outward from the entrance into the energy field, creating a barrier so people could get past the shields without having to shut them down. But the hood had been retracted in preparation for the assault. Edenrise had been buttoned up to hopefully keep the enemy completely out.

A series of explosions sounded in the distance, visible to Nathan from his position. The last of the cluster rockets sank into the ranks of trife, marked by fireballs close to the horizon.

The head of the trife river wasn't as far back as Pyro's attack. Not anymore. The front line of demons had converged two klicks out. While Nathan had held out hope the trife from competing nests would attack one another on sight, he wasn't surprised when they continued his way en masse.

They were within a kilometer now, a group so large and dense it appeared as though a black sea spilled over the land, the flood headed right for them. He had never seen anything like it before, and judging by the looks on the faces of the soldiers around him, he wasn't the only one who was afraid.

He opened his comm to every soldier who had one.

"Get ready," he said.

Rifles went up in a ragged line, every soldier leveling their weapon in the general direction of the incoming tide. The alien hissing was like the roar of an engine echoing across the landscape, the thousands of pounding clawed feet a backbeat from hell.

Nathan could hear his heart thumping in his ears. He could almost feel the flow of his blood moving through his veins. Every emotion seemed to coalesce. Fear, anger, impatience. Excitement even. He was a clone of the greatest Space Force General who had ever lived. War was in his genes, and right now he had a choice to either shirk from the coming violence or embrace it.

He decided he would embrace it.

"Steady," he said. "Hold your fire unless they breach the shields."

Nathan glanced up as the dropship shot overhead, banking to circle the field. By the time he looked down again the trife had broken into an all-out charge.

"Here we go!"

The creatures hissed even louder as they ran, rushing at the wall with reckless abandon, their vocalizations drowning out all other ambient noise. Steady on the wall, the USSF soldiers shifted their aim to follow the demons as they crossed the relatively open terrain, their feet kicking up clouds of dust and debris.

Nathan grabbed the rifle from his back, checking the feed before hoisting it in one powerful hand. He had nearly twenty boxes of ammo waiting in the back of a truck directly behind him. All he had to do was jump down from the wall, reload and hop back up to resume shooting.

He still hoped there wouldn't be a need.

The entirety of the USSF army held its collective breath as the first of the trife began to reach the shields. They watched as the demons hit the barrier, creating bright flashes as the shield blasted them with crackling energy.

By the tens, then by the hundreds, they threw themselves into the barrier , causing the entire side of the shield to glow brightly.

It didn't matter to them how many of their number died. They continued to charge, pushing one another out of the way to be the next to burn alive.

Ten seconds passed. Twenty. Nearly five thousand trife had already succumbed to the energy barrier, forcing those behind them to claw their way up the growing pile of corpses, only to die too when they reached the shield.

Thirty seconds. Forty. More trife went up against the shield, joining the mass of corpses at the base. Some of them toppled and rolled back down while some stayed forward, splayed out against the barrier. Trapped in place.

Nathan found his attention fixed on those trife. Glaring at the bodies at the bottom of the pile, he could see how the continued contact with the shield was cooking the dead, turning their flesh and bone into a charred mess. It shifted the smell in the area from bad to worse, the scent of the dying and the dead becoming nauseating

Still, not a single trife had gotten through the shield. Not a single shot had been fired. There had to be more than ten-thousand dead along the wall.

Maybe it could absorb the assault after all.

"General, we have a problem," Lieutenant Burke said as if sensing his growing hope and choosing that moment to crush it.

"What is it?" Nathan replied without taking his eyes off the awful scene below him.

"Goya in engineering says the spire convertor is overloading because of the constant, escalating drain on the system."

"They're building up on the walls like water against a dam," Nathan said. "How do I get them clear?"

The reply wasn't immediate. Burke relayed the question to Goya, who relayed his answer back.

"Sir," Burke said. "According to Goya, we can't do a damn thing."

Nathan had expected the engineer to say that. He still didn't like hearing it.

"How long do we have?"

"Three minutes. Maybe less."

Nathan looked out at the army of trife. They were still coming, still dying against the shield, with no end in sight.

In three minutes, Edenrise's shields would go down.

In three minutes, forty thousand trife would have unfettered access to breach the walls.

In three minutes, the world was going to end.

If he was going to die, then he wanted to go down fighting.

He was about to get his chance.

27

Nathan

Nathan didn't get three minutes.

He barely got thirty seconds.

The trife continued throwing themselves into the energy shield, the pile rising, the drain on the shield critical. The smell itself was almost intolerable. He could hear some of the soldiers on the line coughing and vomiting, sickened and weak from the odor and the sheer volume of death. The trife were taking his people out of the fight without doing anything more than sacrificing themselves on the shield.

"Burke," he said, contacting his Lieutenant in the control room.

"Yes, General?"

"Tell Goya to turn off the shield."

"What?"

"You heard me, damn it! Turn it off."

He switched to the global comm. "Space Force, fire at will."

The order seemed to snap the soldiers out of their sickness, forcing them to focus on the defense or wind up in even worse shape. Nathan felt the shield begin to subside, a pressure he hadn't realized was there, lifting away from him. The pile of dead trife tumbled inward, knocking the living front of the wave off-balance and throwing them forward into the base of the wall. The front line of soldiers aimed straight down off the edge, hundreds of guns firing into the masses.

The wall shook from the sound and force, and thousands of trife died in the first few seconds, torn apart by the massive barrage. Nathan didn't waste his rounds shooting into single trife below. Instead, he aimed further out, launching large rounds at the enemy powerful enough to rip through multiple targets before their kinetic energy was spent. He kept a steady stream going, adjusting his aim and killing hundreds on his own.

It was impressive.

It also wasn't enough.

The demons surged forward with renewed effort, hissing more loudly as they began latching into the crushed metal of the wall and began to climb. The soldiers executed well, the front line dropping back to reload as the back line came forward, rotating firepower so there was never a break. Thousands of trife died at the base of the wall, but thousands more were there to back them up.

Nathan jumped down off the wall to reload from the truck, quickly changing out his ammo box for a fresh one. He leaped back up, making it just as the first of the trife came over the top, hissing and lunging at Colonel Daw. The Colonel barely flinched before shooting the first demon in the head.

Nathan started shooting again, firing downward now to cut through the climbing trife. He took out entire rows at once, but the slick was like a rising tide against the bulwark, still pressing forward and threatening to overwhelm them.

He heard his first human scream a moment later, as someone on the line was grabbed by a trife and thrown from the wall, down into the mix. The same thing happened again and again, —his people beginning to die.

"Pyro," Nathan said. "We need support."

"Already on it," she replied.

The dropship streaked toward the field. With its load of cluster rockets spent, Pyro fired the four plasma cannons, the large bolts shooting into the middle of the dark army, killing dozens.

A trife climbed over the wall right in front of Nathan. It rushed him, mouth open to rip him to shreds. Nathan met it with a metal fist. He broke its neck and threw it back off the wall. A second appeared a moment later, killed by a bullet from Colonel Daw.

"General," Lieutenant Burke said. "The southern flank is strained. The enemy is about to break through."

"Daw!" Nathan snapped. "Move the platoons down to cover the flank. Thin out the center. I'll hold it."

"Yes, General," Daw replied, still shooting as he sent out new orders.

"Burke, call up the reserves. They need to hit anything that gets over the wall."

"Yes General," Burke said.

Nathan's heart started pumping harder. They were standing firm, but there was just too many of them.

The soldiers began shifting on the wall, moving laterally to shore up the weakened flank. It left fewer fighters around him, putting pressure on him to hold the middle and keep the trife from breaching the gates.

Nathan glanced at the status display inside his helmet, noticing he was nearly out of ammo...again. He fired one last barrage into the climbing trife before jumping backward, using his armor's jets to land smoothly next to the truck. He dropped the used box and grabbed a new one, needing only a few seconds to reload. The dropship soared overhead, completing another strafing run along the line of aliens.

Nathan heard a scream, and Colonel Daw's body dropped from the back of the wall, three trife still biting and clawing at him. "Damn it!" Nathan cursed, more trife leaping down from the wall. Another group began hitting the gates, hissing and clawing at them to pierce the metal. "Burke, I need reinforcements on the gate!"

"General, the reserve is en route, but you need to hold until they can get to you."

Nathan fired at the demons coming over the wall, killing a few. Another of his fighters was thrown to the ground beside him, dead.

Had he made the right decision to relocate forces away from the center to shore up the flanks? Was it possible the trife had shifted the intensity of their attack from the outside to the middle with such precision?

He knew it was possible. The creatures were smarter than they seemed. He had to do something, or it would be his fault when everyone in Edenrise died.

His eyes landed on the ammo truck. It was a risk, but he had to take it.

He swung his rifle around to his back where it snapped to the bulge of the power supply. Then he crouched down, getting his hands under the ammo truck and lifting. The powered armor made him strong, but it was still a strain to lift the heavy vehicle, and more of a strain to keep it balanced. He managed to get it positioned over his head, and he started walking it toward the gate.

Trife were breaking over the wall as he carried the truck, a few dozen clearing his area and breaking toward the city. He regretted losing the people they would kill, but they would lose a lot more if he didn't take drastic action.

He made it to the gate and threw the truck down behind the rows of bars, hitting the barrier with a loud clang. The trife barely reacted. They were so intent on cutting through the bars they hardly noticed. A number of the crossbars were already sliced through and a few of the demons were attempting to squeeze through the gaps.

Nathan grabbed his rifle again as he backed away. He switched to the secondary trigger, still retreating.

Then he pulled it.

A soft thunk and a dark round ball shot from the lower barrel of the gun, hitting the truck a moment later. It didn't rebound, instead sticking there, a small LED quickly flashing red.

Nathan pulled the trigger again, and the ball exploded out of the muzzle.

Firing his jets. he was already leaping skyward, arcing for the top of the wall when it detonated. The explosion set off the rifle rounds inside the truck and blew all of the trife back from the gate.

Scores of trife hands reached wildly through the twisted bars and around the smoking remains of the truck. Hundreds of trife were killed immediately and more continued to fall as slugs slammed down into them from above, finally cutting a hole in the slick.

Nathan didn't stop there. He ran across the wall, his prosthetic arm outstretched, gathering up as many trife coming over the wall as he could. He let them bite down on his metal arm and dragged them to the opposite edge of the wall. There, he pulled them down with him as he leaped into the vacated hole.

"For Edenrise!" he shouted into his comm, hoping to inspire his people. He hit the ground hard, crushing the trife he had gathered beneath his armor as he rolled over and back to his feet. He started shooting those still moving, turning in a wide semi-circle, his slugs cutting down dozens of demons with each round and keeping the gate clear.

He couldn't hold the horde at bay forever. When he ran out of ammo, it would be all over, at least for him. But if he could buy enough time for the reserves to arrive, maybe they would have a chance.

He kept shooting, cutting down swaths of trife as the seconds ticked past. It didn't take long for his rifle to run dry, and when it did he turned it in his grip, holding it like a club. The trife charged at him hundreds thick. He began swinging his weapon, smashing into them and batting them away. Dozens fell to his assault, but he couldn't keep them back forever. They grabbed his legs and jumped on his back, slashing and clawing at his hardened armor, their claws struggling to break through the Other's material. He grabbed them, crushing their bodies in his powerful hands, fighting to stay upright as they continued to swarm over him.

Suddenly, he was off his feet and on his back. His armored weight and that of the trife coming down on top of him crushed the demons at his back. For an instant before they engulfed him, he caught sight of the dropship coming over for another strafing run. And then all he saw was biting teeth and slashing claws.

28

Caleb

"They can't hold much longer," Caleb said.

Over half the trife are destroyed. It is an impressive display.

"A wasted effort if they all die. They deserve better."

What can we do? We are only one human.

"You saw the shield. They have a QDM. Tell me we can't use that somehow."

We could use it, but we'll never reach it.

Caleb refused to believe that.

You can refuse all you want. It doesn't change the truth.

It was just like Ishek to be negative. It was the aspect of the symbiote Caleb was most glad he hadn't inherited. He had never given up on a chance to save human lives before. Not as a Marine Raider, not as Search and Rescue, not as a Guardian on the Deliverance...

And not now.

He had spent the last thirty minutes waiting at the base of a small hill outside of town for the trife army to arrive. He had stopped there to marvel at the tall spire rising out of the center of the city as if a god had planted a spear in it. The blue tinge to the air around the city and the displacement of the energy shield protecting it. He had expected to find something more advanced and secure than the random villages and settlements he had encountered so far, but this was so much more than that.

Whoever had built the city had somehow come into possession of a quantum dimensional modulator, an energy unit capable of producing a near infinite supply of power through a link to an alternate dimension. It was an Axon invention, the power generator they used for all their energy needs. The aliens were so advanced they produced the complex devices like trinkets, putting them in every ship they made regardless of the precise power requirements. Even so, the units weren't common outside of Axon control. That someone here had discovered one and even more importantly figured out how to put it to use was impressive, and it provided Caleb a measure of hope that just because centuries had passed since Earth was overrun, it didn't mean humankind had given up.

It didn't mean the planet was lost.

It was in trouble though. The massive attack had led the shields to fail, leaving the defense to a line of men and women standing on a makeshift barrier and doing their best to hold back a rising tide. He respected their courage. He had seen plenty of Marines he thought were tougher than nails break at the sight of a handful of trife, nevermind nearly sixty thousand.

"If I get us to the modulator, can you end the fight with it?" Caleb asked.

No guarantees, but the possibility exists.

Caleb rose from his hiding place. He had already spotted the armor he had encountered earlier standing on the wall blowing the hell out of the enemy. Watching it work, he was confident it wasn't a robot, but either the leader of the city or perhaps their top military officer as he had stood in one of the hardest spots to defend and had already dispatched some of the soldiers around it to stall a trife flanking maneuver.

It's a ruse.

Ishek was convinced the flank was a trick and the attack would regain the center. Maybe the Relyeh Advocate was right. Caleb didn't care. He only had one mission now.

Get to the modulator. Save the city.

He found the armor again, holding the center almost alone. He glanced up when he heard the dropship arrive overhead, static for a moment while he watched it blast the trife with plasma cannons. He would have given anything for a craft like that when he was running search and rescue through war zones during the initial trife invasion. Would they have even lost the war if they'd had weapons like that back then?

Yes.

"Shut up," Caleb said. He activated the Skin's projection, changing his outward appearance back into the trife he had scanned. Maybe Ishek was right about that too. Again, it didn't matter. They couldn't change the past.

He sprinted down the slope toward the rear of the enemy lines. Within seconds of reaching the slick, he began pushing his way through, drawing angry hisses from the demons around him. He climbed onto one's shoulders and stomped across them as though they were a living road. Some of them grabbed at him, trying to pull him down, but he hurried over them too quickly for them to get hold of him, his stamina increased by the chemicals Ishek pumped into his body.

He made it halfway to the front inside of thirty seconds, dropping back to the ground among the demons. He paused with them when he heard the dropship's thrusters increasing in volume, signaling the craft was returning. The Skin gave its position on his HUD. It was coming right for him, preparing to strafe the line.

Wouldn't that be ironic after everything you've been through? Gunned down by friendly fire.

Sometimes Caleb regretted his bond to the Advocate. This was one of those times.

I kept you alive when you would have died. Don't forget that.

Caleb had done the same for Ishek. The Advocate shouldn't forget that either.

Completely different circumstances.

Caleb smiled, recalling those circumstances. Only for a moment. The dropship was swooping in, plasma spewing from its cannons. The trife ahead of him were being blasted into the air, burned and torn apart. He didn't want to suffer the same fate.

He crouched, ready to move in any direction. The plasma blasts descended. He broke right, leaping and pushing off the side of a trife, slamming into a second, rolling away from him and springing forward. A plasma bolt hit the ground a few meters away, causing the trife there to scream and die. He felt the heat of the gas wash over him, along with a strong whiff of burning flesh. The force knocked him down, but didn't pierce the skin.

A loud crackling rumble followed—the sound of the armor's rifle rapid-firing. Caleb was closer than he thought. Closer than he wanted to be. He turned toward the origin of the noise as slugs began cutting through the nearby trife, tearing the aliens in half as they sliced past him. Caleb threw himself down, staying low while the barrage continued, tearing the trife nearby apart.

It only lasted a few seconds. The gun ran out of ammunition, and the trife immediately began to close in. Caleb heard the armor moving, and then the cracking of bones and the pounding of flesh. Claws and teeth scraped metal. Caleb got back to his feet, trying to join the press of trife bodies as it moved in on the armored soldier.

The man went down under a pile of trife. Dozens of the demons stayed with him, slashing and biting, while the rest continued through the damaged gates and into the city.

Caleb glanced up. The creatures were beginning to make progress on the walls as well, the soldiers defending them falling at an increasing pace. They had put up a good fight, a brave fight, but the end was coming.

It's too late. We can't save them. We need to leave this place.

Even if that were true, they couldn't leave the QDM to fall into Relyeh possession. The trife army would triple in size within weeks with access to that much energy.

Good point.

Caleb checked the Skin's power supply. Judicious use over the last few months had minimized the drain—it still held seventy percent of its stored energy—but he didn't need to conserve it anymore. There was a QDM only a few kilometers away. The Axon power source could recharge his Skin in seconds.

It still won't be enough to stop the assault.

But it might help him save some of the people, starting with the one in the armor.

He activated the Skin's weapon systems, charging them at full power. The action caused the projection to fall away, immediately alerting the trife to an enemy in their midst. The group closest to him hissed and changed direction, leaping at him with slashing claws.

He threw his hands out, the energy flowing from every nodule of the Skin. The nearest wave of trife was thrown back, a hundred or more killed in the blast that immediately drained ten percent of the power supply but also gave Caleb seconds to reach the armored warrior.

He sprinted forward, grabbing the trife that turned to stop him. Each time his hand touched one of them a shot of energy raced through his palm and into their bodies, killing them nearly instantly. He barrelled through the immediate crowd of trife like a linebacker, shoving the demons aside, jumping over them, and finally making it to the pile. He hesitated a moment, hoping the mech's armor would absorb the blast before sending a shockwave of energy through the trife.

Dozens of the trife died on top of the soldier's armor, leaving him buried. Caleb checked his HUD. He had drained nearly twenty-five percent of his power in a dozen seconds. Ishek was right. He couldn't stop the assault on his own even with the Skin. It was powerful, but it was intended to be worn by an Axon Intellect with a much larger secondary power supply.

"Marine!" he shouted, hoping the person in the armor could hear him. "Get up. Let's move!"

He turned to grab an oncoming trife, throwing it aside. He kicked another and blasted energy at a third, fourth and fifth.

"Marine!" he shouted again. "The city needs you!"

He glanced back at the pile of dead trife. Had his attack inadvertently killed the Marine? Had the trife gotten to him first?

Then the pile began to shift. A dozen dead alien corpses were pushed aside as the armored soldier pushed himself up, first to a knee and then to his full height, towering over Caleb. The armor was badly scratched and gouged, and a deep crack ran along the dark visor, but it was still intact.

They stared at one another for a moment.

"Who are you?" the armored man said, his voice choppy through a single, damaged external speaker.

"Sergeant Caleb Card, United States Space Force Marines. Get me to that spire, and I might be able to help you save your city."

29

Caleb

The armored man regarded Caleb. "General Stacker," he said. "I'm sorry for trying to kill you before, but…"

Stacker? Wasn't he——?

Of course Ishek knew who General Stacker was to Caleb. The Advocate could read his mind. One of the most respected officers in the military during the original trife invasion. The government had tried to get him to leave Earth on one of the generation ships. He had refused to go. He refused to believe Earth was lost. He refused to stop fighting.

But *that* Stacker would currently be over two hundred years old. Whoever this man was, he wasn't the original General Stacker.

It didn't matter right now. They had to survive the onslaught first. Then he would worry about the man's true identity.

"Understood," Caleb replied, not paying particular attention to his apology. "We can save apologies for later, sir. Right now, we need to get to the spire." He spun around, putting his hands together and launching an energy blast into the trife there, killing four of them.

"Follow me," Stacker said. He started running toward the city gates, following the trife. Gunshots rang out in the distance as a secondary city defense began shooting at the incoming demons.

Caleb sprinted behind Stacker, impressed by the speed and agility of his powered armor. They plowed through the trife, coming up on them from behind and staying away from the others at the rear. Stacker grabbed any of the demons he was able to reach on the way past, crushing them in powerful hands and leaving corpses behind.

They reached the damaged gates. So many trife were pouring through, and so many corpses littered the area it had created a jam on the other side. Gunfire sounded close by, and entire lines of trife dropped in front of them, the shooters on the wall refocusing on their path ahead. Stacker had to be communicating with them, sending them orders to help clear the way.

"Ish, can the Skin get into Stacker's comms?"

I have tried. The encryption is improved from your conventional systems. I would almost call it Axon-hardened.

So Stacker knew something about the Axon and had developed hack-resistant comms.

It certainly appears that way.

They made it to the other side of the gate. Stacker plowed through the trife, kicking and shoving bodies out of the way to continue toward the spire. Soldiers were coming down off the walls, forming up on their position to defend. They were a ragged, tired looking bunch, some of them covered in the blood of trife and their dead comrades. It was hard to believe the battle had only been in progress for as little as ten minutes.

Caleb!

Ishek's cry caused Caleb to stumble and nearly fall, the sudden pressure in his head almost overwhelming. He slowed slightly, recovering just in time to bat away a trife that had made it through their defenses.

We have a problem. A big problem. Tell Stacker if he can to get his people out of here, he needs to do it now.

"What's going on?"

Now, Caleb!

Caleb opened his mouth to shout out to Stacker. At the same time, all of the trife seemed to freeze at once. Even the air around them seemed to freeze, the atmosphere signalling that something was very wrong. The soldiers stopped shooting moments later, nearly every living thing on the battlefield coming to a stop. The trife lifted their heads, looking back the way they had come.

Caleb looked back too. It was hard to see past the trife. There was something out there. Something in the distance. Something rumbling and groaning in an alien staccato that made his spine shiver.

"General," he said, echoing Ishek. "If you can get your people out of here, you need to do it now. Right now!"

The trife suddenly started moving again. They charged forward, catching the soldiers by surprise. Only it seemed the battle was suddenly over. The trife no longer paused to attack the humans. They rushed past them, hissing and screaming in fear. Desperate to escape.

Escape from what?

Xaxkluth.

The word meant nothing to Caleb, but it seemed to have plenty of meaning for Ishek. The Advocate was afraid, frightened in a way sixty thousand trife had been unable to scare him. Caleb could have looked into the Relyeh's mind for the reason, but he was sure he didn't want to know right now.

"The spire," Stacker said. "Hurry!"

Caleb and Stacker, joined the fleeing horde of both trife and humans. Everyone was on the move now, fleeing the walls and the unseen horror approaching from outside the city. They could still hear the groans, deep and loud, like a monster rising from the depths of the ocean.

Caleb sped up, getting close enough to Stacker to hear him shouting orders inside his helmet.

"All units, retreat to the naval yard. I repeat, retreat to the naval yard. Board the nearest ship. You have three minutes before we cut the ships loose."

Xaxkluth do not fear water the way the uluth do.

"Then we need to stop them."

You can't stop them, Caleb. You don't have the means.

"Even with the QDM?"

Ishek hesitated to answer. That was good enough for him.

There is no guarantee I can make it work. If we linger, we will die.

Then they would die. He wasn't going to leave innocent people to whatever kind of monster was approaching.

They kept running, the groaning sounds increasing in volume, the new creatures gaining ground. Gunfire began to sound again ahead of them. Someone was shooting at something.

"The trife won't go in the damn water," Stacker barked to him. "They're clogging the escape, and trying to get onto the ships."

Caleb swallowed hard. He hadn't thought of that.

"Drop them and get underway," he heard Stacker order. "I know. We don't have a choice. Do it. All units, keep the trife away from the docks. If you want to save your families, your loved ones, keep them off the damn docks."

There was pain in Stacker's voice. Caleb felt it too. Whoever hadn't gotten onto the ships by now was probably going to die.

Including them.

"Stacker," Caleb said. "Pull your soldiers back, as many as you can, to the spire."

The armored soldier didn't ask any questions. He began issuing the orders. "Clear the docks and fall back."

At least the path to the spire would have them going against traffic.

The dropship swept overhead, plasma cannons firing closer to the water. It passed by and banked hard, preparing for another run.

The race took Caleb through familiar city streets. He had spent time at Quantico to the north during his early career and had come south to Norfolk plenty of times. Crossing paths he had crossed many times before, he was shocked by how much had changed, and at the same time how little looked nearly the same. Some of the old storefronts were still intact, their signage restored at some point to near-original condition. Trees lined the buffers between sidewalk and roadway, and restored-to-like-new cars rested at the curbs.

On one hand, the sight transported him back to that earlier, simpler time before the trife invasion. On the other, it was a stark reminder of the suffering and pain that had followed, especially as the trife crashed through the trees, tearing off limbs, or bounded over the cars, scratching the finish.

It was like watching the start of the invasion all over again—only worse.

The groaning continued to get louder, and Caleb could hear the xaxkluth approaching now, the sound of moist, slapping flesh overcoming the hissing and shouting and gunfire. Stacker turned left at the next street, bringing the spire into view ahead of them, two blocks away. A number of soldiers were already in the area, gathered around the spire. They leaned against one another or huddled against the wall—tired, bloody and sweaty. The ones who saw Stacker coming perked up immediately, coming to attention.

Caleb looked to the left as they crossed the first street, back in the direction of the wall. An echo of tearing metal rose above the rest of the chaotic noise, and he got his first look at the new threat, the first of too many advancing into the city.

"What the hell...," he whispered, slowing slightly as his eyes crossed the expanse of tentacles stretching forward from the gigantic monster.

Xaxkluth. Nyarlath's favorite children. The trife didn't gather to attack this city. They were trying to escape.

Caleb

Caleb followed Stacker to the base of the spire. The groaning and slapping sounds from the xaxkluth pursuing them was louder than ever, the monsters closing on them. The soldiers were all back on their feet by the time they arrived, ready and waiting for orders.

"The control room is inside, straight ahead," Stacker said. "I don't know what you'll be able to do. The system melted down."

A handful of people emerged from the front of the building. Uniformed officers carrying rifles. They joined the ragged group on the steps.

"I'm not sure either," Caleb replied. "What about the QDM?"

"QDM?"

"The power source."

"There are stairs to the left. Descend to the bottom and go through the door. We'll hold them off for as long as we can."

"Roger that. Aim for the eyes on the central mass. It'll slow them down."

"Where did you come from?" Stacker asked, surprised Caleb knew anything about the creatures.

He didn't, but Ishek did. "Long story," Caleb replied. "We can get a beer when this is over."

Stacker grunted out a laugh. "It's on me."

"Roger that."Caleb said as he rushed past Stacker and up the stairs into the base of the spire. "Which way?" he asked Ishek. "The energy unit or the control room?"

Control room. Let us see what we can accomplish.

As Caleb ran through the open door just ahead of him, he heard gunfire begin behind him. The change in pitch of the xaxkluth's groaning signalled its rage as it came under attack. He knew he didn't have much time.

The control room was standard military design. Stations. Terminals. Displays.The largest hung across the front of the room. Most of the computers were offline, including the large display. The smell of burning circuits hung thick in the air.

"Stacker said the system overloaded," Caleb said.

That terminal is operational.

Caleb looked at the station in the corner. Its display was still active. He hurried over to it and sat in the task chair, pulling it forward.

Give me control.

Caleb breathed in, closing his eyes and trying to relax. The pressure in his head built as the Relyeh Advocate seized his mind, taking full ownership of it.

Ishek opened his eyes, staring at the display. Humans were so easily weakened without their sight. They relied on vision for too many operations.

We haven't had hundreds of thousands of years of evolution. If you ask me, Relyeh are primitive relative to their age.

Ishek wasn't going to argue with Caleb. Not right now, anyway. He began tapping on the control surface, using

Caleb's understanding of computer systems to navigate this one. He needed to understand how the spire's energy shield functioned before he could determine if he could use it as an offensive weapon.

He pulled up the schematics. The spire had dense carbon crystals mounted at the top. Diamond silicate, its many facets refracted the energy around the city. It wasn't so much a shield as a web, with gaps too small for anything larger than a rodent to squeeze through.

The crystals were mounted to adjustable arms, the web able to be repositioned if necessary. It didn't seem the technicians in charge of the spire even knew that. But they weren't the ones who had created the tech, were they? Only the caretakers.

Of course, the wiring connecting the modulator to the system at the top of the spire was human-made and couldn't withstand the sheer power required to keep it running while it was under stress. The link was damaged somewhere and there was likely no way to fix it.

But the system hadn't failed. It had been turned off. Shut down before it broke completely. Ishek smiled. The humans had done something smart for once.

Does that mean you can use it?

He could use it. But they would only have one shot, and the spire would likely be destroyed.

With them in it.

"I'm not eager to die," Ishek said.

You'll die anyway if we don't stop the xaxkluth.

Ishek sighed. He couldn't argue the truth of the situation.

"There is one way we might survive, but we'll have to leave the modulator behind."

Whatever it takes, Ish.

The Advocate sighed again and began tapping on the

control surface. He entered the reflector controls, quickly programming in a series of positioning alterations.

He glanced up when he heard activity near the door. General Stacker entered the room, trailed by nearly a dozen shocked soldiers.

"Sergeant, this is all we have left," Stacker said. "I hope you have a plan."

The building shook as the xaxkluth slammed into it, trying to get inside.

"I have a plan," Ishek said. "Stay as close to me as you can."

The survivors came forward, huddling around him. Ishek tapped on the controls, his finger hovering over the power transfer switch that would turn the system back on.

"Let us hope the system doesn't fail."

His finger came down on the button. A sharp hum immediately filled the room, a massive spike of energy flowing from the modulator up to the top of the spire. The display changed as it did, showing the output of the energy and the movement of the reflectors.

"What's happening?" Stacker asked.

"If we're lucky, the xaxkluth are dying."

The building continued to shake. A deafening roar sounded from outside, along with groaning screams. The seconds ticked past slowly.

Ishek watched the progression of the programmed route on the display. Seventy percent complete. The building continued to shake, and the screen started flashing red, the system overloading and beginning to fail.

Come on, damn it.

"Come on," Ishek said, echoing Caleb's urging.

The side of the building cracked and started to crumble, a giant tentacle ripping away at the stone, still trying to reach them.

Ishek tapped the control surface, increasing power through the system.

Increasing?

"Stay close," he said. "Timing is everything."

The display flashed and began to spark and smoke. The soldiers around Stacker were terrified, their eyes wide and faces pale. Ishek drank in their fear, feeding on it. There was no reason not to take advantage of the situation. They needed it to survive.

A second tentacle pushed through the crumbling building, reaching out for them. The display went dark. The humming increased to an ear-splitting scream.

Something popped, followed by a bright flash of light. Ishek activated the Skin's shields, using the rest of its stored power to push it out past the gathered survivors, encasing them in a cocoon of energy.

The building exploded.

31

Nathan

Nathan was sure he was going to die. That's what a loud pop and a flash of light usually meant for anyone close enough to be blinded by it.

Then again, this was the seventh or eighth time in the last hour he was sure he was about to die, and yet here he was—somehow, still standing—in the spire control room with a featureless black humanoid figure who claimed to be a Space Force Marine.

If he hadn't watched the figure save his life, he probably wouldn't have believed any part of that story. Even now, he wasn't so sure.

But he wasn't going to question it. Not when Caleb Card was trying his best to save his life and the lives of thousands. He didn't have to be here in the city. Nathan had fought him earlier and chased him off. But why had he run? If he was human, why hadn't he revealed himself then?

Maybe he hadn't realized Nathan was human too. The powered armor did give him more of a mechanical,

185

robotic countenance. Either way, he hoped it was a simple misunderstanding.

One he wasn't sure they would have the chance to clear up.

The building shook violently around them, the ceiling beginning to collapse at the same time a flash of energy washed through him, stopping his breath for an instant. He could see the slight hue of the shield suddenly hovering just in front of his face, enveloping him and his surviving Space Force soldiers. Only a dozen of those who hadn't been able to escape to the ships remained alive..

Out of over five thousand.

The reality hit him like a punch to the gut. So many lives gone. So many still to save. But had they saved them? Was he going to get out of this alive? Did he deserve to?

The groaning of the monster outside the control room changed in pitch and Nathan turned his attention to the pair of tentacles. They thrashed violently in the hole the creature had made in the wall while it screamed outside.

His soldiers shouted as a large piece of cement hit the top of the shield, expecting it to crush them instead of rolling off to the side. They cried out again as more of the building came down, smashing into the shield and shedding away. Dust and debris filled the air, the tearing, cracking, and collapsing noises drowning out the dying alien outside. An extra loud crack shook the entire room, and then the ceiling vanished into open air, the upper part of the spire falling sideways. It broke away from its roots, toppling laterally like a tree. Nathan didn't see the impact, but he heard the breaking windows and rending metal as the top of the spire crashed into it.

"Up and out," Caleb said, the shield fading away almost as quickly as it had come. There was something different about the man now. His whole posture seemed off. Uncanny. It shifted suddenly, returning to normal. Had he imagined it?

"Come on," Nathan growled, activating his jump pack and launching himself up to the top of the rubble pile. He turned and bent down, taking his people by the hand and helping then onto the crumbled stone.

Caleb quickly scaled the rock, joining him at the top and helping recover the rest of the soldiers.

"Armageddon," one of them said.

Nathan looked up for the first time, quickly scanning the city. Whatever Caleb had done with the spire had made a mess of Edenrise. The buildings were cracked and smoldering, the vehicles were thrown from their positions and burning, and there were corpses everywhere. Trife mostly, with a few humans mixed in here and there, along with at least a dozen of the odd giant tentacled aliens that had assaulted them.

"Pyro, do you copy?" Nathan asked, activating his comm. It crackled inside his helmet, but she didn't respond. He looked up, searching for the dropship. It was impossible to see through the cloud of dust.

A loud groan sounded to the east, followed by a second. At least two of the monsters had escaped the massacre.

"We didn't get all of them," Nathan said.

Caleb looked at him. He was trying to hide the truth behind his expression, but Nathan wasn't an idiot. The creatures were tailing the ships. If they managed to catch up to the carriers…

Damn it.

Nathan knew they should all be dead. Caleb had tried to save them. All of them. It wasn't his fault the plan had fallen short.

"We need to get out of here," Caleb said. "In case they come back."

"Come back?" one of the soldiers said. "What for? Look at this place. An hour ago, this was a safe haven. My home." He was distraught. "My wife. My children. I hope they made it to the ships. Or maybe I don't." The man put his head in his hands and began to sob.

"What do we do now, General?" one of the other men asked. "Where the hell do we go?"

"I don't know yet," Nathan replied. "We'll figure something out."

"What the hell are those things?" A third soldier said. "Why are they here?"

"Yeah, I thought the trife were bad news," the second replied.

Nathan looked at Caleb. The so-called Marine Sergeant knew something about these creatures. He had told him how to disable them.

His attention caused the rest of his soldiers to divert their attention until all eyes were on the black humanoid.

Caleb reached back behind his head to the base of his neck. and pulled the hood back over his head and down, proving that there was a human being underneath.

"I'll be happy to tell you everything I know once we're someplace safe," he said. "Everything I've told you is true, Stacker. I'm not convinced you've shown me the same courtesy."

"Like you said, we'll settle this someplace safe. Pyro has to be up there somewhere. We need to get into the open for pickup."

"What about those two monsters out there that got away?" the sobbing soldier asked.

"We'll catch up to them and we'll kill them, Hotch.

That's what we do. Get your shit together. You can mourn when we're on the dropship."

"Yes, General," Hotch replied, straightening up and wiping at his moist eyes.

"Follow me," Nathan said, guiding them down off the rubble to a clearing in the street.

They headed west, away from the shore. The groaning sounds faded into the distance, but he was sure he heard the faint sound of screaming through the suit's sensitive microphones. It made him sick.

They came across another of the monsters, severed nearly in half beneath a piece of a damaged building. Two of its tentacles were still twitching, the teeth at the ends opening and snapping closed. Nathan stopped a meter away from it to stare. He understood the trife and the Others. This was something else altogether.

What was this thing? Why was it here? And why now?

He hoped like hell Caleb had answers.

"Pyro, do you copy?" Nathan asked again, still trying to raise her. The armor had taken a beating. There was a good chance his comms were damaged.

A deep groan caught his attention. He looked up in time to see a tentacle reach over a slab of rubble. Another followed, and then the creature's central mass and huge mouth began to rise. It was oozing a dark liquid, and half its eyes were punctured.

Injured but still very much alive.

He glanced at his survivors. Only a couple of them were still carrying their rifles. He couldn't come down on them. He had lost his too.

"Caleb, can you take it down?" he asked.

"Negative," Caleb replied. "The Skin's out of juice."

The creature saw them, groaning even louder in

response. More tentacles came over the slab as it maneuvered to attack them.

"Back," Nathan decided, waving his people away from it. "The other way."

They turned around. Caleb took the lead, coming to a quick stop when a tentacle appeared from around the corner of a building. "Shit."

"Don't these damn things die?" Hotch whined.

The two monsters were trying to box them in, but they weren't out of options. "East," Nathan said. "Back to the gate."

They ran toward the second monster, turning at the next street and cutting east. The two creatures gave chase, one moving more quickly than the other. It swung around the corner behind them, its body carried forward in an awkward slapping gait. It was the smaller of the two but still towered over them, each tentacle nearly twice Nathan's formidable size.

The gate was visible ahead, though it hardly resembled a gate anymore. Between the fighting and explosion in the spire, the metal barrier had been torn apart, leaving huge gaps and torn metal scattered around the area. The hundreds of trife corpses were hardly recognizable, leaving only a field of dark earth and ash and the awful stench of death.

Nathan didn't want his soldiers added to it, but what could he do? He had no weapons save the strength of his powered armor—finite compared to the many limbs of the enemy. Even so, if he could delay the creature for a few minutes he could give them time to get away.

"Damn it, Pyro. Where the hell did you go?"

He slowed down, letting the others get ahead of him. Caleb noticed almost immediately, and he turned his head, looking back. It was the expression that told Nathan the man was who he said he was. A warrior. A Marine. Caleb was ready to sacrifice himself—the same way Nathan was —to make sure they all made it out. No indecision. No hesitation.

Nathan couldn't shake his head in the armor, and he didn't want to call out to Caleb to let him do what he had to do. He had to trust the man would lead his people to safety. He had to know that if they both died, they would all die.

Caleb turned his head away again.

Nathan pulled to a stop and turned around.

The monster was a hundred meters back, and it groaned loudly when it saw Nathan stop, lowering its body into a more aggressive posture.

"Come on then," Nathan said, increasing the power output to the armor's artificial muscles. He punched his right fist into his left palm, crouching slightly to wait.

Someone started shooting behind him, a pair of rifles sending what was left of their ammunition over his head and into the creature. Nathan looked at his HUD, noticing his men had all stopped moving. What the hell were they doing?

The creature groaned in response, raising two of its tentacles to protect its many eyes. The bullets sank into its flesh, slowing it slightly.

Nathan took a step toward the alien. Another round hit it, but not from the rifles behind him.

From the air.

Plasma rained in on the creature, round after round striking the tentacles trying to protect its central mass. Nathan looked up as the dropship swooped in from the smoke cloud above, slowing and sliding laterally as it moved into position behind him.

Nathan began backing away. The second creature was

coming, turning the corner behind the first. The dropship continued firing, keeping the enemy at bay while Nathan turned and ran under the craft as it came to a low hover , its rear ramp already down.

"Let's move!" Nathan shouted. He didn't need to tell his people twice. They rushed the ramp, helping one another aboard.

Caleb came to stand with Nathan at the bottom of the ramp. "Taxi service is a little spotty out here," he said.

"Better late than never," Nathan said, sharing a grin with Caleb.

The ramp was already coming up as the two of them walked up it into the dropship. The craft immediately began ascending, climbing out of the creatures' range and blasting away.

32

Isaac

"Activating fold generator in five...four...three...two... one..." Able reached forward, tapping the button that would send them across four light years in a matter of seconds.

Isaac knew what to expect. He had been through it once before. The ship's generator began emitting enough energy to pull at space and time, twisting it out of shape around them and piling one part of the fabric of the universe on top of another. While the fold on the way to Proxima had been nearly invisible, this one was a bit different. It turned the universe ahead into a spiral pattern, shaping the stars in such an odd way that Isaac's stomach immediately began to complain.

He wasn't alone. Rico grabbed at her mouth with her free hand, and Able shut her eyes, turning her head away. Looking somewhere else didn't help the nausea. It continued to increase as the ship guided itself into the fold, an unexpected force pressing in on them and spinning the ship as if it were an amusement park ride. Isaac was thrown sideways by the sudden shift, hitting against the bridge's port bulkhead.

Able was yanked hard into the back of her seat and then forward into her straps as was Rico at the command station.

"What the hell?" Drake shouted through the comm. The rest of the Organization soldiers were in seats in the common area in front of the bridge. They hadn't buckled in. Traveling through folded space was usually a smooth affair.

The ship redirected again. Isaac barely grabbed onto the side of the command station to keep from being thrown into the rear wall and then dumped forward toward the primary display.

It was over in seconds, the ship becoming serene again as the fold generators deactivated and space flattened out on the displays. Isaac reached out to balance himself, his mouth filling with saliva as his body threatened to rebel.

He closed his eyes and swallowed, fighting the urge to vomit. He opened his mouth to take in more air, noticing the others on the bridge were doing the same. For a second, Isaac thought he was safe. Then a new sensation washed over him, and he dropped to a knee to puke on the floor.

He coughed when he was done, his stomach immediately beginning to settle. The door to the bridge slid open beside him.

"You too, eh?" Drake said, looking down at him. "Hell, Able. You just made half my team wretch."

It took Able a few seconds to answer while she overcame her own nausea. "It was the new algorithm. I don't know what that was exactly, but I don't think any of us liked it all that much."

"Did we get to where we were trying to go at least?"

"It looks like it," Rico said. "Ship's computer puts us about five AU from Earth. We're closer than we expected."

"Updating ETA," Able said. "Looks like we'll be there in eighteen hours."

"Haeri said they thought we would arrive in two days. That's a huge win."

"Let's hope it's not the only one we get," Drake said. "Ike, there's probably a bucket and mop in one of the storage compartments back aft."

"Isaac's a VIP, " Rico said before Isaac could reply. "Lucius is the rookie. He's got puke duty."

Drake laughed. "I'll make sure to tell him it was your orders."

"You do that."

Isaac got back to his feet. "I made the mess," he said. "I'll clean it up. I'm a Space Force Marine, not a delicate flower."

"That may be true," Rico replied. "But we have other business." She looked back at Drake. "Lucius cleans the puke, Spot drives the ship. Got it?"

"Yes, ma'am."

"Able, once you get us tracked for Earth, I want you and Bennett with Ike and me in the conference room."

"Are we in trouble?" Able asked.

"We're all in trouble. I lost Austin over this, and I want answers. I think Ike deserves to hear them too."

"Copy that, Major," Able said.

"I'm not a major. Special Officers don't have ranks, and I was a sergeant before I resigned from the CSF."

"That may be true, but we have to call you something. Ma'am is too formal, Rico is too informal, Special Officer is a mouthful and Specoff sounds downright dirty. You're part of the Organization now, and Haeri put you in charge of this mission."

"Major it is," Rico said. "You okay with that, Ike?"

"It's fine with me," Isaac replied. "But we didn't ask to be part of the Organization."

"Do you want to stop the Relyeh from enslaving humankind?" Able asked.

"Yes."

"Then why wouldn't you want to be part of this?"

"I didn't say I didn't want to be part of it."

"So what are you saying?"

Isaac stared at the older woman. He had only known her a short time, and she already tended to make him feel like he was arguing with his mother.

"Maybe we should head to the briefing room," he replied.

She returned a condescending smile. Was she doing it on purpose? "Give me a minute to lock the path. I'll meet you there."

"I'll give you five," Rico said. "Come on, Ike."

She took the lead off the bridge, heading back along the port side corridor to the room immediately behind it. The briefing room was small, with a single round table and eight chairs surrounding it.

"How well do you know Able?" Isaac asked as they entered.

"That depends on how you mean it," Rico replied. "She's been in Centurion Intelligence since before my model existed."

It was still hard for Isaac to think of the clones as clones, and the statement made him uneasy. "How long ago was that?"

"The first Rodriguez came out of replication twenty-four years ago. I'm sixteen."

"What is that like? Being a clone?" He paused. "I'm sorry. Maybe that's a rude question?"

"It's okay, Sergeant. I know who and what I am, and

I'm comfortable with it, even if some people on Proxima aren't. Honestly, it isn't all that much different from your experience as a human. The memories are randomized for uniqueness and implanted, so while I know I've only existed for sixteen years, in my mind I've got twenty-eight years of life to look back on. An entire childhood." She smiled. "A pretty good one too."

"But you were made to be a soldier, right?"

"A Centurion Space Force Marine," she corrected. "And I've loved every minute of it."

"Because you were designed to love it."

"I suppose."

"That doesn't bother you?"

"Why would it? It isn't torture to do what you enjoy doing whether you were called to it or made for it. As long as you're fulfilling the purpose you're supposed to fulfill."

"I'm sorry if I'm being forward or rude." He waved his hands. "Everything about this is so new to me. I'm trying to process it all."

"I get it," Rico said. "I really do. You can't offend me. I want to help you get acclimated. I'd have to say I think my situation is easier to handle than yours. To wake up after two hundred years...you're a strong man to still be sane."

"I promised my wife I would never give up on Earth. That promise, her memory, those are all the motivation I need."

"You're a good man, Ike."

"I try to be."

The door to the room opened. Bennett and Able walked in. They stood at attention inside the door, waiting for Rico to respond.

"Relax," she said. "Have a seat." She waited a few moments while they found a place around the table. "We can loop the rest of the team in as necessary, but I didn't want either of you withholding anything from me or Ike that may be classified to the others. I'm sure the Organization has plenty of secrets."

"We do," Able admitted.

"So tell us how deep the rabbit hole goes."

33

Isaac

"It's probably one of the best-kept secrets in the universe," Able said, her eyes dancing from Rico to Isaac and back. "Incredible, considering it's a human endeavor."

She paused, collecting her thoughts.

"We don't know when the Relyeh first arrived on Earth," she continued after a moment. "We have a little better idea about the Axon, but only because we found one of their ships. And because Tinker found one."

"Who?" Isaac asked.

"Tinker," Able repeated. "Does the name John Stacker mean anything to you?"

Isaac nodded. "He was a USSF General. He refused to be part of the Generations program because he believed we could overcome the trife."

"That's right. Depending on when you went into stasis, you might not know he ended up splitting with the USSF, along with about fifty-thousand assorted military personnel. They weren't ready to give up on Earth."

"I might have joined him if I were awake at the time."

Able smiled. "I bet you would have. In any case, he had

a wife and they started a family. That family turned into Tinker." She looked at Rico. "It also turned into a lot more than that."

"What do you mean?" Rico asked.

"John Stacker's wife Mary was a scientist. She was the first person to manage a successful adult replication with an intact memory stack."

"She invented cloning?"

"Yes."

"From Earth?"

"That's right. John wasn't completely wrong about his ability to manage the trife. He set up a base of operations in Norfolk, Virginia and started launching missions against them. He managed to clear about a hundred square kilometers around the city."

"That sounds familiar," Isaac said.

"Hayden," Rico said.

"That's right," Able replied. "Sheriff Duke isn't the first person to try to create a safe zone for survivors. John Stacker did it two hundred years ago, and his offspring held it for a while. But the trife are hard to keep back forever. They recovered all of the territory except for the walled-in portion of Norfolk. Until Tinker came along."

"What made him different?" Isaac asked.

"He was a scientist first, a soldier second. He focused on solving the trife problem from a higher level, which led him to his discovery of the Axon's presence on Earth. He recovered one of their ships from the ocean and harnessed the power of its energy source to create a shield around the city, which he renamed Edenrise."

"Hayden told me some of that story," Rico said. "After Austin died. They got tangled up with Tinker and a clone of John Stacker."

Isaac glanced over at Rico, surprised by how the two

stories were becoming interwoven the more Able spoke. But there was something there he couldn't quite put his finger on. Was there some truth she didn't want to admit?

"An unfortunate circumstance," Able said.

"Austin's death was more than an unfortunate circumstance," Rico snapped, suddenly angry.

"I'm sorry," Able replied. "A poor choice of words. Austin was a good man. A great Centurion. But he was loyal to the CSF. Too loyal to trust with our secrets. It wasn't my call to make, but yes, his death was a result of that fact, and I am sorry for that."

Rico leaned back in her seat without responding. Able continued.

"The Organization spent years in trade with Tinker, shipping him raw materials in exchange for advanced weaponry under the auspices of the Trust. He never knew our goals, and we never knew his. But he was allowed to keep some of the weapons he made. It was all preparation for the day when the Relyeh truly arrived, and we figured Earth would be more ready if they had a man like Tinker doing what he did best. We never guessed his real motivation until it was almost too late."

"And Hayden saved your collective asses," Rico said.

"And at the same time might have cost us a chance to escape Relyeh attention. Would they have been so interested in coming to Earth now if Tinker had succeeded?"

"They were already on Earth," Isaac said, getting Able's attention. "They were already interested. They have been for years."

"Oh?" Her eyes shifted to Rico. "That wasn't in your report."

"I may have omitted some details," Rico replied.

"Care to tell me about it, Ike?" Able asked.

"Not really," Isaac replied. "You know the pertinent

parts, and the rest was dealt with."

"And Sheriff Duke is trying to form an alliance with the Axon after he stopped Tinker from doing the same."

"From what I understand, Tinker was a madman," Rico said. "Hayden isn't. In any case, we've gotten off-track. I want to know the history of the Organization, not a rehash of how you've screwed things up."

"Us?" Able said.

"You mishandled the situation with Stacker. You nearly got Ike here killed. I'm sure you've screwed up more than that."

"If Riley Valentine was part of the Organization, she's at least partially responsible for the death of my son," Isaac said. "It was her research that got him killed. Her research that put me in stasis. And it was her research that nearly gave a Relyeh Ancient a foothold on the planet. I'm willing to bet her recklessness is the reason we're here today."

"You can't blame one scientist for everything," Able said.

"To hell I can't," Isaac replied. "You do understand the Relyeh communicate with one another through a quantum tunnel to another dimension, right? They're all connected, so when one learns something, it can share that knowledge with the rest. Valentine opened a portal to an Axon world the Relyeh were in the middle of trying to conquer. You can't tell me that action hasn't affected the narrative since then."

"Can we all just stop for a second?" Bennett said, speaking up for the first time. He got to his feet. "We can throw blame around until we all pass out from exhaustion. It doesn't change the here and now. A Relyeh ship is on its way to Earth. We have to stop it. It's important to understand the history because yes, it is important that we trust one another, if only because it's equally important that

Hayden Duke trusts us when we arrive. We need to work together on this. All of us." He looked at Able. "Including John Stacker."

The room fell silent. Isaac glanced at Rico. She stared at Bennett, her eyes soft. Affectionate. He knew she saw her late husband in the clone's outburst.

"Ryan's right," Able said. "Let's put everything related to the present aside while I start over from the beginning. Okay?"

Isaac nodded. "Agreed."

"Go ahead," Rico said.

Able took a few seconds to reset herself. "We don't really know when the Relyeh first arrived on Earth. It was before the trife ever showed up. At least a century, maybe more. We only really started to understand they were here when they started getting into scrapes with the Axon."

"What do you mean, scrapes?" Isaac asked.

"The Axon and the Hunger are enemies. The Axon were already here. When they discovered the Relyeh were also here, the two factions fought. Of course, they were smart enough not to get caught for a long time. They dealt with one another in secret. Dark alleys, deserted highways, in the middle of the rainforest. Underwater. That kind of thing. Until they didn't."

"You're saying that the entire time I was a child, to when I became a Marine, to when I was put into stasis in Dugway, the Axon and the Relyeh were here on Earth beating on one another?"

"That's right."

"Why didn't anyone know?"

"Someone did know. The Organization was born out of the team assembled to deal with the situation. Capture and control. Only the Axon turned out to be impossible to capture, and the Relyeh were often difficult to control. We tried. Mistakes were made. In the end, we went in for the kill."

"And started an intergalactic war," Rico said.

"Not quite. The Organization recognized that if there were alien agents in our midst, it was only a matter of time before they came to our planet in force. After all, if it was peace they were after there was no reason to lurk. But both the Relyeh and Axon see us as barely civilized inhabitants of a world they both want to possess. A world we now know sits almost directly in the middle of the borders of Axon and Relyeh claimed space. That's one of the reasons we're concerned about Sheriff Duke's interaction with the Axon. Whatever deal he's trying to make, there's a good chance it'll end badly for us."

"It's a risk," Isaac admitted. "But a necessary one. If what you're saying is true, it's more necessary than we thought."

"Of course it's true. But you can't count on the Axon to help us. They don't want to help us. They want our planet as a buffer between them and the Hunger."

"You had all these years to stop the trife? It didn't stop them from landing here and destroying our world."

"What we knew only scratched the surface. Yes, we had an Axon ship. Yes, we captured one of their Intellects. But figuring out how to take advantage of all that? We didn't have half the tools we have today, and they still aren't enough. We have cloning, but we can't reproduce as quickly as the trife. We have space fold, but we can't travel across the galaxy as efficiently as the Axon. A Relyeh can infect a person, forcing that individual to act according to its will. The Axon can project a perfect likeness of anyone, not to mention cause people to hallucinate. We're fighting blindfolded with one hand tied behind our back. And it's a fight we can't afford to lose."

Able paused. She was clearly upset, not only at having to defend the Organization but at the truth of their situation. All of this time and they were still so far from their goals.

"When the trife arrived, we had to make a judgment call," she said. "Maintain the status quo or try to change the outcome. Riley Valentine was an accomplished geneticist as well as a former Marine Raider. Like Sheriff Duke, she also wasn't afraid to take risks. We gave her a team and set her loose." She looked at Isaac. "I'm sorry if her actions cost you your son, but we had a whole planet to think about. We still do."

"What about Valentine?" Isaac asked. "What happened to her?"

"When the generation ships launched, the Organization launched with them. Every ship had members implanted across the populations, in and outside of the military. They all had specific orders for when they arrived. Valentine and her team were on one of the ships. The Deliverance. Her orders were specific and unique."

"The Deliverance never arrived at Proxima," Rico said.

"No, it didn't."

"And Valentine had something to do with that?"

"She did."

Isaac shook his head. "What the hell did you people do?"

"We engaged in a war to save our planet. We lost. Like it or not, we have to try again. It won't only be Earth we lose this time. The enemy knows about Proxima. They know about the settlement, and they know where in the universe to find it. Either we stop the Hunger or the Hunger will end all of human life as we know it."

34

Caleb

"This isn't over yet," Stacker said, stomping across the cargo hold of the dropship.

Caleb looked around the open space. The other soldiers were leaning against the bulkheads, heads down and breathing hard. Exhausted.

"Not over?" he asked.

"Those things are going for the carriers," he replied. "We have to stop them."

Nathan reached a machine resting against the side of the hold, turning and stepping backward into it. Four robotic arms immediately began moving around him, unscrewing the connections holding his armor together and pulling the large helmet off his head.

Caleb was surprised when he saw the man behind the armor. He was almost as much a machine as the protection he wore.

Even more confusing—he really did look like General Stacker. How could that be possible?

Clone or stasis.

Leave it to Ishek to reduce it to something logical. But the Advocate was probably right. Which one was it?

"I think we both have questions," Stacker said, noticing the way Caleb was looking at him. "We can figure each other out once the ships are safe."

"We're going back?" Hotch asked, lifting his head.

"Of course we're going back," Stacker said. "The city may be done, but the people aren't." He headed away from the group, up a flight of stairs leading out of the hold.

Caleb hurried after him, reaching the top of the steps as Stacker vanished down a short corridor to the left. He gave chase, closing the gap. Stacker noticed him but didn't slow down, going to a sliding door that opened when he put his wrist to the control pad.

It was closing when Caleb reached it. He shoved his hand in to stop its movement and then stepped inside as it opened again, finding himself on the bridge. Stacker was already dropping into a raised chair in the back, and he noticed there was a woman at a station in the front. Displays revealed the landscape around them in a panoramic view of the world beyond the craft. A wave of nausea washed over him as he tried to take in the entire scene.

"Don't try to look at every display at once," Stacker said. "It takes some adjustment. Look at the floor."

Caleb looked down, regaining his sense of place, the nausea passing.

"Never been in a dropship before?"

"I've been in a starship before. A few, actually. But not like this one."

"You aren't from Proxima."

Caleb lifted his head, excited by the statement. "Are you?"

"General," the pilot said. "We're coming up on them."

Stacker's attention went to the primary display. Caleb turned to look at it too. He could see the dark gray vessels against the blue water, moving slowly away from the pier and turning northeast toward the Atlantic Ocean.

A pair of xaxkluth trailed behind it, their tentacles spreading out and then pushing back to propel them through the water toward the ships.

Caleb could see the people out on the deck of the trailing carrier. They had noticed the creatures chasing them, and while most were running for shelter, some were standing at the stern, watching the monsters' approach.

"Pyro, do we have comms to either of the ships?" Stacker asked.

"Affirmative, General. Connecting."

White noise flooded the bridge from hidden speakers.

"U.S.S. Bush, U.S.S. Truxton, this is General Stacker. Do you copy?"

The white noise vanished. "This is the Bush. We copy, General."

"This is the Truxton. We copy."

"You have a pair of bogeys on your tail," Stacker said. "I want all available units armed and on your aft decks immediately."

"Available units, sir?" the Truxton replied. "We're loaded with civilians."

"There isn't a single soldier on board your ships?" Stacker barked. "I find that hard to believe, but if there isn't, then you do it yourself. Go into the population, grab volunteers and give them guns. Get them up on the damn deck, or you're all going to die."

"Uh. Y--y-es, s-sir." the Truxton's comm officer stammered. The voice that answered in kind from the Bush was a bit steadier. "Yes, sir," she replied.

Stacker smacked his control pad angrily, closing the comm. "Do we have to do every damn thing ourselves?"

"It seems that way, General," Pyro replied. She glanced back at Caleb. "I'm Pyro. Nice to meet you."

"Caleb."

"Nice suit." She winked at him.

Caleb felt his face warm as he glanced down at himself. The Intellect Skin fit like a second layer, sitting tight against his body, only a half step above naked.

I think she likes you.

Caleb refrained from telling Ishek to shut up out loud. Nobody had noticed the slight bulge of the Relyeh wrapped around his upper arm, and he preferred to explain it under less tense circumstances.

"Do we have enough power remaining for the plasma cannons?" Stacker asked, his voice level again.

"Affirmative, General. The reactor is at ninety percent and purring like a kitten."

"Then let's roar like a lion," Stacker said. "Target the lead creature."

"Roger. Coming around. Caleb, better grab a seat. There's one next to me." She turned her head back and smiled at him. "USSF soldiers. You have ten seconds to secure."

The warning came out through the speakers, likely across the entire craft. Caleb made his way to the other station, dropping into the seat and strapping in. He had barely gotten himself secured when the dropship broke hard to the right, pulling him against the restraints. The craft took a wide vector north over the land before turning hard south again, descending hard toward the water. Caleb smiled in response to the action, reminded of his previous life in search and rescue and the unit he had served with. His Vultures.

They were all gone now, either dead or on the other side of the universe.

But he was still here. Still alive. Still able to fight. But right now, he was only an observer.

He watched as Pyro opened fire with the plasma cannons.Energy bolts launched from the ship, vaporizing the water around the the lead xaxkluth and then hitting it as the airship closed on its target. . The Relyeh whipped its tentacles up toward the craft. It was too slow and they were traveling too fast and too high, passing safely overhead.

"We need to come in slower," Caleb said. "You'll never do enough damage to them flying this fast."

"Oh?" Pyro replied, eyes whipping toward him in a sharp glare. "Are you a pilot?"

"Marine Raider," Caleb said. "Special Forces. I never did the flying, but I have plenty of experience in the field, especially at the other end of air support. If this ship is an evolution of the USSF Wasps, you should be able to go half as fast and still stay airborne."

Pyro glanced back at Stacker. "Is he for real?"

"It seems so," Stacker replied. "Try it his way."

"Roger."

Charming. You have a way with the females of your species.

Caleb didn't have time to be gentle. There were lives at stake.

The dropship turned around for another strafing run. The first xaxkluth had almost reached the Bush , its central mass closing to within fifty meters as civilians poured onto the aft flight deck with rifles in hand. The small arms wouldn't do much to hurt the creatures, but they would distract them.

"Here we go," Pyro said, easing off on the throttle and adjusting the vectoring thrusters to lower the craft's airspeed. The dropship shuddered slightly in response, threatening to lose its lift. "Are you sure about this?"

"Positive," Caleb said. "You can do it. Just don't get too low."

Pyro watched the display, hands soft on the controls. The civilians started shooting down at the xaxkluth as it approached the ship's stern, reaching up with a long tentacle.

The plasma cannons started firing again, powerful bolts hitting the water and the Relyeh, causing it to thrash and howl in pain. Pyro continued to slow the dropship, easing it in toward the monster and slamming it with rounds.

"That's it," Caleb said. "That's it. Keep it steady."

Pyro smiled at the success of the attack, pouring on the firepower. The tentacles retreated, and the creature vanished beneath the surface as they passed overhead.

"Nice work!" Caleb said. "Circle back and hit it again."

"It's retreating."

Xaxkluth don't retreat.

"It isn't. Speed up and circle back."

"How do you know so much about these things?"

"I've fought the Relyeh before."

"Do what he says," Stacker said.

"Roger."

They went up and around for a third pass. The xaxkluth had re-emerged by then, still getting closer to the destroyer. A half-dozen limbs hung limply behind it, floating dead along the surface. The other creature was approaching the carrier and would be on it before the first target was neutralized. How many civilians would die if that thing got onto the vessel?

"General, don't the ships have anything on them with a little more punch?" Caleb asked.

"The Bush does," Stacker replied. "What it doesn't have is anyone to use it. We had all active units on the wall. Reserves aren't trained in heavy ordnance."

"What kind of heavy ordnance?"

"There's a Badger in the hold. A mech. It was there when I took over the city. Nobody knows how to use it."

Caleb grimaced. The USSF had tried mechs against the trife. It was a disaster. The humanoid machines carried plenty of firepower, but they were too slow and clunky to survive long against any decent-sized slick, and they expended their firepower way too quickly. He was surprised any of them were still around.

It may be an effective weapon against xaxkluth.

"I don't know." Caleb wasn't convinced, but they had to do something. "Is it armed?"

"Armed and operational, as near as my engineers can tell."

"Pyro, go in as low and slow as you can. And keep shooting."

Caleb unbuckled himself and stood up.

"Where are you going?" Stacker asked.

"I know how to drive a Badger. Just get me close."

"We don't have any jump equipment on board. You'll never survive the fall, even at minimum velocity."

You'll survive the fall.

"It'll hurt, but I'll live," Caleb said. "Just do it."

He hurried off the bridge.

35

Caleb

Caleb passed the surviving soldiers on the way to the drop-ship's hold. They had made it up to the seats ahead of the bridge, were strapped in and looking sick from Pyro's hard, tight maneuvers. They perked up as he ran by, watching him hit the stairs and drop to the lower deck.

A Badger. Caleb could hardly believe one of the machines had lasted through the centuries.

And he was about to jump out of a perfectly good dropship to pilot one.

The fear will be intense, and I hunger.

Caleb didn't know how Ishek could hunger again. The level of fear in Edenrise should have left the Relyeh satiated for months.

I'm never satiated.

Caleb crossed the hold to the rear ramp. "I'm in position," he said, uncertain if Pyro could hear him on the bridge.

"Standby," she replied, her voice crisp through a nearby speaker. "Approaching the Bush, and opening the rear door in three...two...one."

A flashing light warned of the ramp's imminent motion. Then a loud clang sounded and the rear of the craft began to drop. Cold air rushed into the hold, flowing over Caleb's head and rushing down his spine. He shivered as he edged out onto the descending ramp, looking out over the edge until he could see the aircraft carrier and the xaxkluth behind it, an alien kraken about to wreak havoc on the ship.

He would feel better about all of this if the Skin still had power. What were the odds he would even survive the fall?

We will survive.

At least one of them was confident.

Caleb dropped to his knees at the edge of the ramp, which came to a stop level with the craft. Wind buffeted his face as he turned around and dropped his legs over the edge, still sliding back until he was gripping the end of the platform in his hands, his legs and body dangling over the chaos below.

The dropship slowed a little more, and it shook slightly as the plasma cannons started firing again, this time casting bolts up ahead at the xaxkluth attacking the Truxton. He couldn't see the shots land, but he had witnessed Pyro's skill with the craft already. He was sure she wasn't missing.

Pyro came in lower and slower than Caleb had expected. As she eased the dropship over the Bush's aft deck, Caleb gauged his drop to the deck at only twenty meters.. He had to time his release right or he would wind up overshooting and landing in the water, a sitting duck for the xaxkluth. His body tensed as the deck of the carrier drew even nearer and then holding fast. Just a few more seconds…

Now!

Caleb reacted instantly to Ishek's harsh command, his

hands releasing the ramp. Then he was falling, dropping in an arc toward the deck of the carrier, far enough forward to avoid the civilians gathered near the stern. He felt the hormones begin pumping through his system, Ishek changing his body chemistry to numb the pain of the landing. The deck was a gray blur under his feet, the stern approaching too quickly.

He wasn't going to make it.

Yes, you are.

Caleb's feet touched down on the deck, and he pitched forward, tucking his left shoulder under as he hit the deck, the impact still dislocating his shoulder. He lost all sense of direction as momentum sent him rolling across the deck. Thankfully, he lost most feeling too. He finally slammed into the steel cable taffrail at the edge of the deck, hitting it with the opposite shoulder and adding a broken arm to the damage to his body.

Waves of pain shot through him despite Ishek's best efforts, the crash landing more violent than he had expected. There was no time to linger. No time to nurse his injuries. Caleb forced himself up, stumbling across the deck.

Civilians ran toward him, eager to help and amazed he was still alive, never mind able to stand. They froze when he got to his feet, stopping to stare in amazed surprise.

One of the people didn't freeze. He was the only one in a uniform, though he was dressed more like a tech than a soldier in stained blue coveralls. "Wait. You need a doctor."

"No time," Caleb said, turning his head. "I need the Badger."

This is going to hurt.

Caleb's shoulder wrenched, a loud pop sounding as it

slid back into the socket. Burning pain went up from the area, and he clenched his teeth, taking it in silence.

The tech hesitated, unsure what Caleb meant.

"Badger," Caleb repeated. "Big metal thing, guns for hands."

The tech smiled. "Oh. You just jumped from the dropship."

"I know. I was there."

"You should be dead."

"I'm not that lucky. If you don't mind, I need that damn Badger. Now."

"It's on the lower deck, but the elevator is lowered. The stairs are that way." The tech pointed to the carrier's island.

"I'll take the shortcut," Caleb replied, already familiar with the layout of the carrier. This wasn't his first time on board the George H.W. Bush. He had toured the carrier during one of his trips to the city over two hundred years ago. "Keep firing at that thing until I get back. Aim for the eyes on the central mass."

He began running away from the civilians, toward the carrier's elevator, limping at first as Ishek worked on healing the damage to his muscles.

This will hurt again.

Caleb slowed as his other shoulder spasmed and jerked back into place. He cried out this time, grunting from the pain.

Infant. It hurts me as much as it hurts you.

Caleb doubted that.

He was at a full sprint by the time he reached the edge of the elevator, already positioned at the lower deck. He found the emergency access ladder, hurrying to it and expertly sliding down.

The deck below wasn't as empty as he thought it would

be. Hundreds of civilians were crowded across it, huddled together near the interior bulkhead. His sudden appearance took them by surprise, and he could taste their fear as he breathed in.

Delicious.

It wasn't the time or place, but Caleb couldn't argue. His symbiosis with the Advocate gave him the same reaction.

A group of civilians came toward him from his flanks as he started scanning the deck for the Badger. They held their rifles awkwardly, unaccustomed to carrying or using the weapons.

"Who are you?" one of them asked. An older man in black pants and a white shirt that was stained with sweat, grease and blood. He had an open cut on his cheek.

"Sergeant Caleb Card, Space Force Marines. A xaxkluth is closing on the ship. I'm going to fight it."

"A what?" another of the civilians asked.

"Alien," Caleb replied. "Where's the Badger?"

"What's a Badger?"

A loud clang disrupted them, followed by another. The ship shuddered, and the people up top started to scream, their gunfire intensifying.

"Big humanoid mech, guns for hands," Caleb said again. He could taste the increased intensity of the fear. It was more potent than anything he had sampled since he had bonded with Ishek.

They were running out of time.

The man nodded. "This way." He ran past Caleb, toward the civilians. "Move aside! Move aside!"

The people scattered, mothers grabbing their children and lifting them away, wounded men and women hobbling to the side. Their effort revealed the Badger sitting against the back bulkhead on its knees and leaned forward with its hands splayed to the front as if it were bent in prayer.

It wasn't. The machine was in its default rest position, aligned to make it easy for the pilot to enter the cockpit in its head.

"You need to get these people out of here," Caleb said, approaching the cockpit. A control pad rested on the side of the large, squarish head, and he tapped on it to activate it. The machine was locked.

"And go where?" the man asked. "We're on a boat."

"It's a ship, not a boat," he said, returning his attention to the Badger, quickly entering the access codes he knew. It took three tries before the heavy faceplate of the machine slid open, revealing the chair behind it. He jumped into the Badger's cockpit, dropping into the chair. He looked back at the man. "Find an interior hatch. I don't care where, but you're all open targets down here."

"We aren't here because we want to be. There's no more room. The ship is full, Sergeant."

Caleb stared at the man. Up top, the clanging continued, the sound reverberating on the ceiling above as the xaxkluth gained the upper deck. The gunfire had lessened somewhat, the shooters succumbing to the monster's attack. He had to hurry or there wasn't going to be anyone left up there.

So many civilians. Why didn't Stacker have more soldiers? "Just do what you can to get everyone out of my way, okay?"

The man nodded and hurried toward the nearest crowd of gawkers "Back up!" he shouted. "Back away from the mech!"

Caleb snapped his feet into a pair of actuators at the base of the unit and slid his arms into two raised slings that ended in a set of control sticks.

Interesting machine. Horribly inefficient.

"Tell me something I don't know."

There were eight buttons at the end of each control stick. Sixteen in total that controlled every command for the machine. Caleb tapped in a three button sequence, and the front faceplate slid closed, the interior of the semi-transparent material lighting up with a large heads-up display ahead of the world outside. Another few taps and the machine came out of its rest position, torso lifting the head up and back. Caleb brought the monster all the way up from a knee, putting Caleb five meters above the deck.

It had been a long time since he had driven a mech. He took a couple of tentative steps forward, working the actuators cautiously as the muscle memory returned.

There was no time for caution.

A line of tentacles dropped over the edge of the deck.

36

Caleb

Caleb turned his hands in the slings, the arms of the Badger executing the same move. Each arm of the mech ended in a large swappable pod.

He had noticed this one was armed with the same munitions on both sides—a plasma cannon in the center, a pair of railguns on the top and bottom and a set of machine guns on either side. Ammo ran to the pods through the arms from a central store on the back, which was protected by extra thick armor. The feeding mechanism was the weakest link of the machine, the mechanism allowing the rounds to flow through the armored limbs—regardless of their position—overly complicated. It would have been better to lock the arms straight or stick with energy weapons that utilized flexible wires and wouldn't run out of rounds. But desperation and loss of top engineers had led to bad decisions and underthought, overengineered and hastily produced designs. It was all part of the trickle down effect that had started with the deadly virus and ended with the loss of the war.

And the planet.

Caleb picked up the pace, stomping forward toward the tentacles while the civilians filled in behind him, hiding behind the mech. The gunfire had stopped on the deck above, the only sound the wet slapping of the xaxkluth as it slid to the edge of the ship.

A pair of large reticles floated on the HUD in front of him, each one featuring smaller crosshairs for each specific ordnance. Caleb lined up the railgun crosshairs on the tentacles, slid his thumb over to the control stick and pressed down on the trigger.

Titanium flechettes spewed from the four barrels in rapid fire, the first salvo cutting off six of the hanging limbs in less than a second, the ammunition count on the left side of the HUD reflecting the decrease. Caleb stopped shooting as the tentacles dropped to the deck, oozing ichor and still twitching. The xaxkluth groaned loudly above, slamming its other limbs on the upper deck in anger and pain.

The civilians behind the mech cheered in response to the outcome, their shouts getting louder when the remaining tentacles retreated.

"That was easy," Caleb said.

Didn't I tell you xaxkluth don't retreat?

He could hear the Relyeh moving across the upper deck, headed toward the carrier's large island. If there was no more room for people down here, how many were hiding up there?

Caleb moved his feet, working the actuators to run across the deck. He headed onto the elevator and looked up in time to see the rear tentacles of the creature vanish from sight. He pivoted his body, the motion reflected by the Badger, twisting to find the controls for the lift.

The man in the white shirt was already there. He

tapped on the control pad. A loud clunk followed, and the elevator started to rise.

Caleb stood in the center of it, turning to face the island as it rose. He lifted his arms, bringing the guns up and over his head in anticipation of the moment he had visual on the Relyeh.

The Badger's head cleared the upper deck, and Caleb found the xaxkluth waiting for him. It was still facing away, but it had backed up a few meters and its rear tentacles lashed out, one of them wrapping around the mech's arms and pulled them askew. It yanked him sideways as he started shooting. His rounds went wide of the mark, the powerful tentacles nearly lifting the mech as it took him off balance.

Caleb cursed, his shoulders hurting as the motion outside was reflected inside, bringing his arms out wide. He gritted his teeth as he pulled back, trying to overpower the creature and get the reticles back in line.

One arm was more successful than the other, and he loosed a barrage from the left-hand machine guns as the reticle crossed the xaxkluth's flesh. Bullets chewed into the back of the creature's central mass, distracting it just long enough for him to bring the other arm back in. He fired from both sides, forcing the alien to let him go. Momentum threw the Badger sideways, and his feet danced on top of the actuators while he tried to keep himself upright.

It didn't work. The mech toppled sideways, the fall jolting him in his restraints. He tapped on the controls, commanding the machine to reset its position by calculating the movements needed to return to rest. The action took seconds he didn't have, and the xaxkluth closed on him again, whipping its tentacles hard around and catching the mech in the side. The force threw him across the deck, metal scraping metal as he flailed, trying to get the machine upright again. He turned his head to get visual on the creature, which appeared to have gotten bigger from the time it was in the water.

It feeds, and it grows.

"Awesome," Caleb replied. And he had thought the reapers were bad.

He turned the mech over, planting an arm and using it to push the machine closer to upright. A dozen tentacles were racing toward him. He opened fire, sending bolts of plasma and flechettes into the oncoming limbs. The defense tore through the xaxkluth's arms, removing four of them in rapid succession.

But there were still eight more.

They grabbed the Badger, wrapping around the legs and pulling him onto his back. The mech hit hard, jolting Caleb and eliciting a painful grunt. He tapped the controls to get the machine back into a sitting position, only to have two more tentacles wrap around the body of the mech, holding it still while a second pair again grabbed the arms.

The xaxkluth flipped itself over the mech, the central mass hovering above him. Half its eyes had been blown out during its approach, leaving oozing holes across its disgusting face. Its mouth was a dark, gaping cavern directly above the cockpit, its hundreds of grinding teeth threatening him as another pair of tentacles reached for the protective faceplate.

"Any ideas?" Caleb asked.

Yes, but it might kill us.

"We're going to die anyway if we do nothing."

Very well.

Caleb winced ahead of the pain he presumed would come.

It didn't.

The xaxkluth howled instead, as a half dozen bolts

poured into it from the sky, tearing deep into its limbs and central mass. The pressure on the Badger lessened. Caleb gathered the mech's feet and kicked the Relyeh's central mass. It knocked the xaxkluth back and off him, limbs releasing as it tried to back away.

"You said they don't retreat."

They don't.

Caleb looked up. The dropship was swooping in, low and slow, still firing on the xaxkluth.

Too low and too slow. The creatures was bunching itself on its tentacles, preparing to jump.

"No!" Caleb shouted, charging forward.

He aimed and fired, pounding the xaxkluth with everything he had. Large gouges tore out of the monster, flesh and blood spraying away from it. The creature groaned in response, shoving itself into the air, tentacles stretching for the dropship.

Caleb shifted the mech's left arm, firing the railguns in a sweeping movement across the line of its tentacles, cutting them off one by one. He targeted the center of the creature, continuing to rip into it with every weapon in its arsenal.

Its reach for the dropship missed, but only because the limbs were no longer there. It hit the top of its arc before falling limp and crashing back to the deck, the disgusting mess of oozing wet flesh remaining still.

Caleb stared at the creature, heart pounding, body tingling. He kept the guns trained on it, waiting for it to move again.

It's dead, Caleb.

Caleb exhaled sharply, suddenly exhausted. "Too close." He looked up. The dropship was circling back around, approaching the carrier's deck to land. The Truxton was on his right, headed toward open water.

There was no sign of the other xaxkluth. It had to be dead, too.

He wanted to relax. He wanted to celebrate the victory. He couldn't.

This new war—this new invasion—was only beginning.

37

Nathan

Nathan waited for Pyro to button down the dropship's systems and set the reactor to begin its power-down sequence before leaving the bridge. He knew he was keeping Caleb waiting outside, but he needed the time to come down from his battle high. To shake off the fury that roared through him at the destruction the alien creatures had caused, at the lives that had been lost.

And at the loss of Edenrise.

His city. The shining star of the planet. The symbol of hope for a future free from trife. It had offered shelter for almost a century, and just like that it was gone.

He could shake off the battle high, but he couldn't shake the anger. It was his job to protect the city. His mission, handed down from the original General Stacker across generations of clones, and from the last Stacker to him. Edenrise should never have fallen.

But it had. There was nothing he could do about that. Not right away. At least the evacuation had gone according to plan. At least the ships had gotten away. How many survivors were on board? How many of the thousands had escaped? No matter the number, it was too few.

He clenched his hand on the armrest of his chair, the augment crushing the padding and bending the metal. The trife were a threat he had learned to manage, but these new creatures had changed the game. Why here? Why now? And under whose orders?

He would find out.

And then vengeance would be his.

"We're all set, General," Pyro said, slipping out of her seat and standing in front of him.

He didn't look at her right away. He breathed out some of the fury. He couldn't change the past. He had to move forward. They all had to move forward.

He stood up, looking down at her. "You did exceptionally well today."

"Thank you, General," she replied. "I feel a little sick."

"Me too."

He led her off the bridge. The surviving soldiers were already gone, having hurried from the dropship to search for their families. He descended into the hold, glancing at his armor as he headed for the open ramp. It had taken a beating and would need some repairs.

"Pyro, once we get organized, we need to see if we can round up any of your team to look at all the armor."

"Yes, General," she replied.

His eyes trailed along the bulkhead and down the ramp to the deck of the carrier. He could see some of the survivors standing outside, lined up and waiting for him. Each face was a reminder of a face that hadn't made it. A family member who had died. His failure.

"I don't know if I can go down there," he said.

"Nathan, you did everything you could possibly do,"

Pyro replied. "And then some. They aren't there to blame you."

She took his hand and squeezed it before letting go. He glanced over at her, and she urged him forward.

He sighed again, trying to release some tension as he started down the ramp. More people were waiting for him than he initially thought—hundreds of weary, ragged survivors.

He was halfway down the ramp when someone in the crowd started to clap. It was a solitary, lonely sound, but only for a few seconds. Someone joined the first and then more joined the second. By the time Nathan reached the deck, the entire gathering was clapping and cheering.

"See?" Pyro said beside him, smiling.

The reaction didn't salve his anger. It intensified the fury and added a layer of guilt. He waved to the crowd, accepting their desire to cheer for him, but rejecting his worthiness of the accolades. He had too much work to do to get caught up in their relief.

"Where's Card?" he asked.

The Badger was in rest position at the back of the group. The carcass of the alien creature was a hundred meters behind it, closer to the island. The people were staying well clear of it, and he didn't blame them. The acrid smell of it was intense enough at this distance.

"I don't see him," Pyro replied. "He has to be here somewhere."

The cheering began to die down. One of the survivors came forward. "General, what are we going to do now?"

"We need to re-organize," he replied. "Re-establish chain-of-command. Put the word out. I want all surviving USSF members here on deck in one hour." He looked at Pyro. "Head to the ship's bridge and make sure the Truxton gets the message as well."

"Yes, General," she replied, immediately breaking away.

"I'm here, General," Hotch said, appearing from out of the crowd. "What can I do?"

"I need a team to begin taking care of the dead. Gather the bodies, see if you can get them identified, and prepare them for burial at sea."

Hotch's face paled. It wasn't the task he was hoping for, but he recovered quickly, recognizing the severity of the situation. "Yes, General," he said, snapping off a smart salute. Then he turned to the people closest to him in the crowd and began recruiting them.

Nathan continued forward. The survivors were beginning to thin out, some going with Hotch, others dispersing to deliver Nathan's message. He still didn't see Caleb Card anywhere.

"Where did you go, Caleb?" he whispered.

He scanned the deck, wondering if he had gone back down below. It didn't make sense for the Marine to avoid him.

His eyes landed on the alien, the sight of it turning his stomach. It was a monstrous thing, like something from the darkest nightmare. Made for destruction.

There. He found Caleb on top of its central mass, behind its many eyes, a number of which had been shot out while it approached the ship. He was cutting into the thing's head with a knife, digging into it like he knew exactly what he was looking for.

Caleb already knew so much more about the creatures than Nathan could believe. Where had the man come from? And how did he know so much? And what the hell was he doing now?

Nathan crossed the deck, climbing over the alien's thick

tentacles and wrinkling his nose at the smell. He also had no idea how Caleb could stand the odor.

"Card!" he shouted, trying to get Caleb's attention. If the Marine heard him, he didn't react. "Card!"

Caleb still didn't pay him any mind. He put down the knife and laid flat against the creature's head, reaching into the central mass, confusing Nathan even more.

He stopped moving, watching in grotesque fascination as Caleb's eyes closed and he remained pressed against the dead creature, his arm inside it to the shoulder, his posture as if he were falling asleep against a lover.

"Attention all hands." Pyro's voice sounded through the ship's loudspeaker. "Attention all hands. General Stacker requires all USSF on the aft hangar deck immediately. I repeat. General Stacker requires all USSF soldiers on the aft hangar deck immediately."

Nathan smiled, looking past the alien to the carrier's island. Pyro must have sprinted full-speed across the deck to get to the bridge that quickly. He appreciated the effort.

"Stacker."

Nathan turned back toward Caleb. The Marine was on his feet on top of the creature, a tense look on his face. His arm was dripping with blood and guts, but he didn't seem to notice or care. He slid down the side of the corpse, walking over to where Nathan was standing.

"What were you doing?" Nathan asked.

"Gathering intel," Caleb replied. "We need to talk."

"Agreed. I'm organizing the survivors. I'll have logistics straightened out within the hour. In the meantime, I can bring you down to the showers and find you a change of clothes."

"No. An hour is too long. We need to talk now, General. What happened to your city was only the beginning. It's going to get worse. A lot worse."

Caleb's conviction sent a chill running down Nathan's spine. "How do you know?"

"The enemy told me."

38

Nathan

"The enemy told you what?" Nathan asked. "And how?"

"It's a long story," Caleb replied. "Too long to go into detail now. How much do you know about the Hunger?"

"The Hunger? I've never heard of it."

"What about the Relyeh? The Axon?"

"No," Nathan replied. "I know the trife. I know the Others. Are you naming other aliens?"

"Others? Describe them to me."

"That armor you're wearing. The Others wear the same thing. Faceless humanoids, who use holograms and hallucinations to manipulate people."

"That's the Axon," Caleb said. "Intellects. Artificial intelligences. The trife are foot soldiers of the Relyeh, who also call themselves the Hunger. They're an ancient race that believes it's their destiny to conquer the entire universe."

"The whole universe?" Nathan replied. "That's crazy."

"Not to them. They've been at it for hundreds of thousands of years."

Nathan's heart started pounding. "I can't even wrap my

head around that." He paused. "Maybe we can talk somewhere else? The smell here is overwhelming."

Caleb nodded. "Right. I forgot about that."

"How do you forget a smell like this?"

Caleb opened his mouth, closed it again. He started walking away from the dead alien, leading Nathan back toward the dropship. "Your craft has a head on board, doesn't it?"

"It does."

"I'll clean up while we talk." He glanced at Nathan. "General James Stacker would be over two-hundred-fifty years old. You aren't him."

"No. It's a long story of its own. I'm a clone, made from Stacker's genetic code. My name isn't James. It's Nathan."

"Then why did you tell me it was James?"

"We don't have time for the minute details. The short version is that I took over Edenrise from another Stacker clone after he went insane."

"Define insane."

"He followed a man named Tinker, who wanted to bring the Others to Earth. He believed they could save us."

"They won't."

"They couldn't if they wanted to. Tinker managed to open a portal to one of their worlds. It was already destroyed."

"The Relyeh are at war with the Axon. They have been for thousands of years. Logistically, Earth is stuck in the middle of the two sides. Valuable to the Hunger because of the nature of humankind. Valuable to the Axon as a buffer planet."

"Then why aren't the Axon doing more to stop the Hunger from taking it?"

"You probably noticed they're already losing the war.

They're on the defensive, fighting to keep what little they have left. They don't have the resources to deal with the Relyeh here."

"Neither do we."

"I've come too far to give up, Nathan. I've been through too much."

"Where did you come from? And how do you know General Stacker?"

They reached the dropship. Nathan followed Caleb back on board. The Sergeant had seized control of the situation, taking command of the conversation and delivering orders with practiced ease.

"Is the reactor offline?" Caleb asked.

"I didn't think we'd need it again so soon," Nathan replied. "I can restart it."

Caleb nodded. "To answer your question, I was here on Earth when the trife invasion started."

"You said you were a Marine Raider," Nathan said, remembering Caleb's statement. "Special Forces."

"That's right. Here on Earth, before the invasion. Before the virus. Before the trife. Before everything fell apart. My unit was one of the first into the infested zones. Areas overrun with trife. We were purely offensive at first. Direct combat, until we realized it was impossible to defeat them head-on. Once the work got underway on the generation ships, my unit was converted to search and rescue. We went back into the cities to pull survivors out. What few there were to save."

Nathan paused at the bridge, entering and leaning over the pilot's station to restart the reactor. "How many people did you rescue?"

"I don't know. I lost count. Hundreds. VIPs mostly. Scientists, engineers, people the USSF decided we needed on the new worlds we were supposed to inhabit. After my last mission, I was ordered to join one of the colony ships headed to space. The Deliverance. I volunteered as a Guardian."

"Guardian?"

"My new job was to keep an eye on things during the trip across the stars, cycling in and out of stasis. It was supposed to be boring and tedious, but things didn't go according to plan."

"I take it the Hunger had something to do with that?"

"The Hunger, the Axon, and the USSF. Nathan, you have to idea how deep all this shit goes."

"I wouldn't be too sure," Nathan said, leading Caleb off the bridge and toward the stern. The ship was humming again, the reactor churning. "The head is this way."

"The layout's pretty close to the old Wasps," Caleb replied. "A little posher than we had it." He smiled. "And probably a lot better in zero gravity."

They entered the bathroom. As a Centurion dropship, it was designed to support up to fifty people on the week-long journey between Proxima and Earth. There were multiple stalls, multiple sinks, and a larger common shower.

"So you're saying you were on the generation ship Deliverance?" Nathan asked.

"That's right."

"But now you're back here."

"Also right."

"How?"

"I came through an Axon portal."

"On purpose?"

"Yes."

"Why?"

"What do you mean?"

"You had to be able to imagine the best case scenario for the planet, and know that it would still suck. If I were you, I would have assumed humankind was lost."

"Maybe, but I knew humankind wasn't lost."

"How?"

Caleb pulled at his body armor, separating the alien material at his chest and bringing it down to his waist. Nathan's attention immediately went to a dark, worm-like growth around the Marine's upper-right arm.

"The Hunger communicates across the vast distance of their domain using an inter-dimensional quantum network called the Collective," Caleb explained. He lifted and rotated his right arm.

Nathan's breath caught in his throat. The motion revealed that the growth wasn't a growth at all. A pair of small, dark eyes looked out at him from the end of the creature's body, regarding him with an intelligence that made his skin crawl.

"This is Ishek. An Advocate. They're Relyeh symbiotes. One of the races they conquered and further engineered, modified to both control and enhance a human counter-part. Typically, the Advocate takes what we humans refer to as the alpha position in the relationship, but I managed to get the better of this one." He paused and smiled. "Though of course, he doesn't agree with my assessment. His name is Ishek."

Nathan stared at the creature. It shifted slightly on Caleb's arm, a soft chittering squeal escaping from somewhere.

"I see," Nathan replied, jaw clenching as he fought to control his sudden anger. "Tell me something, Sergeant. How the hell am I supposed to trust a damn thing you say when you have an enemy alien parasite sucking on your arm?"

39

Nathan

"That's a good question," Caleb replied.

There was no worry in his voice. No concern that Nathan might be able to hurt him if things went sour. That lack of nervousness gave Nathan pause.

"That's why we're here," Calab continued. "I don't need a shower, but I wanted to show you Ishek in confidence. The other survivors, they'd see an alien wrapped around my arm and lynch me before I could say a word, especially after what just happened with the xaxkluth. I didn't need to show him to you, but I want to earn your trust. I know we can help one another."

Nathan continued to stare at Ishek. The sight of the thing made him nauseous. He shifted his eyes, meeting Caleb's. "Okay. I'm listening."

"I came back here for a reason. To deliver a message."

"What kind of message?"

"A solution to the trife problem. A means to wipe them out."

"We already tried that," Nathan said. "The poison killed people too."

"What?"

"Sorry to disappoint you, Card. But you're not the first person to come up with that idea. We've had over two hundred years to work on it, and we couldn't get a solution that didn't also kill humans."

"This one might be different."

"It might. It might not. Have you tested it?"

"The trife are specifically engineered for each planet and species they're deployed against. The only way to test it was to bring it here. I can't believe my source would send me back with a solution that would kill both human and trife."

"You said it, but you don't sound convinced."

Caleb paused, jaw flexing, eyes dropping. "Damn you, Valentine," he whispered, shaking his head. He looked up at Nathan again. "Fine. In all honesty, I'm not one hundred percent sure it isn't the same solution. All I have is a datafile jammed into my brain. I'm not even sure how it's supposed to be extracted."

"Where did you get it?"

"Doctor Riley Valentine. Class A Bitch. But she sacrificed herself to get her research back to Earth, so there's that. I'm supposed to deliver it to Proxima."

Nathan's eyes narrowed. He didn't trust anything having to do with Proxima. "Anyone in particular?"

"I don't think she knew anyone specific who lived over two hundred years," Caleb replied flatly.

"So how do you know who to give it to? How do you know you can trust them?"

"I always assumed I would hand it over to whoever's in charge of the planet, or whoever's in charge of their military."

Nathan shook his head. "Not a good idea."

"Why not?"

"Let me tell you something about Proxima. The Proxima government decided Earth is a shithole converted into what they consider an alien ant farm and populated by ignorant savages. They see this place as a testing ground for their experiments, not their home away from home if you know what I mean."

"They gave up on Earth?"

"That's right. Big time. Except where it suits them. Edenrise, for instance. We've been trading with them for over half a century, even though their own laws make the trades illegal."

"Trading what?"

"They bring us raw materials, and we turn them into weapons. High-end, high tech weapons. We keep some of them for ourselves and pass the rest back."

Caleb's eyebrows lowered. "Wait a second. I was just out in the field with you. Other than your powered armor, I didn't see any firepower we didn't have two hundred years ago. Your plasma cannons carry a bit more punch, but it's not an innovation."

"We never kept our cache inside the city. Too risky if our contacts ever decided to renege on our agreement and found a way to get past the shield."

"You could have used those weapons today."

Nathan sighed. "Tell me about it. Nobody figured on some giant tentacled monsters showing up behind every damn trife this side of the Mississippi. Maybe we should have."

"You couldn't have known. Your shield took a hell of a beating."

"I'm glad we got some people out in time. With your help. You saved a lot of lives today."

"Good. I hope that helps you trust me. who reprogrammed the shield to kill the xaxkluth. Not me."

"I knew you seemed different. Now I guess I know why. I'm going to trust you, Caleb. I don't have much left to lose, and I'm desperate for someone who knows what the hell is going on out there."

"Thank you. I—"

"I wasn't done," Nathan interrupted. "You need to trust me too. Whatever's happening out there, whatever your mission is, you can't just go running to Proxima with everything you know. Like I told you, the government doesn't care about Earth, and any problems we cause down here and bring to them are usually met with stiff reprisal. Do you understand?"

Caleb nodded.

"Good. There's another faction on Proxima called the Trust. They're a crime syndicate. Bad news. They're the group we've been trading with all these years. Like I said, illegal. But it gets better than that. The Centurion Space Force and the Trust are both headed up by the same man. General Aeron Haeri. I don't quite have that bastard figured out yet, but he's the reason I'm down here instead of up there."

"You're originally from Proxima?"

"Affirmative. I was a Centurion Space Force pilot until I got too close to something the Trust didn't want me to see. They tried to kill me. Fortunately, I'm a hard man to kill."

"I get that feeling. My orders were to deliver the data to a military dark ops group that was dealing with the Relyeh and Axon invasions before the trife ever came to Earth. Does that mean anything to you?"

"Are you suggesting there were aliens on Earth before the trife arrived?"

"That one threw me for a loop too, but yes. That's what I was told."

Nathan stared at Caleb in silence. He could hardly believe it. "If there's a dark ops branch on Proxima, they never made themselves known to me."

"That's who I want to talk to, but we don't have time right now."

"You said things were going to get worse. Worse how?"

"The xaxkluth who attacked your city were only one group. As near as we can tell, there are thousands of them emerging planetwide."

"What?"

"That's not the worst part."

"You're kidding."

"The Relyeh are divided under twelve siblings born of the first Relyeh hundreds of thousands of years ago. It's their responsibility to carry out the destiny of the Hunger and conquer the entire universe from end to end. Earth is a prize they all want to claim because whoever controls it will have a better foothold against the Axon. From what Ishek and I have been able to learn, we're confident that one of the most powerful of the Relyeh, Nyarlath, is making a move on the planet. The xaxkluth are her vanguard."

"Vanguard against what? Have you seen a lot of the planet, Sergeant? Other than Edenrise, there's only one other place I know that can put up even a hint of a fight."

Nathan froze as soon as the words left his mouth. His heart thundered in his chest.

"What is it?" Caleb asked.

"I have to warn him."

"Warn who?"

"I need to find Pyro. We leave in forty-eight minutes. Right after I talk to my soldiers."

"Roger that, Nathan. Warn who?"

"Sheriff Duke," Nathan said, turning to leave. He

glanced back over his shoulder. "And you're wrong, Sergeant. You do need a shower. You're covered in alien guts, and no offense, but you stink."

He hurried from the head, across the dropship and out through the hold, sprinting across the deck at full speed and leaving a very confused Caleb Card behind.

40

Hayden

Hayden looked out through the open side of the Iroquois, watching the city of Sanisco approach below. It was like most of the cities in the area. Ravaged by war, beaten and crumbling.

But not broken.

The outskirts were lined with streets filled with dilapidated buildings and rusted wrecks of old cars, shattered glass, chunks of rock and other debris left over from the first invasion. Vegetation crept in through the cracks of worn asphalt, cement and concrete. In some places the weeds took on a surreal beauty that captured Hayden's imagination every time he saw them. To the north, the detonated halves of the Golden Gate Bridge rested on opposite shores while the central expanse poked up from the bay. To the east, the Oakland Bay Bridge was in a similar state, the overall destruction cutting the city off from trife attack on three sides.

His eyes turned toward the northeast section of the city. Toward home. The destruction lessened, the vegetation faded. The buildings, while old, showed increasing signs of stability and improving conditions. A wall had been erected along the perimeter, composed of concrete and old cars, tracing Interstate 80 from the Bay Bridge to Route 100, and following it north to Black Point. It was all that remained of the city, and it was more than enough for the survivors who lived there.

Or it had been enough. The loss of Haven and Lavega had brought thousands of refugees north, and he could see them too, camping just inside the walls. They had crews working overtime to test the stability of more buildings to renovate for the new residents to have safe places to live. It wasn't a fast process, especially considering the size of the influx. It would take months to get them all adequately housed. Maybe years. Not that any of them were complaining. They had been lucky to escape north with their lives and were fortunate to be in one of the only two places Hayden knew had walls of any kind.

There was another benefit. A lot of the refugees wanted to be UWT Law Officers. They wanted to learn to defend themselves, their families and the rest of the survivors. They wanted to stand up and fight against the threat that had chased them here and for the cause they had come to believe in.

Hayden's cause. Peace. Security. Justice. Freedom. Simple tenets that were easy to name and harder to achieve. But they were working on it.

The helicopter started its descent, dropping among a handful of buildings under repairs and landing in the street beside the tallest of the intact structures. Old documentation had informed them the building used to be called the Transamerica Pyramid. Two-hundred sixty meters tall and shaped the way its name suggested, it rose above almost everything in the city, the newly restored light in the crown jewel at the top a beacon for the refugees to follow. It was the home of the United Western Territory government, the main headquarters for Law, and the most extensive and advanced science and research center on the west coast of the former United States, if not the entire globe.

Of course, the trife problem wasn't localized to the States, but Hayden had enough to worry about here to give too much thought to the rest of the planet. Judging by the Relyeh interest in this part of the world, he had a feeling they had fared significantly better than some other places. It was a mixed blessing to be sure.

Deputy Fry was waiting at the landing area when the chopper touched down. He hurried over to the helicopter, staying low to avoid the diminishing downwash so he could meet Hayden and the others as they exited. A second group of deputies waited nearby to take the bodies of the fallen.

"Sheriff, Chief Deputy Hicks," Fry said in greeting as Hayden and Hicks climbed out of the helicopter.

"Deputy Fry," Hayden said. "Where's the Governor?"

"In the lab."

Hayden shook his head. "Doc Hess told her to stay out of the lab."

"Sheriff, I think you'd have better luck pacifying a trife."

"Solino, you're with me," Hayden said. "Hicks, get your people rested. I'm not sure what comes next, but I want you ready when it happens."

"Roger, Sheriff," Hicks said.

Hayden and Solino headed away from the helicopter and up the steps of the pyramid while Hicks took the Rangers to the armory to shed their equipment and then to the barracks for some downtime. The ride north had been quick but tense, the entire unit stressed by what they had experienced. Hayden didn't blame them. He was stressed too. The new aliens were one thing. The strange hologram was something else. Its threat of war and its arrogant confidence had left him shaken. For as much as the UWT had accomplished against the trife, they had no chance against the true might of the Hunger.

But the might of the Hunger was coming, and sooner than he had expected.

Inside the building, the two men crossed the lobby to the bank of lifts at the rear. Hayden tapped the control pad and a set of doors slid open, one of the cabs already waiting. They boarded and descended to sublevel three, exiting into an underground parking garage that had been converted to a research and development lab. Dozens of computers and displays of various shapes, sizes, and ages sat on tables spread across the open floor, while bundles of wires snaked away toward the corner. A handful of engineers perched on an assortment of seats, from an aluminum stool to an old wooden dining chair. Some ran programs that sifted through data stores while others used small tools to try to repair more of the machines. Almost all of it was made before the war, scavenged by the UWT's collectors or acquired from scavengers via trade. More equipment was always coming in, assessed and either rebuilt or used as parts to restore other devices.

Hayden didn't see Natalia with the other engineers. He turned toward the southern section of the lab. His eyes crossed over a cluster of computer terminals fronting a half-dozen large machines that Doctor Hess and Natalia had been using in recent biological and genetic research and testing. And then his gaze passed over a makeshift divider to a terminal resting beside a motorized chair salvaged from a dentist's office. The divider was composed of individual wood crates, each one containing a mechanical limb, augments similar to Hayden's arms, while the terminal and chair were used to install and program the prosthetics.

Another machine rested to the right of the botter station that Natalia called a neural interlink. From the outside, it was little more than a metal frame wrapped around a plastic seat, but the exterior simplicity hid the interior complexity. Originally designed to allow humans to communicate with the goliaths, it was the result of years of work by some of Proxima's brightest scientists. They still used it for the goliaths, but now they had a secondary—it was a dangerous but potentially invaluable—use for the technology.

HAYDEN SPOTTED Natalia in the seat and reacted with a deep sigh. Dismayed but not surprised, he glanced at Solino, who knew to wait while Hayden approached the interlink. Wires ran from a box at the side of the frame to electrodes attached to different parts of Natalia's body beneath her clothes. A wired cap and a pair of bulky goggles hid most of her face, leaving only the tips of her short black hair, small turned-up nose and jaw exposed.

Chief Engineer Sean Lutz was sitting at a computer terminal across from the interlink, monitoring the output from the system. A tall, rail-thin man with wild hair and a scruffy face, he stiffened when he noticed Hayden approaching.

"Uh...Sheriff Duke," he said. "You, uh...you're back early."

"I radioed that I was on my way," Hayden replied. "I thought Nat would be waiting outside."

The system output froze. Natalia reached up, grabbing the goggles and lifting them off her head. She looked at Hayden with apologetic brown eyes.

"Hayden," she said. "Before you say anything, I have a good reason for being here."

"Do you?" Hayden replied, unconvinced. Natalia hung the goggles on a waiting hook and removed the cap while he knelt beside her, reaching under her shirt and tenderly peeling the electrodes off her skin. "I almost lost you the last time you used this thing."

She leaned over, putting her forehead against his. "I know. I wasn't using it. We were collecting some diagnostics."

"Preparing it for use," Hayden translated.

"Caught," Natalia admitted. "It's been weeks, Hayden. I'm fine now. Back to normal."

"I'm not eager to see that change again anytime soon."

"We may not have a choice, all things considered."

Hayden stood and offered his hand. Natalia took it, letting him pull her out of the interlink. They embraced for a moment.

"Does this mean I'm not in trouble?" Lutz asked. "I was only following the Governor's orders."

"We'll see," Hayden replied. He locked eyes with Natalia. "We need to talk."

41

Hayden

"Nick, can you go upstairs and tell Heather I'll be up in another hour or so?" Natalia asked.

Deputy Solino smiled and glanced at Hayden, who nodded his approval. "Of course, Governor. I'd be happy to."

"Thank you."

Solino turned and hurried for the stairs, not wanting to wait for a lift.

"He seems pretty eager," Hayden said, watching him go.

"He and Heather are seeing each other."

"By seeing, you mean…"

"Yes, Hayden. You sound like such an old man sometimes."

Hayden smiled. "Kids these days. If they aren't out teasing trife, they're making out in the shadows of ruined buildings."

Natalia punched him playfully in the arm. "Like we never ran into the splits to make out."

"Feels like ancient history."

"Because it is. I'm sorry about Nan, Cortez, and Rollins. They were good people."

"They were."

"Do you want me to come with you?"

"We can notify their families after we talk. We have a problem, Nat. A big problem."

"I know, you told me before you headed up from Tijuana."

"And you reacted by going to the lab to prep the interlink. That's a separate problem in itself."

"Somebody has to do it."

"It doesn't have to be you." They reached the lift banks. Hayden tapped on the pad. The one he had taken to the garage was still waiting, and they stepped in. "What floor?"

"Let's go to forty-two."

"Are you sure?"

"They just finished the rebuild last week. I know we talked about keeping the UWT offices down on ten, but I've been thinking a lot about that. We need to go back up, if only to show we won't be cowed by adversity."

Hayden tapped the floor on the control pad and looked at his wife. The last governor of the UWT had died up there during an attack that had cost nearly fifty lives and left most of the floor in ruins. It was still a painful memory for a lot of people in Sanisco.

"You know I appreciate the symbolism. But can it wait until we figure this crisis out?"

"If that's how the Sheriff wants it."

"It is."

Natalia smiled. "Okay."

"So, the interlink," Hayden pressed as the lift ascended. "It doesn't have to be you. Let Lutz calibrate it from the hot seat while you run the diagnostics."

"I'm impressed. You almost sounded like you knew what you were talking about there."

Hayden laughed. "Come on, Nat. I'm serious. That thing nearly killed you."

"Which is why it has to be me. I'm not putting someone else in that seat to die. I can't ask anyone to do something I won't do myself. And besides, I already have experience in the Collective. I spoke to Shub-Nigu. And I survived. Even Doc Hess said by all accounts I should be dead."

"That's not something to be proud of."

"But it still means something. My mind is strong enough to withstand the pressures of the Collective. That seems to be more important than ever, considering what you encountered out there. New aliens that make the trife look like pansies?"

"Ugliest things I've ever seen. And they grew so damn fast. I'm nervous to think what would happen if one of them had gotten to a nest."

"Ironic that they're trife-eaters, isn't it?"

"I think they'll eat anything they encounter. Besides, you know the Relyeh feed on fear. Those things were definitely frightening."

"But you killed them all."

"I killed one deposit of them. Their mother made it sound like there are plenty more."

"Their mother?"

The lift stopped, the doors sliding open. Hayden and Natalia stepped out onto the forty-second floor. It still had a smell of fresh plaster and cement, and the windows Proxima had provided still glistened in the light of bright LEDs.

"They did fantastic work," Hayden said, scanning the room. "They picked all this up from books?"

"We have some really talented people in the city," Natalia replied. "But it wasn't without some trial and error. The flubs were cleaned and redone."

The room was open and large and led back to a second office and a conference room adjacent to an open-air patio. Natalia led Hayden toward it.

"I skipped over that part during the ride. I was still processing the whole interaction. It was strange, Nat. Real strange." He reached into his pocket and withdrew the projector, holding it out to her.

"A projector?" she guessed, surprising him with her ability to identify it.

"You've seen something like it before?"

"No. But the crystal in the center gave it away."

"I didn't even notice a crystal," Hayden admitted, looking closer at it. "The hologram was a middle-aged woman dressed like a lab tech. Maybe like someone who worked in the building where we found the egg sacs. But she spoke to us like she was in the present, only kind of stilted."

"Stilted?"

"Maybe that's not the best word for it. I don't know. It was like she learned to speak by watching old movies. Bad dialogue. Does that make any sense?"

"Not really, but it probably doesn't matter." They reached the glass doors to the patio, which slid open silently at their approach.

"It matters because it was out of the ordinary. And it matters because of what she said and how she said it. She was arrogant. Confident."

"If she's a Relyeh like Shurrath, why wouldn't she be both of those things? Especially if you're right about there being more of those creatures."

"Exactly. Like I said, a big problem. And we have no

idea what the consequences are or what we're about to come up against. I don't think it begins and ends with tentacled monsters."

They walked across the patio to the edge of the building. The air was cooler up high, and the city small below.

"What do you suggest, Sheriff?" Natalia asked, looking out over the city. "How do we keep these people safe?"

Hayden shook his head. "I've been thinking about that since I got on the chopper. I don't have an answer, and it pisses me off."

"I've been thinking about it too," Natalia said. "Which is why I was working on the interlink. Caleb Card," she said, almost to herself.

"What?"

"Do you remember? When we connected to the Collective. Caleb Card was there. A human on the Relyeh comm network. He's here on Earth somewhere."

"You don't know that."

"I'm pretty sure. He was close. I could sense it."

"Let's say you're right. How will finding him help us?"

"For one, he must know quite a bit about the Relyeh to be on their comm network, don't you think?"

"Pozz."

"For another, he still has access to it, which means he has access to information. Maybe he can tell us more about what the Hunger is planning."

"We know what they're planning."

"I mean how. Like you said—beyond tentacle monsters. That can't be all there is."

"Assuming you're right on both counts, we don't know how to find him."

Natalia took Hayden's hand, turning to face him. Their eyes met. Hayden didn't like the look in hers.

"Yes, you do."

Hayden shook his head. "Nat, you have no way of knowing if that'll work. You could wind up dead, and still no Caleb Card. And considering we're making some big assumptions on his usefulness, that's not worth the risk."

"I hear you, Hayden. I do. But what are our options? We barely handled the last problem. We aren't equipped to deal with this. Look at what we've built here. And think about what we already lost. These people depend on us. We can't afford to play it safe. You know that. I know you do. And I understand. Hallia, Ginny, they give you something, but they also take something away. You want to play it safe. You want to stay away from risk. But living on Earth isn't a promise of anything. We could have gone to Proxima. We decided to stay here. We have a responsibility."

Hayden nodded. "I do know that. And I'm willing to make any sacrifice necessary to protect these people. Except you."

"We don't have room for exceptions. Love doesn't change that."

Hayden sighed, turning to look out at the city. She was right. When wasn't she?

"We'd need to find a Relyeh with a bi-directional communications structure. A full ick. Hess said a trife won't do. They can only receive."

"The Relyeh all went into hiding after I took out Shurrath."

"They can't survive here without feeding, and you're the Sheriff of the United Western Territories. There has to be a lead somewhere you can follow."

"Right. I'll put Solino on it."

"Put Hicks on it," Natalia suggested.

"Why?" Hayden smiled, remembering Heather. "Oh. Yeah, I guess he deserves a little break. I'll ping Hicks when we get downstairs." Hayden looked down at his blood-stained armor. "I need to get out of these clothes. I can only imagine how bad I smell."

"It's pretty bad," Natalia admitted. She put her hand on his face. "We'll do this together. I won't let anything tear down what we've built here."

"Me neither," Hayden agreed.

"I know. We have some hard business to take care of, and then you owe me the rest of the night."

"The pleasure is mine, Governor. It's just a shame it has to be mixed with so much pain."

"That's life, Hayden. Especially here."

"Pozz that. Let's go."

42

Hayden

Hayden changed in the Law Office, trading his stained and worn armor for his typical Sheriff's uniform—a dark blue collared shirt, black pants, tan leather boots, ammo belt around his waist and two revolvers holstered beneath his arms—all under a long leather duster. He pinned the silver star-shaped comm to his shirt collar. A larger, slightly melted plastic star was already pinned on the outside of the duster. That star had been given to him by a homeless, hungry, desperate child, and was a constant reminder to him of who and what he was fighting for.

He asked Hicks to begin looking into recent reports for a potential match to a khoron modus operandi. Like all Relyeh, the worm-like parasites required the pheromones and chemicals emitted during high-stress situations to survive, and there was a good chance they would do something illegal to achieve that.

The only question was whether or not anyone would report it.

Hayden and his deputies had worked hard to create a system of trust within the UWT, but too many years of lawlessness and martial control had made a lot of the people cautious. Sometimes too cautious. Hayden didn't blame them for that. They had reason to be afraid. But they also had reason to hope. He was doing his best to guide them in that direction.

Hayden and Natalia went from the barracks out into the city. Many of the residents outside waved and said hello as they passed or walked with them a ways to talk about the city or the UWT as a whole. Some asked for things, and some just wanted to say thank you. One survivor from Lavega cursed them for their misfortune and the loss of her home and was quickly brought aside by other residents looking to help comfort her. Natalia broke away from Hayden then, joining the group to deal with the heartbroken woman while he continued through the city.

As Governor, it was difficult for her to manage all of the people who had lost something but most handled the loss with resignation. It was rare for someone to lash out, but Natalia said she preferred it to silence. It was a symbol of the hope they were trying to bring to the survivors. A display of the belief that their lives shouldn't end so easily or have so little value.

Three dead officers typically meant three grieving families, but Cortez had no one besides his brothers and sisters in Law. Nan and Rollins both had families in Sanisco. Nan had parents and a brother, while Rollins had a wife and child. Hayden knew his family would be harder to face. Not only for their loss but also for the reminder of what it could cost his family.

He entered the apartment building three blocks from the pyramid, climbing the stairs to the third floor. A couple of people there offered somber greetings. They already knew if they saw him in one of the apartments alone or with Natalia it meant someone in Law had died. It left him feeling more depressed than usual. He was like the angel of death, coming to deliver the worst of news. But somebody had to do it, and these people were his responsibility.

He found Nan's apartment and knocked on the door. Most families in Sanisco lived together, at least until marriage and new families pulled them apart. Nan's brother Carlo opened the door.

"Sheriff Duke," he said, his face beginning to pale the moment he saw Hayden.

"Carlo," Hayden replied, his chest constricting. "Are your folks here?"

"Yes." He moved aside. "Come in, Sheriff."

Deputy Nan's mother heard her son, and she came out of her bedroom with tears already in her eyes. Hayden fought to hold back his emotion. He would rather face a thousand trife alone than do this. Nan's father emerged behind her mother. He was more stoic, his face flat.

"I'm sorry," Hayden said. He didn't need to say much more than that. They knew why he was here. "She died to save her fellow deputies. She died a hero."

Mrs. Nan came over to him and threw her arms around him, sobbing into his chest. He held her while she cried. Mr. Nan stood in front of him, watching them, fighting to bury his emotions and mostly succeeding. But not completely.

Carlo put his arm over his mother's shoulders. He had tears in his eyes. "What happened, Sheriff?"

"A trife queen attacked us," Hayden replied.

"A queen?" Nan's father said, surprised.

"That's right. We lost two others in the fight."

"You're lucky you made it out alive."

Hayden heard the accusation in the man's voice. He didn't blame him. Why should he be alive when his daughter was dead? Hayden asked himself that question all the time.

"We made it out alive because of Kyrie," Hayden said. "She gave her life for us."

"Thank you for coming yourself," Carlo said, gently trying to pull his mother away. "I'm sure you have a lot of other things to do."

"I wish I didn't," Hayden said as Mrs. Nan released him. "Of course, you have the full support of the UWT. Whatever you need, please don't hesitate to ask."

"Thank you, Sheriff," Carlo said. "Goodnight."

Hayden nodded, backing toward the door. They were going to be pissed at him for a while. He understood. He left in silence, closing his eyes when he heard Deputy Nan's mother begin to wail.

He wiped away the tears as he headed back down the stairs and out into the street.

43

Hayden

"Dad!"

Hayden smiled and knelt as Ginny rushed over to him, taking her in his arms. She hugged him tightly and kissed his cheek.

"Good to see you too," Hayden said. He looked past Ginny to the sofa, where Hallia's caretaker Heather was sitting with Hallia asleep in her lap. Deputy Solino sat beside her.

"I think they're in love," Ginny whispered into his ear.

"I think you're right," Hayden replied. "How are you, little darlin'?"

"Good. You should bring me on your next mission with you. I'm useful."

"I know you are. But you're more useful here. Did any trife attack the city today?"

"No."

"See. All you."

Ginny laughed. "I'm serious."

"So am I."

"You both look very serious," Natalia said. "Thanks for staying late, Heather."

"Of course, Governor," Heather replied. She was young and a little pudgy, with a pretty face that glowed when she smiled, and the perfect, patient demeanor for dealing with an infant and a precocious tween. "Anything I can do to help."

"I'll take things from here," Natalia said, going over to her and picking up Hallia. "Why don't you and Deputy Solino go enjoy the rest of the evening?"

Deputy Solino laughed. "Are you suggesting these two aren't enjoyable?"

"Not at all. But adults need a chance to enjoy adult things too."

"I'm an adult," Ginny said. "Close enough, anyway. And if you're talking about the adult things I think you're talking about, there's nothing you can say I haven't already heard, and probably a lot of it I've already seen."

Hayden glanced at Natalia. It was easy to forget Ginny had practically raised herself on the streets of Dego. She had also risked her life to save Hayden's. Not the average twelve-year-old.

"Right," Deputy Solino said, face turning red. "Well, that wasn't what I had in mind. But they are showing Star Wars at the rec center." He looked at Heather. "Interested?"

She nodded. "Sure."

"Engineer Lil fixed a projector someone brought in," Solino explained. "High definition for the first time."

"Sounds great," Hayden said.

"Can I go?" Ginny asked, looking at him.

It also still took him by surprise when she asked for permission to do things. She technically didn't need permission. He and Natalia weren't really her parents. But she had chosen them, and she wanted their approval. She wanted to feel cared for and about.

And he did love her.

"Try to stay out of Heather and Nick's hair," Natalia said, laughing.

"I'll find someone else to bug," Ginny said.

"And be back by ten," Hayden said. "Got it?"

"Pozz." She looked at Heather and Deputy Solino. "You two coming?"

Heather laughed and got to her feet, joined by the deputy.

"We'll keep an eye on her," Solino said. "Or maybe she'll keep an eye on us."

"Bye mom," Ginny said. "Bye dad. I love you."

"Love you too," Natalia and Hayden replied.

The trio left the apartment. Natalia sat down with Hallia on her arm. Hayden sat next to her, putting his arm around her. She leaned into his chest.

"Do you hear that?" Hayden asked.

"No."

"Exactly. I don't get enough quiet time with my wife anymore."

"It's nice, isn't it?"

"Pozz." Hayden kissed the top of Natalia's head. "In case I haven't told you lately. I love you."

"I love you too, Sheriff," she replied. "Always have. Always will."

He put his free arm around her, putting his hand on Hallia's back. They sat in comfortable silence for a while.

"You know," Natalia said, shifting slightly. "Hal should sleep for a couple more hours. We have some time to ourselves."

"What are you suggesting, Governor Duke?"

"Political scandal? Governor found in bed with Sheriff."

Hayden laughed. "I want to. More than anything. Especially now. But I'm beat, Nat. And you deserve better than that."

She nodded, putting her head back on his chest. "You need to tell the Relyeh to stop sending tentacle monsters to kill you. Tell them it leaves you too drained to make love to your wife."

"You'd be the one to tell them," Hayden replied. "Do you think it would work?"

"Somehow, I doubt it."

"Why don't we put Hallia to bed? Maybe I'll find a second wind if we relax together for a while."

"I'm fine with whatever we do right now, so long as we do it together. Just don't lose hope, Hayden."

"I won't if you don't," he replied.

"Deal."

Hayden stood up and took Hal from Natalia, carrying her to her room beside the master, at the back of their apartment. They lived inside the pyramid on the ninth floor and had a view of the bay and the Golden Gate Bridge. He laid his daughter in the crib, leaning over and kissing her forehead. "Daddy loves you."

Hallia didn't react. She was sound asleep.

"Mommy loves you too," Natalia said, kissing her from the other side of the crib.

They turned and headed out of the room together.

The badge on Hayden's collar flashed.

"Sheriff Duke," Hicks said. "Do you copy?"

"I copy," Hayden said, glancing at Natalia. "Do you have something?"

"I do."

"That was fast," Natalia said.

"Sorry to bother you," Hicks said. "I know you wanted some downtime with your family."

"What have you got?" Hayden asked.

"A farmer came in about ten minutes ago. Says his wife is missing."

"Trife?" Natalia asked.

"Governor Duke," Hicks said, hearing her voice. "We don't think so. He says he didn't see, hear, or smell anything. But he did find what looks like a torn strip of cloth from her shirt out in the field where she was tending crops. I can look into it, Sheriff. I just thought you should know."

"No," Hayden said. "I'm in. Contact Bronson. We'll meet at the chopper in twenty."

"Roger that, Sheriff. Hicks out."

Hayden looked at Natalia. "Sorry, love. Even if it isn't a khoron, if he didn't find a body she's probably alive and in trouble."

"I know. I want you to go. Just be safe, okay?"

"You know me. Tell Ginny and Hal I'm sorry I didn't have more time for them. If we can wrap this up quick, maybe we can salvage a few hours."

"One thing at a time, Sheriff."

"Pozz." Hayden kissed her. "Maybe we can salvage something too. Something newsworthy."

Natalia laughed. "I'll look forward to it. Now go."

Hayden kissed her again and hurried out the door.

44

Nathan

Nathan had just enough time to find his own shower and fresh clothes before the hour was up. Fortunately, one of the officer's quarters on the carrier had already been designated for his twin and stocked with both utilities and dress uniforms for the General of Edenrise.

He emerged from the island of the U.S.S. George H.W. Bush with five minutes to spare. Pyro walked beside him, dressed in combat armor and carrying her helmet against her hip. A small selection of soldiers walked behind them in combat armor of their own—the most elite of what remained.

They marched across the deck, past the rotting corpse of the xaxkluth to where the rest of the surviving soldiers had gathered, only a short distance from the dropship. There were only about a hundred of them in total, a depressingly small group of men and women, many of them sporting bandaged arms or foreheads, or other minor injuries. Even so, they came to stiff attention when Nathan approached, standing proudly for their leader.

Nathan walked past them, climbing onto the back of

the resting Badger to be seen by all. He had a comm in his ear that would broadcast out to Pyro's helmet, which in turn would transmit to the Bush's comm across to the Truxton. She had managed to locate two surviving engineers to help her set the system up, as well as check on Nathan's armor and effect simple repairs.

A similar number of soldiers on the other side waited for his instruction. He looked to his right, finding the other carrier floating half a kilometer away. Both ships were still cruising toward open water, and from there north to what he hoped might become a temporary safe haven.

"Space Force!" he snapped, getting their attention.

"Hoorah!" they shouted back in reply. It was pitiful compared to their last muster when nearly six thousand soldiers were organized across the field.

"I'll keep this short and simple." He looked out at the soldiers, able to pick them out by faces. "We lost a lot of good people today. Both members of our family and citizens of our city. We're tired. Hurting. On the run. But we're here. We're together. And with your help, we can restore Edenrise."

"Hoorah!"

"Early counts show six thousand here on the Bush, another two thousand on the Truxton. Eight thousand survivors. Eight thousand people who are still depending on us to provide protection and leadership in the days ahead. I can't tell you those days will be easy. As you've seen, the enemy is upping the ante and escalating the fight. You know what we say to that."

"Fight back!" the soldiers shouted.

"That's right. We'll fight back. We'll protect our own, and we'll rebuild. I see Lieutenant Locke. Lieutenant!"

"Sir, yes, sir?" Locke said, remaining at attention. He was short and muscled, his uniform bloodstained, a bandage over his left eye. Wounded but present, and eager to serve.

"From what I can tell, you're the second ranking officer on this ship. That means the Bush is your responsibility."

"Yes, sir. Thank you, sir."

"Captain Koi is the ranking officer on the Truxton. He's in charge of both his ship and the entirety of the settlement. Understood?"

"Yes, sir," Locke replied.

"As you know, both ships are home to well-equipped armories. It is the duty of every remaining Space Force soldier to continue to defend these ships with their lives. They are our home for the immediate future. Locke, Koi, I want you both to designate units to begin conscripting from the civilians and teaching them how to use our available weapons. The only people who are exempt are those too injured or elderly to fight, and no more than one parent or potential caretaker for any children who are newly orphaned. Understood?"

"Yes, General," both Locke and Koi replied.

"Good. Your orders are to head north. Stay well clear of the shore. These new alien creatures aren't affected by water the way the trife are and will likely attack if they get visual. We're relatively safe out to sea, but we can't stay out here forever."

"Sir," Locke said. "What about the weapons cache?"

Nathan expected the question. "As you can see, I have a unit suited up and ready to go. I'll be joining them in a recon of the weapons cache. If at all possible, we'll begin to recover some of the ordnance to assist with defense."

"Yes, sir," Locke replied. "How long will you be gone, sir?"

"I don't know. As long as it takes." He paused a moment, waiting to see if anyone else would ask any questions. They didn't. "Most of you came to Edenrise from outside, because you were looking for something better than mere survival. Losing the city and the protection of the energy shield is a blow to all of us. But Edenrise is bigger than a place. It's bigger than a shield. Its value is in its people. All of you. If you think of something that should be done, bring it to Locke or Koi. If you see something that needs to be done, do it. It's vital that we remain focused on the tenets that made Edenrise great. Loyalty, honesty, trust, freedom. I'm counting on all of you."

"Hoorah!"

"Locke, you have the ship."

"Sir, yes, sir!" Locke said.

Nathan jumped down from his perch on the Badger. Locke was already shouting orders, finding his next in command and reorganizing the soldiers into units. He smiled as he headed to where the unit he'd gathered was standing. Pyro came up beside him as he walked.

"Nice speech, General," she said.

"I didn't know I had it in me," Nathan replied. "Liberators, with me."

He passed the unit, led by Sergeant Walt, a broad woman with a large tribal tattoo over the left side of her face. It was a new designation, one he had based on the USSF logo and its meaning to him. Freedom, perseverance, strength, power. He hoped the small group could live up to the name.

They filed in behind him, tailing him into the dropship. Caleb was already waiting for them in the cargo hold. He had cleaned up well, a model physical specimen in the utilities he had found.

"Sergeant Card," Nathan said. Caleb came to attention, submitting himself as subordinate to him. Nathan motioned to the cart Private Jeffs was pushing. "I've got combat armor for you. I trust you know how to use it?"

Caleb smiled. "Yes, sir."

"Good. I'm also promoting you to Colonel. We need a clean chain of command."

"As you say, sir," Caleb replied, a slightly amused look on his face.

"Liberators, you've already met Colonel Card out in the field. He saved all of your lives."

"Yes, sir!" the Liberators replied.

"Welcome to the team," Sergeant Walt said.

Caleb stared at her for a moment, hesitating before nodding. "Thank you, Sergeant."

"Time's wasting," Pyro said. "Welcome back aboard, Colonel Card. General, permission to prep for launch?"

"Granted. Sergeant Walt, get your gear stowed and ready. Colonel Card, with me."

Caleb followed Nathan up the stairs to the main deck.

"What's the situation, General?" Caleb asked once they were clear of the unit.

"The soldiers below know me as General James Stacker. I prefer it to stay that way."

"Roger that."

"They also don't know about Sheriff Duke. I can't keep them from finding out, but I prefer to leave them in the dark as long as possible. I don't expect trouble under the circumstances, but it's better to be discreet."

"Agreed."

"We'll head to the weapons cache first. With any luck, the area will be clear and we can recover some of the more advanced ordnance before heading west. We used to have a comm link to Sanisco, but it went down with the city."

"Understood, General." Caleb paused.

"Is there something you want to say?" Nathan asked.

"A couple of things," Caleb admitted. "I sensed another human on the Collective a couple of months back. A woman, I think. I couldn't quite reach into her to tell who she was or where she came from. Do you know anything about that?"

Nathan shook his head. "I barely understand what the Collective is. But if it requires any kind of technical know-how, it probably originated in Sanisco. Sheriff Duke's wife Natalia is one of the smartest people I've ever met. What's your other question?"

"It's more of a statement. Sergeant Walt is a khoron."

Nathan froze, staring at Caleb. "What exactly does that mean?"

"It means she's infected by a Relyeh creature similar to Ishek. The Advocates were engineered from the khoron. An evolved iteration. I'm not sure what it's doing here or what its intentions are."

"Does it know about Ishek?"

"I don't think so. Fortunately, we learned how to block out the nascent connection to the Collective. It's sort of like putting a password on a computer network."

"Then how did you recognize it?"

"Like I said, Ishek is an evolved version. We're a little more sensitive. We could probably break into it and determine its motives."

"Or we can drop her out of the hold from ten kilometers up," Nathan said. He had decided to accept Caleb based on what he had done to help Edenrise. He wasn't ready to start taking in every Relyeh refugee they came across.

"It's better to be discreet," Caleb replied, using his words against him. "She can't cause any trouble without me knowing it, and I'd prefer a chance to talk to her. I just thought it was important that you were aware."

"I understand." Nathan nodded, then hesitated a moment, considering. "I'll follow your lead on this, Caleb. You know a hell of a lot more about it than I do."

"I appreciate your trust."

"Pull Walt aside when we lift off. It'll take about an hour to get to the weapons cache."

"That far away?" Caleb asked.

"You can't just leave your most advanced ordnance sitting out in the open where anyone can find it, now can you?"

"No, sir."

"You have my permission to handle Walt however you need. Find out what you need to find out. Whatever it takes."

Then he turned and walked away.

45

Caleb

Caleb was sitting next to Sergeant Walt in the bow of the dropship as it lifted off from the U.S.S. George H.W. Bush, ascending rapidly enough to press him back into his seat. He smiled subconsciously at the liftoff, remembering the many times he had made similar maneuvers on the. way to or from an infected zone.

The quick acceleration only lasted a dozen seconds before the ship leveled off, the ride flattening out.

"ETA forty-eight minutes," Stacker said over the loud-speaker.

Caleb glanced over at Walt. She was staring straight ahead, a slightly sick look on her face. "First jump?" he asked.

She looked at him and nodded. "I've never been airborne before."

"You get used to it. The secret is to remember to breathe."

"That's all? Just remember to breathe?"

She doesn't need to breathe.

That wasn't entirely true. The khoron inside her could keep her alive for an extended period without breathing, but not indefinitely.

"Simple. In any case, we're level for now. You're safe until we drop."

"I can't wait."

"I was hoping we could head somewhere to talk in private," Caleb said. "I'm new to Edenrise. Actually, I only arrived while the city was under attack. I could use some debriefing on how things work around here."

"You seem like you've already got in pretty good with the General," Corporal Hotch said, overhearing him. "He made you a Colonel so you could boss us around."

"And so you would show some respect," Caleb said, sharpening his tone of voice. "Why don't you drop and give me fifty, Corporal?"

"What?" Hotch said. "Now?"

Caleb pointed to the space between the seats. "Right there. Right now."

Hotch's face paled, but he slid out of his seat and started doing pushups while the other Liberators laughed.

"I can help you out," Walt said, unbuckling herself from the seat. "There's a small debriefing room behind the bridge. I'm sure General Stacker won't mind if we use it."

"Lead the way," Caleb replied.

He got up, following her past the bridge to the small room, which featured a table and six chairs organized behind a terminal and display. He closed the door behind him as they entered.

"So, how did you end up outside Edenrise during the attack?" Walt asked, turning to face him. "General Stacker said you're a Centurion?"

Tell me when Caleb.

"I was tracking the trife," Caleb replied. He wasn't ready to push her just yet. He wanted to see how she responded to basic questioning. "I followed them north. I was hunting them."

"Alone?"

"Mostly."

"But you were a soldier once. That much is obvious. The way you speak. The way you stand."

"What about you? How long have you been in Edenrise?"

"Only about a month. I lost my last home. I was looking for something new to believe in."

"And you already made Sergeant."

"I scored well on their entrance tests. I know I look a little meaty, but I've got moves." She laughed. "Do you want to sit, sir?" Caleb pulled out a chair. Walt sat opposite him. "I don't know how much help I can be to you, Colonel. I'm pretty new to the area myself, and with everything that just happened, it's kind of screwed up the established norms."

She's already trying to brush you off.

"Fair enough. Maybe you can give me a quick briefing on the rest of the Liberators?"

"I don't know any of them. General Stacker pulled us together last minute."

"There has to be something of value you can share with me."

Walt shrugged. "I can't think of anything, sir."

"Where are you originally from?" Caleb asked.

"Sir? I'm not sure how that matters."

"I'm just trying to get to know my subordinates, starting from the top down. Did you have family in Edenrise?"

"No, no family. I guess I'm lucky in that."

"Do you have family anywhere?"

"None to speak of, sir."

Any time now, Caleb. This is getting us nowhere.

"I feel like you're intentionally stonewalling me, Sergeant. I'm wondering why."

Walt leaned back, eyes narrowing. "Sir? Is it a requirement I tell you my life story to be part of this team?"

"No, but it goes a long way toward earning trust."

"And you don't trust me?"

"Should I?"

"Yes."

"Based on what criteria?"

Walt's face flushed. "I'm a member of General Stacker's Liberators. That should imply trust."

You're getting them worked up. I like it. Makes it easier to crack them.

"The tattoo on your face. It's an interesting symbol. What does it mean?"

"It doesn't mean anything. I designed it myself."

"You're lying."

Walt's jaw clenched. "How dare you," she hissed, standing up. "I don't know who you think you are, but I'm not about to take this bullshit. I—"

"Sit down," Caleb said, at the same time Ishek pushed on the khoron inside Walt.

Her eyes widened, and she started to shake as she dropped back into the seat. "You…"

"I'm like you," Caleb said. "Only better." Ishek kept the pressure on the khoron. "I ran into another of your kind when I first arrived here. And I've been bumping into your kind ever since. Who do you serve?"

Walt stared at him, trying not to answer. Ishek pushed on the khoron, forcing her to speak.

"No one," she replied.

"All khoron serve a master," Caleb said. "Who do you serve?"

She winced as Ishek increased the pressure. "No one. I swear. I used to serve Shurrath, but Shurrath is gone."

"Gone?" Caleb asked.

"Yes. I don't know where or how. I used to feel him. But not for months."

"And you're sure you don't serve Nyarlath?"

Walt shook even harder. "No. I was trying to escape her. That's why I came to Edenrise."

"What about your hunger? How have you fed it?"

Walt didn't respond.

Tell me.

Caleb closed his eyes as images filled his mind, passing from Walt's khoron to Ishek over the Collective. Dark places. Dark vices. Consensual torture.

"Enough," Caleb said, pushing the memories out of his head. He stared at Walt. "You're a danger to this mission."

"No more than you."

"I can resist Nyarlath. Can you say the same?"

"Yes."

"You couldn't resist me."

"I've realized that this planet is the end. Not only for humankind but for anything that comes here and thinks to control it. That is its place in the universe. The end of all things. The Old One may have seen the spread of the Relyeh across the universe, but it will not come to pass. I'm convinced of that. If it doesn't matter which master we serve, then it's better to serve the master who makes no demands. Who asks for loyalty and earns it."

"Until you have no choice."

"It's been months. I've felt no compulsion."

"Nyarlath is coming."

Walt shuddered again. "Who told you this?"

"Multiple khoron loyal to her. She's had agents here for some time. And when she arrives, if she aims to compel you then you will comply."

"I'll resist."

"And you'll fail like you failed with me."

"I'll resist long enough to kill myself. Or for you to kill me."

Caleb leaned back in his seat. He wasn't sure she would or could. At the same time, he was hesitant to remove her.

They needed all the help they could get, even if it was from another Relyeh.

"You'll remain open to me," Caleb said. "No resistance."

"Yes, Colonel."

"When Nyarlath comes, if you and your khoron are not strong enough to defy her, I will end your life. Do you understand?"

"Yes, Colonel."

Caleb stood up. "Take a minute to compose yourself, and then meet us back up front. We've got twenty minutes until we drop."

"Yes, Colonel."

Caleb left the room, heading next door to the bridge. He didn't have security clearance, so he knocked on the door. It slid open a moment later, and he entered.

"General," he said.

"Well?" Stacker asked.

"It's an asset worth utilizing. At least until it isn't."

He nodded. "Carry on."

Caleb ducked back off the bridge, returning to the front of the dropship. Sergeant Walt rejoined him a minute later, avoiding eye contact.

That went well.

Keeping her was risky, but it was a risk they had to take. If nothing else, she might serve as an early warning against Nyarlath's arrival.

And against Nyarlath, every second would count.

46

Caleb

Caleb moved to the front of the Liberators as Stacker descended the steps into the cargo hold.

"Liberators. AH-TEHN-SHUN!" Caleb snapped.

The rest of the unit moved into place behind him, and they all came to attention as Stacker reached the group.

"We're almost in position," Stacker said. "Grab your gear. We drop in five."

"Yes, sir!" they barked back, immediately going into motion. Most of the Liberators had already finished organizing. They were dressed in full combat armor, plasma rifles strapped to their backs and helmets resting nearby.

Caleb was nearly ready too. He had left the Skin behind, stashed into a small compartment near the reactor for safe-keeping. He wore the combat armor Stacker had brought him instead, comfortable in its familiarity. He had snapped on the helmet and connected to the unit's subnetwork a few minutes earlier, the action momentarily bringing him back over two-hundred years to his former life as a space marine. For a moment, he wasn't in the dropship with these new squadmates. He was prepping for action with his Vultures: Sho, Washington, Banks, Habib. They were all gone now, except for Washington.

And he was hundreds of light years away.

"What kind of ordnance are we looking to recover, General?" Caleb asked, following Stacker over to the side of the cargo hold and the robotic arms that held his powered armor.

"We've got all kinds of munitions," Stacker replied. "But I'm most interested in the scuzz rockets and the enhanced plasma rifles."

"Enhanced plasma?"

"About ten times the heat density and charge of the P-90 on your back," Stacker said. "They use mineral components mined from the asteroids outside Proxima to manage the heat load without exploding in your face. The plasma cannons on board use an older version of the tech." He stepped back into the center of the arms, which immediately went to work placing the powered armor over him.

"What about the rockets?"

"Essentially mini-nukes. One warhead separates into one hundred delivery vehicles, similar to the cluster bombs we used earlier, only about a hundred times more powerful. They were designed as anti-spacecraft weapons, in the event the enemy utilizes swarm tactics or high volumes of air or spaceborne targets. Considering the trife, that idea isn't too far fetched." He paused while the arms dropped the large helmet over him, screwing it to the rest of the armor. The front visor slid open. "We never wanted to use them here, but we kept some of them because we knew we might not always have an option. If what you say about these xaxkluth is true, we're probably going to need them."

"Roger that, General," Caleb said.

"We have other weapons inside. Nearly fifty years worth of munitions we've held back from Proxima. Enough to put up a good fight."

"Enough to win?"

"Not on our own. That's part of the problem. Whatever Proxima thinks about Earth and the people who live on it, none of us are going to make it through this without working together. And even then, the odds are bad. There's no point trying to pretend they aren't."

"Agreed. They were bad the last time I was here too. We aren't extinct yet, and both the Hunger and the Axon do have weaknesses. It's up to us to exploit them."

"I like the way you think, Caleb." The arms finished assembling the armor. Stacker stepped forward out of the machine, turning back to grab his large rifle from its mount on the bulkhead. He snapped it to his back, keeping the visor up as he crossed the hold to the rear ramp.

"Liberators!" he snapped. "Line up."

Caleb grabbed his helmet and joined Stacker at the head of the line, while the other Liberators filled in behind them, two by two.

"Are we going in hot, General?" Caleb asked.

"Lukewarm," Stacker replied. "No positive identification of any obvious threats, but all things considered, I'm assuming the worst."

"Yes, sir."

"Buckets on. Sound off."

Caleb dropped his helmet over his head, hearing it click into place, connecting to the rest of the combat armor. The HUD activated in front of him, and he waited until his connection turned green before speaking.

"Liberator One, check."

Sergeant Walt was next. "Liberator Two, check."

"Liberator Three, check," Corporal Hotch said, a nervous quiver in his tone.

"Liberator Four, check," Corporal Dane said, his voice like gravel.

"Liberator Five, check," Private Yasko snapped, her response sharp and eager.

"Liberator Six, check," Private Ki replied, his soft inflection more like a meditation.

"Liberator Prime," Stacker said. "Check."

"Parabellum," Pyro said. "Check. We're closing on the target. Skids down in thirty seconds. Still no sign of alien activity, trife or otherwise. General, there's a small group of nomads camped about two klicks from the main. We're going to draw their attention."

"How many?"

"Twenty or so, and their horses."

"Six, Five, you've got guard duty," Stacker said. "They get too close, scare them off."

"Yes, sir," they replied.

"Twenty seconds," Pyro said, counting down. "Fifteen seconds."

Stacker hit the control pad for the ramp. It clunked and began to drop, letting the air start rushing in.

"Ten seconds."

"Wedge formation," Stacker said. "I've got point. Nice and easy."

The ramp continued to drop. Caleb could feel the sharp downward motion of the craft, controlled enough to keep them on their feet. He could see the landscape approaching through the newly open space.

Is that?

His heart started to race, old memories flooding back.

It is, isn't it?

"Five seconds," Pyro announced.

Ishek was right.

"General," Caleb said. "I know this place. This is where the Deliverance was built. This was home."

47

Caleb

The skids hit the ground, absorbing the impact as Nathan charged down the ramp. He didn't reply to Caleb's comment, remaining focused on the mission.

Caleb pulled himself back to the moment, only a step behind as they evacuated the dropship, the Liberators running off behind him. He quickly scanned the terrain, confident they had touched down at the launch site of the Deliverance, half a klick from the excavated hill where the massive generation starship had been assembled. The hangar was destroyed during the launch, and the evidence of the side of the incline's collapse was evident beneath the regrown vegetation. But so was evidence of a newer, smaller excavation—a break in the landscape revealing dirt and rock that had been moved back and forth. There were crush patterns in the grass as well, suggesting a dropship landed here regularly.

Taking the lead, Nathan raced toward the disturbed. Liberators Five and Six stayed further back, tailing them at a slower pace and keeping themselves oriented toward the nomads Pyro had pointed out—a red arrow marking them on the HUD.

"Looks like our nomads are more curious than afraid," Pyro said, monitoring them on the dropship's more powerful sensors. "They're headed our way."

"Liberators Five and Six, you know what to do," Caleb said.

"Roger, Liberator One."

The rest of the unit followed Nathan to the side of the hill. He came to a stop beside a large rock, kneeling in front of it and digging at the ground with his armored hand. He pulled up the earth, revealing a control pad beneath it a moment later. He tapped in the access code, and the vegetation to his right faded away, revealing a blast door behind it.

Caleb smirked beneath his helmet. A projection and a fake potential door.

Clever.

Nathan approached the door, reaching for the control pad mounted on the right side. His hand paused before he touched it. "Something's wrong," he said.

Caleb instinctively grabbed his rifle from his back in response to the statement. "General?"

Nathan's hand continued to hover over the control pad. The seconds passed like hours.

"General?" Caleb repeated.

He checked his HUD. The nomads were near enough his ATCS painted them each individually, closing quickly on Yasko and Ki. The two Liberators started firing, a few warning shots that hit the ground ahead of their horses.

Something's wrong.

Ishek echoed Nathan's statement. Caleb was inclined to agree.

The warning shots hadn't slowed down the nomads at all.

The two Liberators stopped shooting. They were still as the twenty horseback riders thundered toward them.

What the hell was going on?

Yasko and Ki turned to face one another, raising their rifles slightly.

"Axon," Caleb said, recognizing the action right before the two Liberators discharged their weapons into one another. Both of them fell at the same time, just as the riders reached them. "Retreat!"

Caleb started firing, launching bolt after bolt into the riders. He cursed as the rounds passed right through what were obviously holograms.

"General, we have to get out of here!" Caleb said. "Parabellum, we need immediate evac!"

The dropship whined behind them, the thrusters powering up. Nathan turned back toward the control pad, his fingers moving to open the sealed door.

"No!" Caleb said, lunging forward and grabbing Nathan's hand. "Whatever you see, it isn't real. Come on, General!"

Nathan whirled on him, slamming his chest with his free hand and sending him sprawling onto his back. The Liberators closed on him, pointing their guns at his chest.

Except for Walt.

She shot forward, hitting Hotch hard enough to knock him into Dane and sending them both to the ground before they could shoot Caleb. Then she latched onto Nathan's hand, trying to keep him from opening the door.

"They were waiting for you," she said. "General, it's a trap."

Nathan grabbed her by the neck, lifting her and throwing her aside before turning back.

"Ishek!" Caleb shouted.

The Advocate emitted a high-pitched squeal, the frequency enough to momentarily interrupt the Axon's neural disruption.

"General, the Others," Caleb said, hoping the alternate name would help Stacker resist the hallucinations.

Stacker's head turned. The dropship was swooping toward them, spinning to point the open ramp in their direction. The nomads were closing from the left flank, the first rider breaking free from the group.

His rifle came to his hands in an instant. He started shooting, targeting the first rider, his rounds punching through it without effect.

The dropship landed a dozen meters away.

"Go!" Stacker shouted. "Retreat!"

Caleb grabbed Hotch's arm, helping him up. Walt did the same for Dane. The lead nomad raised an old single-shot bolt-action rifle toward them and fired. Dane grunted, his head slumping forward in response.

The other nomads grabbed similar guns from the side of their saddles, preparing to fire on the Liberators. Some of the Liberators slowed, hesitating as they brought up their rifles to shoot back.

"No!" Caleb let go of Hotch, letting him run on his own. He swept his rifle across the line of nomads, looking for the Intellect that was running this show. He had one shot at picking the right rider.

The real one.

His eyes crossed the back of the line. No matter which one he shot at, he was only guessing.

He never got to take the shot. Stacker's rifle crackled beside him, roaring as it unleashed a sudden, massive barrage across the entire row of riders. The rounds went through most of them...

Except one..

Blue flashes erupted from the Axon's shield, the sudden activation causing the holographic projections to fade, revealing the featureless black humanoid mounted on a gray horse. . It jumped from the saddle and gained speed, sprinting toward them faster than a horse could run. Its intent was obvious. Beat them to the ship.

Caleb joined Stacker in firing at the Intellect, hitting it hard with both plasma and projectiles. Walt made the ramp carrying Dane in her arms, with Hotch right behind.

"Pyro, get us out of here!" Stacker bellowed through the comm.

The dropship's lift thrusters fired full-bore on both sides, pummeling Caleb and Stacker with swirling dirt and debris. The craft began to rise before either of them reached it, rising above their heads within seconds. Stacker wrapped a powerful arm around Caleb's waist and jumped, firing his assist thrusters and arcing up into the hold, the heavy landing shaking the dropship.

He released Caleb, reaching for the ramp controls. A sharp blue bolt of energy nearly severed his hand, entering the dropship and slamming into the top of the hold, powering through it and burning into the next deck.

"Hold on!" Pyro cried, banking hard to the left. The momentum tossed all of them into the bulkhead and then threw them back as the dropship accelerated and climbed.

The ramp slammed closed, the craft continuing to rise. Caleb pulled himself to his feet, checking his HUD. Dane's tag was red.

"Son of a bitch," Stacker cursed, getting up off the deck. "We need to go back around and hit it from the air."

"You'll never see it from the air," Caleb replied. "Not unless it wants to be seen."

Stacker growled, storming over to Dane's body and

looking down. The Liberator had died as if he'd been shot, but there was no bullet. No wound. The Intellect had convinced his mind of the shot.

"I've never seen one duplicate its projections before," Stacker said. "Or combine the hologram with the hallucination."

"They're learning to fight us more efficiently," Caleb replied. "Now that some of us know to fight back against them."

"Makes sense."

"It knew about the weapons cache," Caleb said. "It was waiting for you to open it."

"It attacked us before I could."

"It attacked us before we could get to the guns inside. You have something in there it doesn't want us to recover. Something that can hurt it and others like it."

"Or it wants a piece of the action," Stacker counted. "Either way, how the hell could it know what we have in the cache, never mind where the cache is?"

"How many people knew this place was here?" Caleb asked.

"Hardly anyone who's still alive. Me and Pyro are the last two."

"What about someone who isn't still alive?"

"Dead men tell no tales, Caleb."

"Except when they're telling them to an Axon Intellect. Don't underestimate them, General."

Stacker stared at him. Caleb could tell the General was trying to guess where the Axon might have learned about the cache. Nathan was worried he had slipped up somewhere. Let his guard down. And maybe he had. There was no telling where the Axon had come from or how long it might have been waiting for Nathan to arrive. It didn't matter anyway. It was there, and it had kept them from getting to the weapons cache. But why hadn't it entered on its own? Even if it couldn't duplicate Stacker's biometric identification, it should have been able to force the door open.

"I know what you're thinking," Nathan said. "Tinker made the lock. Electromagnetic, with a series of eight fail-safes. Even Intellects have limits when it comes to pure force."

He really did know what you were thinking.

"Forget the guns for now," Nathan continued. "We still have to warn the Sheriff that a storm is coming, and the only way we'll survive it is together. Walt, find somewhere to stow Dane's body. Liberators, check your gear and stay ready. As far as I'm concerned, nowhere is safe anymore."

48

Hayden

"I feel like we were just doing this a few hours ago," Hicks said as Hayden emerged from the armory.

He had traded the full combat armor from his last mission for a bodysuit beneath his clothes, and his helmet for his custom-made sunglasses, leaving behind the star-shaped comm and the plastic star that revealed his identity. It was possible he might need to do some questioning or enter a populated area without raising too much suspicion, and appearing as anything more than a solitary wanderer would make that especially tricky.

"We *were* just doing this a few hours ago," Hayden replied, hopping into the helicopter. The rest of the Rangers were buckled in behind Hicks, and they waved to Hayden as he entered. "Let's hope we can avoid anything too crazy this time."

"Pozz that," Hicks said.

Hayden tapped the side of the glasses to activate the comm. "Remember. We need to take the perp alive. If he's got a khoron in him, he's going to be stronger and faster than an ordinary human." He leaned forward and tapped on Bronson's shoulder. "Let's go."

The pilot gave him a thumbs-up and then increased the throttle on the chopper, lifting them into the air. They continued to ascend into the darkness, over the tops of the nearby buildings before vectoring northeast, up and over the bay.

"Tell me more about the situation," Hayden said.

"The farmer's name is Josias Colombo," Hicks said. "His wife's name is Rosa. She's thirty-two years old, slim, big chest." He paused. "His words, not mine. Long dark hair, brown eyes. She was wearing a long-sleeve shirt, brown cotton pants, and a straw hat. He was surprised he didn't find the hat. Went missing two days ago. It took him that long to get down here on horseback."

"What happened to the water taxi?"

"He didn't want to leave his horse."

"His wife is missing, and he didn't want to leave his horse?"

Hicks smiled and shrugged.

"What else?"

"There's a small settlement about ten klicks from his farm. It used to be a winery or something, but now the farmers all go there to drink and trade with scavengers passing through. He was worried she was trafficked through there and already passed back east out of the UWT."

"Toward Salt Lake City?" Hayden asked. "We've got eyes out that way."

"Further north. It seems word has spread that Ports is clear, and Seattle is thinned out."

"There are still nests in Seattle."

"Smaller ones. You know the criminals would rather take their chances with trife than get too close to us."

"Let's add Seattle to our to-do list."

"I think we're out of space on the to-do list."

Hayden smiled. They were perpetually out of resources for everything he wanted to accomplish. One thing at a time.

The helicopter continued northeast, crossing the water and continuing into more open space.

"Is that Alpha?" Jackson asked, pointing out into the distance.

Hayden looked out that way, finding the silhouette of the goliath in the distance. Only the upper half of the giant was visible past the hills.

"Too small to be Alpha," Hayden said, referring to the largest of the creatures. "And traveling alone." He continued staring at the silhouette. "It is a little closer to the city than I would expect. There aren't any trife within at least fifty klicks of here."

"I've seen them this close before," Bronson said. "Usually when their bellies are full. He'll probably grab some shuteye against that hill."

The chopper continued north, leaving the goliath behind.

"Is that it?" Hayden asked twenty minutes later, pointing to a long stone building in the distance.

Large torches were arranged along the outside, while light from LEDs was visible glowing from within. A handful of horses and a group of customized armored cars sat in a circular driveway, around a large, crumbling fountain.

"Looks like it to me," Hicks confirmed. "But since when do farmers have modboxes like that?"

"Is that a bus?" Bahk asked, pointing to a dark area away from the building.

"Confirmed," Hayden said, noticing the vehicle. Like

the cars, it was modified with armored plating and steel spines to help protect it from trife attack.

"I don't like this, Sheriff," Hicks said. "That doesn't look like a farmer's market to me."

"Me neither," Hayden agreed. The setup was suspicious to say the least. "Maybe there's something to Josias' fears about his wife being trafficked. Bronson, bring us in over there. Not too far, not too close."

"Roger, Sheriff," Bronson replied. The helicopter began to descend, coming to rest in the field beside the building a few minutes later.

"Wait for my signal."

"Roger, Sheriff," Hicks said. "We've got your back."

Hayden jumped out of the chopper and ran across the field toward the building. There were no guards stationed outside, and nobody had come out to see them land even though the helicopter was anything but quiet. He understood why as he got closer. Loud, live music was blaring out through the windows, a deep rumbling bass escaping into the night. He could drop a bomb on the place and they probably wouldn't hear it.

What the hell was happening inside?

Hayden made it to the side of the building, crouching low and pressing himself against the wall. He laughed at himself, straightening up a moment later. There was no reason to act like he didn't belong there. He walked right past the open windows, the smell of tobacco, alcohol and cheap perfume wafting out with the pulsing noise. They had landed at the back of the building, and the closest door was around the side. Hayden reached it and tried the handle. It was unlocked.

He slipped inside, nearly bumping into a woman in a short, straight dress carrying a tray of drinks. She gasped and backed up, one of the glasses tipping over and crashing on the floor.

The music was deafening, but somehow a bearded thug nearby heard the glass break and was on them in a second.

"What the hell did you do?" he screamed at the woman.

"It was my fault," Hayden said, getting in front of him. "I bumped into her."

"Is that right?" the man said.

"That's right." Hayden met the heavy's eyes, challenging him.

"You don't look familiar," the man said.

"This is my first time here," Hayden replied, breaking eye contact to look around the room. Wine barrels had been converted into tables, and men were standing around most of them, barely dressed women at one side or in some cases both. They were playing cards. Gambling.

The man smiled. "You got notes?"

"I've got UWT chits," Hayden replied. "Are those good here?"

The man's smile increased. "Hell, yeah. Who told you about the Wheat?"

"Josias. You know him?"

"The farmer?"

"That's right."

"That little shit was supposed to be here tonight, dealing cards. Do you know where he is?"

"Nope."

"Love the sunglasses by the way," the man said. He held out his hand. "Name's Albert. Sorry we got off on the wrong foot. Any cowboy with chits and notes is welcome here, as long as they like good booze, loud music, and expensive women." He laughed.

"The girls are for sale?" Hayden asked.

"Rent," Albert replied. "We bus them in from up north. They belong to Hanson."

"Never heard of him."

"You've never heard of Hanson? Where are you from, cowboy?"

"All over."

"Scavvy?"

"Just a loner."

"You want a drink?" Albert asked, reaching for one from the woman's tray. She hadn't moved since the glass had broken, but two other women had come over to pick up the glass.

"No thanks," Hayden said.

The music was making his head hurt, and the smoke was beginning to clog his lungs. The drinking wasn't illegal. Neither was the gambling or the music, though he was starting to question if it should be. The women? Albert said the women belonged to Hanson. That made them slaves, part of the trafficking Josias had mentioned.

Even if there wasn't a khoron involved with this, it needed to be put to an end.

"I'm not much for the music," Hayden said. "Do you have somewhere a little more quiet to spend some time with one of your girls. Or maybe two or three." He offered his most lascivious smile.

Albert smiled back, putting his arm over his shoulder. "I like the way you think, my friend. What's your name again?"

"Earl," Hayden replied.

"Earl. That's a good ole cowboy name, isn't it? I like it. Show me the money, and I'll show you the goods."

Hayden spread his duster to reach under it, the move flashing the handles of his revolvers. He noticed Albert noticing them, but the man didn't say a word. Not until he produced an entire roll of UWT chits.

Albert's eyes lit up at the sight of them. "Where did you get so many chits?"

Hayden widened his smile. "I do the dirty work because it pays well."

Albert laughed again. "You need to meet Bryant. Follow me."

Hayden trailed Albert as the man led him through the first room and into the next. The music was originating from there—four huge speakers connected to amps, which were connected to the band's instruments and a laptop. Cages flanked the group, women dancing inside them. They were putting on a show, but Hayden could see the fear in their eyes and the tension in their faces.

A dozen men were watching the show, dancing with more girls intermingled among them. The bus probably seated at least sixty, and it seemed to have arrived full.

"How long has the Wheat been in operation?" Hayden asked as they crossed the room, shouting into Albert's ear.

"About six months. You can thank Sheriff Duke for clearing out the trife. He made this all possible."

49

Hayden

Hayden froze in place, heart thumping. *He* had made this possible? He had cleaned up the trife so people could break free of the cycle of violence and mistreatment that had caused Proxima to label them savages. He had done it with the belief that people were fundamentally good, and they wanted to help one another more than they wanted to harm one another.

In one instant, Albert had shaken that belief to the core. This place existed because he had taken away the greater threat. He had allowed human evil to replace alien nature without providing enough oversight to ensure it couldn't happen. He had put his faith in goodness without paying enough attention to the downside.

His eyes shifted to the women in the cages. Maybe if he hadn't cleared out the trife, they would still be prisoners. Perhaps they would be dead. There was no way to know what the alternate future might be. But this was the present reality.

And it was his responsibility to fix it.

How many other places like this existed across the

UWT? How many other laws broken or ignored? Why weren't more people reporting this? Josias had only come to them because his wife was gone, not because he wanted to put a stop to this abuse. Hell, the farmer had been working here.

"Earl, you okay?" Albert asked, noticing he had stopped. "It's cool if you want to listen to the music."

Hayden forced his face to relax. He looked at Albert. "Are they available?" he asked, pointing to the women in the cages.

"Which one?"

"All of them."

Albert smiled. "We can take a break. It'll cost."

"I can pay."

"Consider it done. Wait here."

Albert walked over to another thug near the stage. This one was carrying an MK-10 USSF assault rifle and wearing a military bodysuit like Hayden's. He glanced over and then moved to the first cage.

"They'll meet you downstairs," Albert said. "This way."

He led Hayden out of that room and into a third. A few men were on couches, snuggling with a few of the women. Syringes were spread across the table between them, some used, some fresh. They eyed Hayden as he passed before returning to their activities.

"I've seen other places like this outside the UWT," Hayden said as they approached a set of open wooden doors leading to a stairway. "I didn't think there were any here."

"This may be the biggest one to the north," Albert replied. "Hanson keeps a tight grip on things if you know what I mean. But there are smaller operations across the whole region. He who has the most guns wins."

Albert laughed again. Hayden smiled along. They descended a set of stone steps into the cellar. Old wine barrels filled a portion of it, possibly still full, though it had likely all turned to vinegar by now. He paused and looked back as the four women from the cages filed in behind him, and then the two doors swung closed, helping to block out the noise.

"All for me?" Hayden asked.

"You've got the chits," Albert said.

"I've got a lot more in my other pockets." Hayden smirked. "Maybe I shouldn't have told you that."

"We're businessmen, Earl. Not common thugs."

Hayden nodded. Could have fooled him.

"Ladies," Albert said to the women coming down the steps. "This is Earl. Earl, this is the ladies."

"A pleasure," Hayden said. His gut wrenched when he looked at them. Frightened, but resigned.

"Albert, who have you brought?"

Hayden turned around again. A new man had joined them. Well-dressed, well-groomed, with dark hair and a trimmed goatee. Thin, athletic, arrogant. Blue eyes. Fair skin.

"Bryant, this is Earl. Earl, Bryant. He's a first-timer with a lot of chits to spend."

"My favorite type of clientele," Bryant said, flashing a gold-filled smile. "I see you already made a selection. What's your pleasure, Earl?"

"Pain," Hayden replied. "Fear."

He hated to say it, knowing how the women behind him would react. He understood how things went out there. All of them had probably been raised under the thumb of a tyrant or collected off the streets as kids. Probably long before he had come into the picture and deposed King, the former warlord from Sanisco.

Bryant's smile increased. "I see. Well, we can accommodate any taste so long as the chits are good. In fact, you're welcome to join my private party if you're interested. You can bring those girls with you."

"Sure," Hayden replied. "Why not?"

Hayden followed Albert and Bryant away from the stairs, past the wine barrels to a closed door in the corner.

"You aren't squeamish, are you, Earl?" Bryant asked.

Hayden reached up, grabbing his sunglasses and tapping on the temple six times, signaling the Rangers that it was time to move in. The onboard ATCS had already fed the scene out to their helmets, providing them a full schematic of the building and a look at the positions of the operators inside. Now it was up to Hicks and his team to take out the bad without harming the good.

He held the glasses in his hand, making direct eye contact with Bryant. Either the man was infected by a khoron, or he was the most disgusting masochist Hayden had ever encountered.

Either way, he was going to take him out.

"I'm used to pain," Hayden replied, slipping the sunglasses back onto his face. He squinted his right eye a few times, activating Hicks' feed in the top right corner. The Rangers were running toward the building at full speed.

"I doubt you've seen anything like this before."

Bryant pushed open the door. Hayden looked through. His breath caught in his throat.

He expected to see men and women with whips and chains, tied up and possibly beaten. If he went to an extreme, he expected knives and blood, cutting and choking.

This was worse.

Much worse.

The room was full of creatures that looked like someone had merged a human with a trife. Taller and more muscular than a standard demon, a nearly human head with a mouth full of sharp teeth, and five fingers and toes sporting thick claws. They waited patiently, staring back at Hayden, their mouths spreading into smiles.

"Have you ever seen a reaper before, Sheriff Duke?" Bryant asked.

50

Hayden

Hayden started reaching for his revolvers. The women behind him screamed. Bryant backed away from the door to give the reapers room to maneuver. Albert tried to grab Hayden's arm.

"You should have taken the offer you were given, Sheriff," Bryant said. "The Master is gracious to those who are worthy. And terrible to those who deny them."

The reapers started toward him, baring their teeth and howling. Hayden was already in motion. He slammed his hand into Albert's face, breaking his nose and sending him sprawling backward. Then he backpedaled, grabbing his guns and turning them on Bryant. The first reaper was on him before he could shoot the infected man and he changed targets, quickly pounding the Relyeh creature with slugs from both guns. He emptied the revolvers into it.

It barely reacted.

Hayden brought up his forearm, activating the Axons shield and catching its attempt to slash his face. Claws scraped against the energy shield, the force of the blow pulling Hayden's arm down. A slash from the other side nearly decapitated him as he barely got under it in time.

"Hicks, a little help!" Hayden shouted, throwing himself backward. The women were screaming and fleeing behind him, trying to get away.

"I love the fear," Bryant said. "Don't you, Sheriff?"

Hayden skipped sideways, ducking between a stack of wine barrels and narrowly avoiding another slash from the reaper. Its claws went clean through the barrel, sending old, spoiled wine gushing from the wound and onto the floor.

Controlled gunfire sounded on the floor above, followed by sharper screams. Hayden glanced at Hicks' feed. The Rangers were inside, hitting the targets he had identified earlier. He watched them drop under the quick ambush, shot before they could react.

He looked away, backing down the column of barrels and quickly reloading while the reaper recalibrated, slowing to follow. He aimed a second time. It had caught a dozen rounds in its chest, but he didn't see any of the wounds now—only small stains of blood from the original damage. He had seen quick healing before, but he couldn't believe how fast the creature recovered.

He was about to squeeze the trigger when something hit the top of the barrels above. He looked up in time to see another reaper there, looking back down, wearing a monstrous smile. The distraction was intentional. He returned his attention to the reaper in front of him, getting his arm up again to block its attack, but falling back under the weight of the assault and slipping on the wine that had already spilled. He landed on his back, the reaper looming over him, a sadistic grin spread across its hideous face.

He closed his hand, switching the Axon material from defensive to offensive. Claws sprouted over his wrist, and he slashed at the claws reaching for his face, severing the limb from the reaper. It howled and backed away, giving him a moment to recover.

But only a moment.

Another reaper came in from behind just as Hayden got to his feet. He spun on his heel, firing his revolver in its face, the rounds puncturing its eyes and breaking some of its teeth. It fell back, and he snuck past it, heading down the aisle along the wall. Another reaper chasing behind him.

He looked into the HUD again. The targets the Rangers had dropped were back on their feet, proving Bryant wasn't the only infected.

It was a trap. A carefully laid, perfectly timed trap.

Maybe he should have been suspicious when Josias turned up so soon after he arrived back in Sansico. Maybe he should have guessed something was wrong when he had gotten into the place so easily and brought downstairs so quickly. But that wasn't the way things worked out here. The threats were ever present, but they were never so organized.

"Hicks, it's a trap," he snapped into the comm. "We need to fall back."

"Roger, Sheriff," Hicks replied. "I'll keep the exit clear for you."

"Forget about me," Hayden said. "Get the Rangers out of there."

Hayden froze as a reaper came around the corner in front of him. Another blocked his rear. He turned right, heading down another aisle, but a third reaper moved into his path.

He was boxed in.

They didn't attack. They stood at the edges of his escape routes.

"Now what?" Hayden said out loud. He held his revolvers at his sides, keeping an eye on the reapers flanking him, waiting for them to make the first move.

He glanced at his HUD again. The fighting had cleared the non-combatants from the building, leaving the women scurrying into the open fields around the structure and the men taking to their horses and cars to escape. They had come for the vices, not the violence.

A momentary calm settled over the place. A reset. The music had died out. The silence was thick enough to stop a trife claw. A bead of sweat ran down the side of Hayden's face, cool and heavy.

The chaos resumed all at once. Gunfire sounded above again as the three reapers rushed Hayden.

He aimed and fired both revolvers in both directions, using the glasses to assist. The ATCS had a direct connection to his augments, and it helped him line up the shots, placing them perfectly into two pairs of beady black eyes. Blinded, the reapers on his flanks slowed their attack, waiting to heal. The reaper in front of him left its feet, lunging at him from five meters away and leading with its claws. Hayden dropped a revolver, grabbing the base of the stack of wine barrels to his right and using the strength of his augment to yank it loose. Half a dozen barrels lost their stability, tumbling sideways and hitting the reaper, knocking it away.

Hayden scooped up the revolver, turning back toward the wall. The blinded creatures had yet to recover, and he charged the one on his right, shoving his Axon claws up under its chin and through its mouth to its brain. It slumped against the claws, and he roughly pulled them out, letting the Relyeh collapse and climbing over it while reloading his guns.

He had barely cleared the creature when gunshots

sounded behind him, and three slugs smashed into his back. The force threw him forward, sending him sprawling onto his stomach. He immediately rolled over, finding Albert about to start shooting. He got a hand up in front of his face, protecting it as the bullets continued to rain in, each shot into the bodysuit like a solid piston pounding into him. He aimed with his other hand, guessing the position of Albert's head, and pulled the trigger.

The shooting stopped.

Hayden jumped to his feet. Albert was down, but wouldn't stay that way for long. He had killed one reaper, but there were at least four more. And then there was Bryant. Where had the khoron-infected asshole gone?

"Hicks, sitrep!" he snapped, finding Hicks' feed. The Rangers hadn't retreated the way he had ordered.

"Closing on the stairs," Hicks said. "We're on our way, Sheriff."

"I told you to retreat, damn it."

"That's a negative, Sheriff."

A thunk sounded through the comm, a small silver ball launching from the bottom of Hicks' MK-12. Hayden didn't need to see it to recognize the sound of the powerful rifle.

Two seconds later, the stairwell door exploded.

Hayden watched three reapers dash past the column of wine barrels where he was standing, rushing toward the suddenly obliterated door.

And the Rangers standing behind it.

51

Hayden

"No!" Hayden shouted, rushing down the aisle toward the center of the room. Hicks and the other Rangers opened fire on the reapers, four rifles pounding three Relyeh with slugs. Under different circumstances, it might have been enough. But the reapers weren't ordinary trife. They were spliced with human DNA, making them stronger, faster, smarter and able to take way more punishment.

He made it to the edge of the wine barrels in time to see the reapers collide with the Rangers. Bahk was down in an instant, tackled by one of the creatures, its claws punching clear through the hardened transparency of his visor and into his head. Jackson managed to get out of the way, still shooting at the reaper attacking her and bringing it down. Hicks stood his ground, one of the reapers digging its claws into his arm as he fired a second explosive into its chest. Grunting in pain, Hicks kicked its leg and shoved it aside. The explosive detonated a moment later, sending pieces of reaper splattering across the room.

One down, three to go.

Hayden raced to the stairs. His HUD showed the khoron-infected guards were also recovering from their wounds and coming up from behind, ready to rejoin the fight. The reaper on Bahk finished its work, preparing to lunge at Ivanov, while Jackson's target scrambled back to its feet. Albert was coming around the corner near the back of the room, joined there by Bryant.

Hicks fell to a knee, blood pouring from the deep wound in his arm.

Hayden's jaw clenched. He had told them to retreat, damn it. He closed his eyes. But only for an instant. Just long enough to refocus. He had four rounds in one revolver. Two in the other. He had a pair of augmented arms, one of which had Axon nano cells layered over it.

He had been down before. As long as he was breathing, he wasn't out.

But how the hell was he going to get his people out of this?

How the hell was he going to get himself out?

Six bullets. Two reapers in front. One somewhere to his left. Two khoron-infected behind him, their exact position fed into the combat network by Hicks' line of sight.

He opened his eyes.

Turning sideways. he pointed the revolver with four shots toward the reapers in front of him. The revolver with two shots, he aimed at the khoron-infected behind him. Making all six shots virtually simultaneously would be impossible without the augmented fighting capabilities of the ATCS in his sunglasses, which is why Natalia had made them.

He a crack shot before he had received the gift.

He was even better after.

He squeezed the triggers on both guns, hands twitching

in response to his inputs based on the view of the targets. Four rounds went for the eyes of the reapers near his Rangers. Two went for the two khoron-infected, aimed at the space between the collarbone and neck, a six-centimeter gap in bone that led to the khoron's normal position in its host body.

It all happened in a split-second. The two rounds hit their marks and Albert collapsed. But Bryant was wearing a bodysuit, and the bullet couldn't punch through. But it still distracted him.

The four other rounds hit the reapers, but not where he had hoped. They got their hands up in time, blocking their faces from his attack as if they had seen it coming. Because they had. He used the same attack against the other pair less than a minute earlier, and the information had already passed through their subliminal network, letting them react ahead of him.

Six rounds. Four targets.

Only one of them fell.

It wasn't even close to enough.

One reaper leaped at Ivanov, and she screamed as it tackled her, raising its claws to strike. The other grabbed Jackson's leg, claws digging into it and yanking her to the ground. The third emerged from the barrels next to Hayden, coming his way, while Bryant pulled a gun of his own—a big, arrogant, overly satisfied smile on his face.

Hayden's heart pounded as the revolvers fell from his hands, dropping toward the floor. He couldn't stop the reapers. He couldn't save the Rangers. They were going to die.

He was going to die.

He had done his best. And he had failed.

He rushed toward the reaper on Ivanov. He wasn't sure

he would make it in time, or if the reaper on his left would grab him before he could get that far. Bryant could shoot him in the back of the head. He only saw the Ranger in trouble, and that he was the only one who could help.

Or so he thought.

A strange sensation washed over him, a tingling that caused the hairs on his neck to stand up. At the same time, the reapers suddenly froze, stopping mid-attack. Something hit the building, a wave of heat and energy flowing overhead and into the ceiling, causing a detonation of masonry and wood that sent debris exploding outward.

The force of the sudden attack threw Hayden into the steps beneath Hicks, who was tossed back and into Jackson and the reaper. Bryant was hit just as hard, thrown back into the wall like a rag doll. Dozens of wine barrels splintered and shattered, spilling their contents on the floor.

Hayden groaned and rolled over. A cloud of dust rose into the open hole created by the attack. A large humanoid shape dropped through the center of the cloud. He stared at it in disbelief, heart racing, a small smile turning up the edges of his mouth.

Nathan Stacker hefted his rifle, taking two steps to the nearest reaper, pressing the muzzle against its head and squeezing off multiple rounds. Blood, bone and brain matter sprayed against the floor. Nathan turned and stomped toward Bryant, who started shooting, his bullets pinging uselessly off the Centurion's powered armor. Nathan grabbed the khoron-infected man's head, ready to break his neck.

"Nathan, wait!" Hayden shouted. "I need him alive!"

Nathan froze, shifting his powerful grip and breaking Bryant's legs instead.

Hayden pushed himself up, grabbing Bahk's rifle. The

reapers were still frozen in place as if they were in a trance. He put the end of the weapon to each of their skulls, firing enough rounds to ensure they wouldn't get back up.

It was over in seconds.

52

Hayden

Hayden didn't waste time on greetings. Not right away. He had wounded Rangers who needed attention. He turned away from Nathan and toward Hicks, digging into the Chief Ranger's thigh pocket for a patch before removing his helmet and helping him open the combat armor.

"Ivanov," he said as she shoved the dead reaper off her and rose to her feet. "Help Jackson."

"Roger, Sheriff," she replied, moving to where Jackson was laying on the floor, trying to tend to her own leg wound.

"Hayden," Nathan said, coming up behind him.

"I appreciate you showing up when you did, Nate," Hayden replied without looking. "More than I can express in words. Give me a minute to patch up my Ranger." He tore the sleeve from Hicks' undershirt, revealing the deep gash beneath. "Hurts, doesn't it?"

"Shut up," Hicks replied, smiling. He looked at Nathan. "Thanks for the save, General."

"Any time," Nathan said.

Hayden tore open the patch and placed it against the

left side of the wound. It clung to the flesh on its own, and he pulled at it, dragging it across the wound edges so the skin was joined together again. Then he brought the patch down and put light pressure on the center to seal it.

"You'll wind up with a scar, but otherwise you'll be fine," Hayden said.

"Only fifty more and I'll be caught up to you," Hicks said, half grinning.

"Hayden," Nathan said again.

"Do me a favor," Hayden replied. "Check on Bryant. He might be getting up again by now."

"He won't get up again. Caleb's got him under control."

Hayden froze at the name. His head turned slowly back toward Nathan. "Did you just say, Caleb?"

"Pozz," Nathan replied.

"Sergeant Caleb Card?"

"Pozz."

Hayden's heart started racing. Caleb Card was here? "Shit. You should have opened with that. The whole reason I'm here instead of Sanisco is because I was trying to get a new ick for Nat. She wanted to find him."

"I already found him," Nathan said. "Or rather, he found me."

"What the hell is going on out there?"

"I was hoping you could tell me. Hayden…" Nathan paused. His faceplate slid up, revealing his tired human eye and a weary, sweaty face. "Edenrise is gone."

Hayden felt like he was punched in the gut a second time. Even Hicks reacted to the news.

"What?" the Chief Ranger whispered.

"Gone. Destroyed."

"What about the shield?" Hayden asked breathlessly.

"It couldn't hold. There were just too many."

"Trife?"

"It started with trife. It finished with—"

"Tentacle monsters," Hayden interrupted.

Nathan nodded. "You've seen them."

"Pozz. We killed a big one, and then we found a room full of their egg sacs. Probably a hundred of them or more. We lost good people doing it."

"I lost thousands, Hayden. In less than an hour. Caleb's the only reason any of us survived."

"Who is he?"

"He's got some story to tell, but I'll let him tell it. The good news is, he seems to be on our side."

"I'll take all the good news I can get."

"I don't have much more of it to share. We're in a bad spot, Hayden. And I'm not sure we can get out of it."

"We have to try."

Hayden turned back to the Rangers. Jackson was patched and on her feet, Ivanov helping to support her. Hicks was holding his patched arm against his chest, looking down at Bahk.

"His wife just had a baby," Hicks said.

Hayden clenched his teeth, hit a third time. He knelt beside the Ranger, removing the destroyed helmet. Bahk's face was unrecognizable. "Hicks, your bucket."

Hicks passed it over, and Hayden lifted Bahk's head, sliding the helmet down and clicking it in place. Then he slid his hands beneath the body, lifting it up.

"I take it you have a ship," Hayden said.

"It's parked outside near your chopper," Nathan replied.

Hayden looked past Nathan as Bryant got back to his feet and started walking toward them. Hayden grabbed his revolver, raising it toward the khoron-infected man.

"Wait," Nathan said. "He's not a threat."

Hayden saw it now. Bryant had an empty look on his face, his body shuffling like a zombie. "Card?" he asked.

"Sort of."

Hayden didn't ask him to elaborate. It was better to let Sergeant Card explain for himself. He turned and started up the steps carrying Bahk. The building was in ruins around them, small fires threatening to turn into much larger ones at any moment.

He kicked the remains of the cellar doors out of the way, moving through the room with the stage. Bodies littered the floor, including the thugs the Rangers had downed. The cages had broken free of the beams suspending them, falling sideways to the floor. The dancers were still locked in, trapped and terrified.

"Help us!" one of them shouted.

"Hold on," Hayden said to them. "We'll get you out."

Nathan went over to the first cage, grabbing the top in his powerful hands and tearing it away. The women climbed out as he did the same to the other one.

"Hurry!" Hayden said, directing them toward the exit. The smoke was getting thicker, the fires beginning to spread.

"This way!" Ivanov said, trying to guide them out. "Hurry."

The women ran out ahead of them. Hayden trailed Jackson and Hicks, with Nathan at the rear. They passed through the second room and out into the open, rushing to the field behind the building. The flames expanded rapidly, licking out the windows and enveloping the inside of the winery within minutes.

A group of nearly a dozen women were already in the field, huddled together a short distance from the Centurion dropship, which was blocking Hayden's view of the Iroquois. They were dingy and ragged and bruised. A few were bleeding from open cuts. But they were alive.

"Rosa Columbo," Hayden said, approaching them with Bahk still cradled in his arms. "Do any of you know Rosa Columbo?"

The women were silent for a few seconds. Then one of them emerged from the group—a petite, olive-skinned woman in a short nightgown. "I'm Rosa Columbo."

"I'm Sheriff Hayden Duke of the United Western Territories." He could almost feel the entire group of women relax slightly at the mention of his name. "Your husband Josias told me about this place. And that you were taken. I came here looking for you."

Rosa shook her head. "No, Senor. I'm sorry, but that's not possible. Josias is dead."

Hayden glanced at Hicks before looking back at Rosa.

"No," Hicks said. "He said his name was Josias Columbo. About this tall. Brown hair, brown eyes, similar complexion to you. He described you perfectly."

Rosa continued shaking her head. "That sounds like Josias, but I'm very sorry. That cannot be. Three days ago, a man came to our farm. He murdered my husband and took me. He didn't say why, but he brought me to these animals. They told me if I didn't do what they said, they would torture me. I saw other girls who tried to resist." Tears welled in her eyes. "Josias is dead. I watched the man cut his throat. I watched him bleed to death in the grass."

Hayden stared at her. If Josias was dead, who was the person in Sanisco claiming to be Josias? And who also looked just like Josias?

"Axon," Nathan said.

A chill ran down Hayden's spine. If Nathan was right, everything had just become much more complicated. Why would an Axon lead him into a Relyeh trap? Were the

Axon and Relyeh working together now? That didn't seem possible.

"Nathan, how did you know where to find me?"

"We did a flyby of Sanisco before we came up this way," Nathan replied. "Your people told me where you were. I think your city is fine, Hayden. For now, anyway."

"For now?" Jackson asked.

"If there's an Axon in Sanisco, then nothing's fine," Hayden said. "It got me out of there for a reason."

"I think you should talk to Caleb," Nathan replied. "On the way back to Sansico."

"Pozz," Hayden agreed. "How many can you take in the ship?"

"We've got space for all of them, but I think they're better off here."

"You expect the creatures that attacked Edenrise to attack Sanisco?"

"I think it's inevitable. My guess is the only reason they haven't is because you found their nest before they all hatched."

"We need to warn them," Hicks said. "We need to get them ready to fight."

Hayden activated his comm. "Bronson."

"Yes, Sheriff," the pilot replied.

"Try to get HQ on the line."

"Roger. Standby."

"You aren't going to leave us out here, are you, Sheriff?" one of the women asked. "We don't even have any clothes."

"We're not safe out here," another one said.

"You aren't safe with us, either," Hayden replied.

"They can come back to my farm," Rosa said. "I have shelter there."

"Can you give us a gun, at least?" the first woman said.

"I'll do one better," Hayden replied. "Jackson, how's your ankle?"

"What's wrong with my ankle?" Jackson replied with a smirk.

"I want you and Ivanov to stay with the group. Bring them back to Rosa's farm, make sure everything's clear, and then call Bronson for pickup."

"Roger, Sheriff," Jackson and Ivanov said.

"Sheriff," Bronson said. "The connection's choppy here. I'm getting a link, which means the antenna's up and the equipment is active. It's probably just interference from the hills."

"I can get us there in no time," Nathan said. "But we need to move."

Hayden nodded. "Jackson, Ivanov, get these people to safety. Ms. Columbo, I'm very sorry about Josias. I'll get to the bottom of this. I promise."

"Thank you, Sheriff."

Hayden turned to Nathan. "Let's go."

Isaac

Isaac sat in the small mess at the rear of the Capricorn. A plate rested on the table in front of him, a brown block of flavored protein resting on the plate. He looked up as Rico approached the table with a plate of her own.

"Mind if I join you?" she asked, smiling down at him.

"Be my guest," Isaac replied, motioning to one of the chairs.

Rico sat, taking her fork and digging into the meal. She took a huge bite, chewed, and swallowed before looking at Isaac again. "Not hungry?" she asked, pointing her fork at his plate.

"Not particularly," he said, grimly.

"It's all catching up to you, isn't it?"

"Yeah, I guess." He looked up at her, a small smile tipping up one corner of his mouth. "It's a lot to process."

"Want to talk about it? I'm a pretty good listener."

"You don't really want to hear me whine, do you?" His grin broadened.

"Sure. Why not? Go for it." She took another bite and chewed.

"Over two hundred years in cold storage," he said with a deep sigh. "How do you process something like that, let alone waking up to find I'm nothing more than a curiosity to an ancient alien that wanted to enslave humankind, and that was after it murdered my son. I managed to help defeat that alien and was shipped to another planet, thinking I was going to be treated like something important. Instead, Iwas locked away and had to be broken out of a golden prison, only to come back to Earth in time to warn them about the coming of a massive alien starship and a new invasion." Isaac paused. "All things considered, I feel great."

Rico smirked. "It can always be worse."

"Did I mention that ever since we went through that twisted wormhole I've had to use the bathroom every thirty minutes, and I can't bring myself to eat a single bite of anything?"

"To be honest, this isn't exactly a gourmet offering. Don't be too hard on yourself, Ike. This is only your second experience with space travel. The wormhole left me a little queasy for a couple of hours too."

"It isn't just the wormhole. It's the whole thing. Proxima, the Trust, the Organization, the Relyeh, and the Axon. The incoming ship. Earth is one planet in an entire universe of planets. A universe that has a hell of a lot more intelligent life in it than any of the scientists I ever knew believed. I get pissed when I think about how that truth should be wondrous, and instead it's a total disaster."

"I hear you," Rico replied. "I can't relate, but I empathize. I was made to be a Centurion. Military life is the only life I know. Bred for war, as they say. That doesn't mean I never saw it. Life on the outside. Young couples. Mothers with their babies. The whole normalcy thing. When I finally accepted my feelings for Austin, when I quit the CSF so we could be married, I thought it was my chance to be like everyone else. I thought I could live a happy, civilian life. Clones are sterile, but they're making clone infants now using the parents DNA. I thought I would have a chance to be one of those mothers. But reality didn't let me. We don't get to choose the universe we live in. We only get to choose how we live in it."

"I promised my wife I would never give up. Never stop fighting. But this? It's so much bigger than I ever imagined."

"It's only as big as you let it be. Who you are, what you do, that doesn't change. Fight the small fight. Win the small battle. Work your way up or die proud that you tried. That's what I'm doing. We've been out here for over two hundred years. We're still alive and kicking. I intend to keep it that way."

Isaac smiled. "I can see why your Bennett loved you. You have a lot of wisdom in there."

Rico returned the smile. "No. I'm just quoting an enlistment commercial I saw in the loop station once."

"Bullshit."

They both laughed.

Isaac picked up his fork and stabbed the protein block. He took a piece off and brought it to his mouth, breathing in the smell of it. "Reminds me of Thanksgiving dinner."

"Our Thanksgiving was moved to the day the first ship landed on Proxima. But yes, turkey, gravy, mashed potatoes and cranberry sauce. I smell it all in there."

He put it back on the plate. "It was a good pep talk, but I still can't eat it."

Rico took another bite. "Don't stress about it, Sergeant. You'll get your appetite back. Stop trying so hard to force it."

Isaac dropped the fork. "Yeah, you're right. What about you? How are you feeling?"

"A little nervous. A little excited. A little scared. The usual."

"Are you getting used to having this Bennett around?"

"Still a work in progress, like your stomach. It would be easier if he didn't look exactly like Austin and have all of the same mannerisms, tone of voice, and pretty much everything else except his name. The mind knows the difference, but the heart wants to cling to the familiar."

"I can't relate, but I empathize. If I were in your position, I don't know if I would be able to stop myself from falling in love again."

Rico leaned forward, lowering her voice. "I don't know if I can, either. Haeri might have thought he was buying my loyalty, but he's really messing with my head, and I don't like it."

"I don't blame you. Not to minimize your feelings, but speaking of Haeri, what do you think about whoever tried to have me killed?"

"I think they started with the wrong person. If what Able says about the Organization is true, they aren't going to take this lying down. Proxima has been in a delicate balance since the beginning. A tense peace. This could be the action that pulls the settlement into an underground war. If it does, it isn't going to be pretty."

"It seems like a pretty lousy time to fighting amongst ourselves."

"Yes, it does. It's almost as if the enemy is pulling the strings."

"Do you think there are Relyeh on Proxima?"

"Relyeh, Axon, maybe both. How would we know?"

"There's not much we can do about it, is there? We're banished to Earth."

"For now. Maybe not forever."

"Do you think we'll live that long?"

"Forever? No. Long enough to go back to Proxima? I'm going to fight like hell to make it happen."

"Then I will too. Deal?" Isaac put out his hand.

Rico took it, clasping it tightly. "Deal."

"Rico," Bennett said, entering the mess. Rico leaned back, looking at him with a forced coldness.

"What is it?" she replied.

"We're nearing Earth orbit. Able wants you to take us in."

Rico got to her feet. Isaac stood too.

"I want to see this," Isaac said.

"Then let's go."

54

Natalia

Natalia didn't get time to herself very often. There was always something to do, someone to take care of, time to spend with family or down in the lab. Or going out into the streets to talk to the residents. There were always problems big and small, things that needed fixing, things to organize. And then there was Hayden.

She had loved him for a long time. It had grown into a comfortable love, like an easy breeze on a warm day. Predictable and safe, and she liked it that way. She had proof he would do anything for her. He had already saved her from hopeless despair once, and she wanted more than anything to return the favor.

It was the reason that when she found herself in her apartment with Hallia asleep and Ginny at the movies, she didn't remain fixed for long.

She went into Hallia's room, picking up her daughter carefully enough she didn't wake her and placed her gently in an old rolling crib she had restored. She covered the top of it with a thick material to keep it dark and then headed out of the apartment, down the corridor to the lift, and from the lift, out into the street. The movie theater was a couple of streets over, and she crossed them uneventfully, saying hello to the few people who hadn't gone to see the film.

She still remembered the day they had finally found a bulb for the projector and built a wire to connect it to the old playing device. They had inherited a collection of movie discs from a storeroom of one of the buildings, and scavengers started bringing them more as word began to spread. Now they showed the films a few nights a week, the five hundred seat theater always filled to bursting.

"Governor Duke," Deputy Solace said as she approached the entrance. "Come to see the movie?"

Natalia smiled. "No. I was hoping you could pass a message to Ginny for me. Just tell her to find me in the lab when the movie's over."

"Yes, ma'am. You could have asked me over the comm."

Natalia smiled. "I wanted some fresh air. How's everything looking?"

"Calm and quiet, just like we like it."

"Good. Let's try to keep it that way. Goodnight Harvey."

"Goodnight, Governor Duke. I'll get that message to Ginny right away."

Natalia headed back to the pyramid, boarding the lift and taking it down to the subterranean garage that served as her research lab. Hayden had gone to find her an ick knowing how important it was for them to better understand the appearance of these new aliens and how Sergeant Caleb Card fit in. She knew how worried he was that accessing the Collective would kill her the next time, instead of leaving her with limp she was still dealing with.

She needed to do whatever she could to minimize the danger.

The lab was deserted. Most of the engineers had gone to see the movie, and the rest were probably already asleep, preparing for an early start in the morning. Her people were dedicated, almost as dedicated as she was. They were the reason Sanisco ran as well as it did. So much of everything was over two centuries old. The electrical wires, the water pipes, even the reactors that fed power to the city. It was a minor miracle any of it held together at all, and another that they were able to keep it all running.

Natalia rolled the carriage into the corner near the neural interlink. Hallia was fast asleep, cooing softly beneath the cover. Natalia walked over to the terminal connected to the link and sat down, flipping on the display. She tapped on the control pad, logging into the system and going back to the readings from her first time using the device. From what Doctor Hess had told her, the cause of her near-death experience was an overload of input from the Collective. A simple case of too much data flowing into her brain for her brain to handle. What she needed was a valve—a means to control the flow. In order to create one, she had to better understand precisely how the ick functioned.

It was challenging because she didn't have a real one to experiment with. Instead, she was left with the data captured by the computers during her use. Lutz had been working overtime on building simulations based on that data, and she wanted to check on them now to see if she could continue his work.

She opened the source code, reading through his algorithms. She understood them for the most part, though there were a couple of secondary calculations she would need to quiz him about in the morning. The good news was that since the Collective flowed into her mind through the interlink, a machine, it was reasonable to expect they could gain a measure of control over it. The only question was whether or not limiting the flow would leave the Collective essentially useless to them.

She played with the calculations for a while, bringing over a chalkboard and scribbling different ideas on it, erasing most of them after they didn't fit. Hayden thought she was the smartest person he knew, but she didn't see it that way. She made a lot of mistakes. Too many mistakes. He was the one out there saving lives every day. He was the one with the courage to face every challenge thrown at them head-on. There were plenty of times she wanted it to all go away so she could focus on the family she had fought so hard to build.

Two hours passed in a blink. Natalia leaned back in her chair, staring at the code on the screen. She was missing something. But what? She glanced over at the carriage. Hallia was still out cold. She slept like her father. Natalia smiled, but it faded quickly. Where was Hayden? She should have heard something from him by now.

She tapped on her comm, speaking softly. "Fry, are you there?" She waited a few seconds. No reply. "Fry?" She looked down at the comm. The LED was red. Fry wasn't answering. He was on comms duty tonight. Maybe he went to use the bathroom? But her call would go through to him there.

She stood up and walked over to the carriage. It had to be a malfunction in her comm. It wouldn't be the first time. She would walk it up to the Office and swap it out with another.

She wrapped her hands around the handle of the carriage.

And then the power went out.

"You have to be kidding me," Natalia said, staring straight ahead into the pitch black. She tapped her comm a few times, the LED turning bright white, a mini-flashlight that provided just enough light for her to see her surroundings. They had managed to go three months without a power outage. The timing was awful. "Come on, Hal. We need to see what happened to the lights."

She turned around, wheeling the carriage in front of her, freezing when she saw a ghost.

55

Hayden

Hayden followed Nathan up the ramp into the dropship, still carrying Bahk. Hicks brought up the rear with the zombie-like Bryant. A group of soldiers waited at the top of the incline. Most looked ragged in their combat armor, their postures wilting, their eyes tired.

All except one.

"You're Caleb Card," Hayden said, certain the only member of the team who didn't look like they needed a few days of sleep was the man he wanted to meet. Caleb looked ready for action in his combat armor—physically fit and strong-jawed, with short brown hair and kind but serious eyes.

"Sheriff Duke, I take it?" Caleb replied, looking down at Bahk. "One of yours."

Hayden nodded. "Reaper got him. I want to bring him back to his family."

"I understand. Walt, can you take the fallen and put him in storage with Dane's body?"

"Yes, Colonel," she replied, coming up next to Caleb and holding out her arms.

"He's pretty heavy," Hayden said.

Walt smiled. "I can manage. I'm stronger than I look."

Hayden passed Bahk over to her, and she carried him to the stairs at the back of the hold, vanishing up them a moment later.

"You lost one of yours too," Hayden said.

"Three," Caleb replied. "We were only able to recover Dane."

"What happened?"

"We were trying to re-equip from Tinker's weapon's cache," Nathan said. "An Other was waiting for us. It wanted to get into the cache too."

"How did it know where to find it?"

"Unknown."

"Pyro, everyone's aboard. Let's get this bird in the air."

"Roger, General. Good to hear your voice, Sheriff."

"Chandra, is that you?" Hayden said.

"Pozz," she replied.

"You're a pilot now."

"A damn good one," Nathan said, closing the ramp as the dropship began to slowly rise.

"Thank you for the compliment, General," Pyro said.

"You've earned it."

"ETA to Sanisco is eighteen minutes,"

"Not bad," Hayden said. He looked at Caleb again. "It doesn't give us much time to chat."

"Nathan told me a bit about you on the way over," Caleb replied, putting out his hand. Hayden took it. "It's an honor, Sheriff. I admire everything you've been trying to do."

"I'm just doing my job," Hayden replied.

"So am I," Caleb said. "Sergeant Caleb Card, United States Space Force, formerly United States Marine Corps."

Hayden's eyes narrowed. "Another Forgotten Marine?"

"Another?" Caleb said.

"Sergeant Isaac Pine," Hayden said. "He was in stasis since the trife invasion, up until a few months back. He helped me deal with a problem. He's on Proxima right now, getting cured of a brain tumor. What's your story?"

"I was on the generation ship Deliverance. Went to sleep near Mars, woke up almost fifty light years away. Came back through an Axon portal."

"I assume that's the abridged version?"

Caleb laughed. "We only have time for brief introductions. I'll be happy to give you all the details later. Nathan tells me it was your wife I sensed reaching out through the Collective."

"Apparently," Hayden said. "I'm away from home because I was looking for an ick to harvest so we could find you."

"An ick?"

"That's what we call the organ the Relyeh use to communicate through the Collective. Natalia and our Doctor figured out how to wire it up so we could use it. But one use kills the organ."

Caleb was silent, his eyes glazing over slightly.

"Caleb?" Hayden said.

His eyes came back into focus. "Sorry. You need pheromones to feed the ick, as you call it."

"You mean fear."

"You're familiar with the Hunger?"

"Too familiar. That problem I mentioned? Its name was Shurrath."

Caleb's eyes widened. "You killed Shurrath?"

"No. I sent him to the Axon homeworld as barter."

Caleb stared at him, dumbfounded. "Sheriff...I admired you before I heard any of this. What you've done is bordering on miraculous."

"Tell that to the thousands of people Shurrath killed before I neutralized him. There's nothing miraculous about it, Colonel."

"You killed Shurrath?" Sergeant Walt asked as she came down the steps.

"Uh, sort of," Hayden said.

"How do you know this Shurrath, Sarge?" one of the other soldiers asked.

"Nevermind," Nathan told the soldier. "Sheriff, I think we should continue this discussion on the bridge. Caleb, can you show him up while I get out of this tin can? Walt, you too."

"Yes, General." Caleb motioned to the stairs. "This way, Sheriff." Walt followed on their heels.

"Hicks, wait here?" Hayden said.

"Roger, Sheriff. I'll get to know the rest of our new friends."

Hayden had been on the craft before and was already familiar with the layout. The hatch opened as he and Caleb neared it. The two men entered.

"Sheriff Duke!" Pyro said, looking back at him with a big smile. Hayden walked over to her and put his hand on her shoulder, squeezing it.

"Chandra, you look better than you sound. I take it Nathan's treating you well?"

"No complaints, Sheriff. What happened to Gus' augment?"

"I knew you'd finally notice," Hayden said. "It got ruined saving my life."

"Just the way he would have wanted it."

"Pozz."

Hayden glanced up at the displays around the bridge. They were headed south toward Sanisco, hanging relatively low to the deck.

"I'm sorry about Edenrise," Hayden said.

"Me too," Pyro replied. "But we'll avenge them, won't we, Sheriff?"

"We will."

"Sheriff, I know why General Stacker wanted us to speak in private," Caleb said. "He wanted me to introduce you to Ishek."

"Ishek?"

"The reason I was able to almost communicate with your wife on the Collective. And the reason those reapers stopped short of killing you and your people."

"And Bryant?"

"Yes, though I'm not sure you still need him now that you have us."

"Ishek's a Relyeh," Hayden stated.

"Yes." Caleb unclasped his combat armor, shrugging his arm out of it. Hayden noticed the moist, black band around it immediately, but he didn't react. Like it or not, it wasn't the strangest thing he had seen lately. "I was captured by a Relyeh. He tried to control me with Ishek, a creature like the khoron called an Advocate. I turned the tables."

"How?"

"That's a story for another time. It's important that you understand I'm in control, and I'm loyal to Earth. I went through a lot to get back here."

"Why did you come back?"

"To deliver a message to Proxima. But Nathan tells me I need to be careful who I deliver it to."

"He's right. But I might be able to help you with that. My relationship with Proxima is less illegal than Nathan's."

"I would appreciate that, but we have a much bigger problem to handle first."

"The tentacle monsters."

"They're called xaxkluth. They're Nyarlath's favorite creation."

"Nyarlath. I've heard that name before."

"One of the original Relyeh. One of the most power-ful. She's on her way here, to finish what her brother failed to finish."

"She's been trying to recruit me to the cause," Hayden said.

"Really? Interesting."

The door to the bridge slid open, and Nathan stepped in. "I see you showed him your little friend. Good."

Hayden looked at Ishek, and then Sergeant Walt. "The other soldiers in the hold don't know about him. But you do?" He took a step toward her. "You're also sporting a tattoo I've seen before."

"Shurrath's mark," Walt replied. "I was a follower until he was taken from this world."

"You're khoron-infected."

"Yes."

"All of Shurrath's khoron are supposed to be dead."

"Who told you that?"

Natalia had told him that, but he couldn't rule out that she had made a mistake. He looked back at Caleb. "Why is she still alive? She's probably sending everything we're saying back through the Collective."

"She isn't," Caleb said. "Ishek is keeping an eye on her."

"I hate to say this, Caleb, but how do I know I can trust you? Between the khoron and the Axon, it's hard to know if anyone is who they say they are."

"You can trust him," Nathan said. "He saved thou-sands of lives in Edenrise."

"I did my job," Caleb said. "Like you're trying to do yours, Sheriff. We aren't enemies. I want us to be allies.

We're all going to need as many of those as we can get. The xaxkluth are emerging."

"I can't argue that logic," Hayden said. "If Edenrise fell to the xaxkluth, Sanisco will too. We need to start the evacuation before it's too late."

"General," Pyro said before anyone else could speak. Her tone drew Hayden's attention to the primary display.

"Oh no," he said.

"What the hell is that?" Caleb asked.

"Pyro, get us down there," both Hayden and Nathan said at the same time.

Caleb

"Attention all hands," Pyro said into the comm. "Prepare for emergency maneuvers. I repeat. Prepare for emergency maneuvers." She looked back at Hayden. "You might want to sit

Sergeant Walt left the bridge, hurrying to the seats at the front. The General took his seat at the command console.

"I've got it," Hayden replied, wrapping his augmented hands around the back of her seat.

Caleb stared at the dropship's primary display even as he hurried to the second pilot station and strapped himself in.

I'm not familiar with that humanoid creature.

Caleb had never seen anything like it before either. Not even on Essex, the planet where he had taken the portal back to Earth. It was nearly sixty meters tall, with long, lean limbs and mottled, patchy skin, thinner in places to reveal the cordlike muscle beneath. Oversized arms and hands led to a narrow torso, which went up to a twisted nightmare of a head.

Small eyes peered out from a deformed face, above a mouth that was too large, the jaw hanging toward the base of the neck. The mouth was open, revealing row upon row of grinding teeth, all of them covered in dark stains of flesh and blood from whatever the thing liked to eat. It was naked and sexless, a giant of a thing.

It was also under attack.

Six xaxkluth surrounded it. Two more were on its body, their tentacles wrapping around its limbs, the teeth at the end of edge taking bites out of it. The creature looked like it was groaning, its blood spilling down its legs as it kicked out, catching one of the xaxkluth and sending it rolling away. The alien recovered, bunching itself and then charging forward.

"Goliath," Hayden said beside him. "It looks like it already killed a few of them."

Caleb shifted his attention further out. There were three xaxkluth nearby, their central masses crushed and motionless. "Is that one of the Hunger's monstrosities?" he asked.

"No. One of Proxima's. They made the goliaths to fight the trife. It looks like it's doing okay against the xaxkluth, but it could use some help. Nate, do you have any extra guns?"

"Rifles," Nathan replied. "No revolvers. Sorry, Sheriff."

"I'll make do," Hayden said. "Pyro, take a run at the group on the ground, and then give us twenty seconds at slow speed to disembark."

"Slow speed?" Caleb asked.

"I can take it," Hayden replied. "Can you?"

I think he just challenged us.

Caleb smiled. He liked Sheriff Duke already. "Affirmative."

"Nathan, you with me?" Hayden asked.

"I don't know, Hayden. Maybe we should get back to Sanisco? The xaxkluth are getting closer."

"We can't just leave it," Pyro said. "The poor thing needs help."

Hayden didn't respond right away. He was worried about Sanisco and his family, and he wanted to get back to them as soon as possible. At the same time, Pyro was right. They couldn't just leave it to be killed.

"If we help the goliath now, it'll help us later," he said. "They aren't that smart, but they do remember. But if you can get Sanisco on the comm, I'd be much obliged."

"I'll try," Pyro replied.

"Fine," Nathan said. "Pyro, go ahead and make that run on the aliens and then give us enough time to get down there."

"Roger, General. Hold on."

The dropship shuddered slightly as Pyro guided it into a hard turn, running parallel to the fight for a few seconds to get a better angle of attack. The xaxkluth below weren't as large as the two they had struggled against in Edenrise, most of them only four meters high. They clearly hadn't found as much to feed on as the others coming down from the north.

Thanks to the goliaths, it seems.

The dropship dipped, plasma cannons unleashing fury as they swept down toward the field. The rounds dug into the dirt around the xaxkluth before finding their moist flesh, burning deep into limbs. One of the shots scored a direct hit on the creature's main mass, and it writhed violently in response before becoming still.

Caleb put his hand over the buckle to his restraints, ready to jump up the moment the g-forces eased.

They passed over the xaxkluth at a hundred meters, rushing past the goliath's head as its eyes shifted to watch them. It swung a huge arm downward at the xaxkluth, who managed to crawl away before the goliath's hand smashed into the ground.

"Go!" Pyro said, signaling them to make their move.

Hayden was already headed for the door, almost faster than the hatch could open for him. Caleb hit the release for his belt and jumped up, taking the rear behind Nathan.

The trio raced past the Liberators and Hicks, who hardly knew what was happening. They reacted instantly, getting up and following the group into the hold.

"Sheriff, get the ramp," Nathan said, rushing to his armor and stepping into the machine. "Caleb, guns."

Caleb went over to the crates they had brought on board from the Bush, lifting open the top of one and grabbing the MR-12s inside. He passed one to Hayden as the Sheriff returned from the ramp control, adding three bullet magazines and a grenade magazine.

"What's going on?" Corporal Hotch asked.

"Rescue mission," Hayden replied. "Wait here."

"I want to help."

"We aren't touching down," Caleb said. "You can't make the drop."

"But he can?"

"I've got a pair of cyborg arms and a high pain tolerance," Hayden said.

"I'm coming," Sergeant Walt said.

"Sergeant," Caleb replied.

"You need all the help you can get, Colonel."

"Fine. You're in. Grab a rifle."

"She can make the drop, but I can't?" Hotch said.

"I appreciate your desire, Corporal, but I want you here," Caleb replied. "That's an order."

"Yes, Colonel."

Hotch wasn't happy. Caleb appreciated that too.

"General, better hurry," Pyro said. "There's a xaxkluth headed our way. And it's a big one."

"Let's go," Nathan said, stepping out of the machine.

Caleb loaded the grenade magazine and the first of the bullet mags into his rifle. Hayden and Walt did the same, while Nathan grabbed his larger gun. Then all four of them ran to the ramp.

Caleb looked down as he reached it. They were only five meters above the grass, but still moving at nearly a hundred kilometers per hour. He could hear the vectoring thrusters firing on either side of the craft, helping to keep it in the air at that speed.

He didn't stop moving, jumping right before he reached the edge. The xaxkluth was right there in front of him, about a hundred meters away. The goliath was to his right, still under siege from the other aliens.

He tucked his shoulder as he hit the ground, rolling with the momentum. He hit hard enough to knock the air from his lungs, bouncing a couple of times before sliding to a stop.

Caleb didn't waste any time on the ground, jumping up and spinning around. Hayden was on the ground nearby, slowly pulling himself back to his feet. Walt was close too, already up and ready.

Nathan was the only one spared the crash landing. He floated to the ground on his armor's jets, landing closest to the xaxkluth and already unleashing hell on it. His railgun made a whining sound as it unleashed its ammunition. It raised its tentacles to protect its central mass, trying to close on the General before it was reduced to jelly.

Walt's fire joined Nathan's, and then Caleb added his. Hayden sat back on his knees, mouth open and trying to get his breath as he aimed his rifle and fired a single silver ball from the grenade launcher.

It arced high in the air. Too high, it seemed to Caleb. But it came down a few seconds later, evading the xaxkluth's tentacles and sticking to its center.

Then it detonated.

The xaxkluth's central mass blew out in a mess of gore, the remaining limbs immediately falling still.

Who is this man?

Caleb didn't know much about Hayden yet, but from what he did know, he was glad Sheriff Duke was on their side.

57

Isaac

Isaac entered the bridge of the Capricorn right behind Rico, grabbing the navigator's seat as Spot rose from the pilot's station to let Rico replace her. Able was in her familiar place at the command station overseeing the activity.

Isaac noticed the older woman had changed into a fitted formal uniform, though it wasn't a style he had seen before. A black jacket, black pants and a dark gray shirt—all of it pressed and perfect. No hardware, no name tag, no decorations of any kind—save a single small ring embroidered over the chest in white thread.

She wasn't about to meet with Sheriff Duke without looking like she carried some level of authority, even if it was loosely limited to the people on board.

"Sergeant Pine," Able said. "Have you seen Earth from this angle before?"

Isaac looked up at the displays. The planet was dead ahead—white, blue and green.

Beautiful.

And deadly.

"I got a quick look on the way out," Isaac replied, sitting and strapping in. "This is better."

"It's my first time," Able said. "I've never been outside the Proxima system before. A few trips to the mining rigs, but otherwise I've stuck to Praeton."

"And you volunteered for this mission?"

Able laughed. "Who says I volunteered? But yeah, somebody had to do it."

Rico started tapping on the controls. "Why'd you ask me to bring us in?"

"I thought it was fitting. Plus long-range sensors are freaking out, and I don't know if that's because they're old and broken or because there's something seriously messy going on down there."

Isaac looked at the display on the station in front of him. It was showing the same sensor data as the other two stations. Small red marks covered the planet as if it had measles.

"What does it mean?" he asked.

"The marks are unidentified masses," Rico replied. "Based on prior topographical scans of the surface."

"Unidentified masses? Like large groups of trife?"

"No. The system's algorithms adjust for life forms. They filter out anything that falls within a reasonable variance. It can't be anything living. It would have to be huge to show up on the scan."

"From what I've experienced, I don't think we should rule anything out."

Rico looked over at him. "Let's really hope it's nothing alive. It isn't localized to the Pacific Northwest. Hell, it isn't even localized to the United States. There are marks across the entire planet."

"It can't be anything alive," Able said. "The Relyeh ship isn't here. Where would it have come from?"

"Good point," Isaac replied. "But if it isn't alive, then what is it?"

"We're going to find out," Rico said. "There's a mark almost directly on top of our target."

The dropship continued toward the planet. Rico started slowing them down as they closed on the atmosphere, expertly guiding the Capricorn toward the surface.

"Entering atmosphere in five...four...three...what the —" Rico cut off her countdown as her display suddenly flashed in warning.

Isaac had seen it first, out of the corner of his eye on the starboard display. At first, it appeared to be a small asteroid. A dark, rocky, asymmetrical mass. But then the crumpled rock unfolded, revealing an array of long tentacles spreading out from a round mouth, the sudden alien creature shooting toward them on a direct collision course, already too close to avoid.

"Shit!" Rico cursed, tempted to take evasive maneuvers and realizing she was out of time.

The creature hit an instant later, the dropship shaking slightly as a number of the starboard video feeds went dark, suffocated by the creature's many limbs.

"Keep her steady," Able said, her voice remaining calm and commanding. "Bring us into the thermosphere. We'll see how much that bitch likes the heat."

Rico kept the dropship steady, continuing the drop. Isaac's eyes remained glued to the displays. One of them was directly to the side of the alien's head, in full view of what seemed to be a thousand tiny eyes running along the side of its face.

"What's it doing?" Rico asked, keeping her eyes glued to the primary display and watching her approach.

"It seems like it's hanging on for the ride," Isaac replied.

He spoke too soon. One of the tentacles drew back and then snapped forward, pounding the side of the craft. A second one repeated the motion.

"Not hanging on for the ride," Rico said. "Able, we need to abort the approach."

"Negative. We have no way to get that thing off the ship. Either it burns up on approach, or we smash it into the ground."

"Great choices," Isaac said.

Rico's eyes narrowed, her focus on bringing them in. They hit the thermosphere, the hull beginning to heat up on entry.

The Relyeh didn't burn up. Instead, its delicate tentacles shrank back into the harder material that had disguised it, shrinking its profile but keeping it attached to the dropship like a giant barnacle.

"It isn't going to burn," he said.

"Damn it," Rico replied. "Get the hell off us!"

They continued to drop, through the thermosphere and beneath the outer layers. The Relyeh reacted to the cold, expanding back out of its shell and beginning to pound the craft again. Now that they were within the pull of gravity, each strike threatened to send the ship spiraling out of control.

"We have to do something!" Rico shouted, fighting to keep the Capricorn flying straight. They were still descending sharply, vectoring for the target.

The creature moved, and the entire dropship shook violently, yanking Isaac hard against his restraints. Warning tones sounded on the bridge, the display in front of him showing the damage.

"I think we just lost one of the thrusters," he said.

"What *is* this thing?" Able said. "It's like it was just waiting out there for us."

"Maybe it was."

"How is that possible?"

"Someone tried to stop us from leaving Proxima. What if they were Relyeh?"

Rico shot a look over at him. He didn't want that to be true either, but what if it were?

"Haeri can take care of himself," Able said. "So can the Organization. Our mission is Earth."

"Our mission is getting to the surface alive," Rico said.

The dropship shook again. Another warning tone sounded.

"Damage to the stabilizers," Able said. "Get us on the ground."

"I'm doing my…"

Rico's voice cut off. Isaac saw why. They had broken through a high level of clouds, the ground becoming visible below. Dozens of dark creatures were moving across the landscape from every direction but west, where the Pacific Ocean met the coast.

"There's your mark," Isaac said, barely able to breathe, let alone speak. He was there during the first invasion when the trife had swarmed the cities by the thousands. There were a lot fewer of whatever the dark blobs were, but they were bigger. A lot bigger.

"This can't be happening," Able said.

"There's Sanisco," Rico said, the primary display marking the city with an outline. There were already creatures at the outskirts, smoke rising from just beyond the walls. The aliens were moving through the outer city, smashing large tentacles into the buildings around them.

"Have you ever seen those things before?" Isaac asked, glancing back at Able.

"No," she replied, her face white. "I wish I wasn't seeing them now."

A third warning tone sounded. The ship shuddered again and started to drop more rapidly.

"There goes the other thruster," Rico said. "We've got vectoring nozzles only."

"All hands," Able said. "Brace for emergency impact! I repeat, brace for emergency impact!"

The dropship turned slightly, away from the city and toward the wide highway to the south, Rico somehow managing to steer with no main thrust. The dropship wasn't designed to glide, making the effort even more impressive.

"This is it. Hold on!"

Isaac was thrown forward into his restraints as Rico fired the retro-thrusters, the backward force slowing the craft's momentum in a matter of seconds. That slow-down led to further loss of flight control, the Capricorn's nose dipping as a result. Rico used the vectoring thrusters to push the front back up, leading with the tail as they closed to one hundred meters.

Fifty.

Twenty.

Ten.

"Eat dirt, you bitch," Rico cursed, triggering the port side thrusters and throwing the dropship onto its side. It fell the last five meters, catching the hull and the Relyeh on the top of a building and smashing through, bouncing off slightly and then coming down hard on the pavement.

Isaac held onto his restraints, closing his eyes as they slid along the ground, smashing through abandoned wrecks before hitting something hard enough to launch themselves back into the air. They landed upside down.

The craft spun multiple times, shoving him around before finally coming to a stop.

Isaac opened his eyes, looking over at Rico. She was looking back at him, hanging upside down in her seat. They both glanced back at Able. She was alive too, a dark scowl on her face.

"Let's haul ass," she said. "We're sitting ducks out here."

Isaac released his restraints, holding them and using them to flip himself over and drop. Rico and Able did the same.

Something hit them again, shaking the ship violently enough to knock them all from their feet.

Isaac looked back at the displays. Only one was still active, cracked as it was. He could see the Relyeh creature hovering over it, preparing to hit it again.

"I think we should stay inside," he suggested. "Wait for it to decide we're dead."

"What if it never decides we're dead?" Able asked.

"If we go out there, it'll kill us. And if it doesn't, they will."

Isaac pointed to the background, where two of the other tentacled creatures were approaching.

Able sighed. "I knew this wasn't going to be easy, but this is ridiculous. Better find somewhere to secure yourself. It's going to be a long day."

58

Hayden

Hayden didn't waste time admiring his shot. He ran past the xaxkluth, racing to get into the real fight.

"Nice shot, Sheriff," Caleb said, coming up beside him, running as if it was no effort at all.

Damn show off.

The goliath was ahead of them, nearly half a klick away. It had managed to kill another Relyeh, but it was suffering under the enemy's assault. Three of the tentacled creatures were on its body, and one was climbing toward its face, positioned on its back where it couldn't reach it with its hand.

"Caleb!" Hayden shouted. "Tell Nathan we need to get those things off the goliath's back." He wasn't wearing combat armor and had no helmet comm with which to contact the General himself, And he didn't dare risk his glasses on the drop. They were the second pair Natalia had made him, and she would kill him if he lost them again so soon.

"Roger that," Caleb replied. "General, Hayden says we need to take down the xaxkluth on the goliath's back."

"On it," Nathan said. He surged forward in his powered armor, taking leaping steps forward and using his thrusters to speed up his advance. He cleared the dead xaxkluth and started shooting again, his rounds hitting one of the creatures on the ground.

Hayden understood why. If the goliath realized they were trying to help, it might turn around to give them a better shot at the Relyeh climbing it. He took a wider vector to get an angle on the enemy, coming side-by-side with Sergeant Walt.

If the Sergeant was a khoron, she was a traitor to her kind. Hayden hadn't thought that was even possible, but here she was, adding her fire to his.

The assault got the attention of two xaxkluth. It also got the attention of the goliath. It looked past the creatures at them, howling loudly as though asking for their help. It raised a large leg, bringing it down to crush the xaxkluth, which moved sideways to avoid the gargantuan foot. The goliath howled again in frustration.

"Hang on! We're coming!" Hayden shouted up at the goliath, not sure the biological construct understood him at all.

He switched bullets for another grenade, launching it across the field at the closest xaxkluth. It was ready for the attack, and it caught the projectile, bending its tentacle to fling it back. Hayden squeezed the trigger again, sending the detonation signal. The grenade exploded, taking the creature's limb with it.

It wasn't a very effective attack, but it did prove to the goliath they shared a common enemy. The giant howled again, turning sideways and giving them a better angle on the creatures biting into its back.

Nathan slowed to take better aim on the creature riding the goliath's shoulder, not letting the xaxkluth heading for him distract him. He opened fire, his rounds crossing a quarter kilometer and pounding the xaxkluth, which seemed to dig in more tightly in response.

Hayden switched his aim, going for the monster heading for Nathan. He squeezed off a few rounds and then dropped the empty magazine, grabbing another and snapping it in without breaking stride. Sergeant Walt pulled ahead of him, but they were both tailing well behind Caleb.

Card shot as he ran, one round at a time, each bullet carefully placed to bypass the Relyeh's undulating tentacles. He hit the central mass, taking out one eye. Then another. And another. Impressive shooting. Hayden followed his lead, conserving ammunition to wait for the best shot. It took him three rounds to hit the first eye, and then he took out three more in rapid succession.

The xaxkluth was almost on top of Nathan before the General could take evasive action. He leaped forward and rose on his thrusters. The Relyeh's tentacles stretched out to reach for him, one of them managing to grab his leg. It dragged him hard to the ground, slamming him into the dirt.

Plasma bolts sizzled from the sky, hitting the creature along its central mass. It groaned as it tried to lift Nathan into the air to bring him to its mouth. Nathan was still clinging to his rifle. He fired it upside down, launching a grenade into the xaxkluth's maw.

The creature's face exploded, and Nathan fell back to the earth.

Pyro continued strafing across the field, buying them time. Hayden switched his attention to the creatures on the goliath, sending bullets into the one on its back, which had almost reached the giant's face. Caleb, Walt and Nathan joined him a moment later, sending so much metal into the xaxkluth it struggled to hold on.

The goliath roared, turning its back on them to let them shoot. It's hand swept down, catching one of the creatures and holding it fast, lifting it toward its mouth. The xaxkluth struggled in its grasp, writhing violently as the goliath brought its hand to its face, releasing the creature into its huge maw, its rows of teeth quickly taking the xaxkluth in and devouring it.

Hayden kept his attention on the creature struggling to remain on the goliath's back. A few more rounds and it was destined to fall.

He dropped his second empty magazine, loading the third, still advancing. They were only twenty meters from the goliath now, shooting almost straight up at its back. He caught sight of the two xaxkluth attacking the goliath's legs. They were pulling themselves off the giant, preparing to intercept them.

"Caleb!" Hayden shouted over the roar of gunfire, getting the Marine's attention. He saw the xaxkluth too, immediately shifting his aim.

The two Relyeh broke free and charged. They were already so close, they would be on them in seconds.

One last round poured from Nathan's gun, hitting their primary target. It was the winning shot, and the xaxkluth finally succumbed, the last of its tentacles breaking free of the goliath's back. Its body tumbled to the earth while Nathan slapped his depleted gun to his back and pivoted to face the oncoming creatures.

Caleb's gun went dry too, and he switched to grenades, firing ball after ball into the rapidly approaching creatures. The rounds hit and detonated, taking a tentacle with each shot. It wasn't nearly enough. Hayden fired furiously, emptying his rifle in seconds and following Caleb's lead, dumping grenades into the xaxkluth. But the Relyeh had adapted to the attack, and they caught the balls, smothering them and sacrificing a limb to continue their assault.

They were nearly out of ammo, and the two xaxkluth remained. Hayden found the dropship descending toward them, about to make another run.

Pyro was too late.

The xaxkluth rose on their tentacles, stretching out above them and preparing to pounce. Hayden closed his right hand into a fist, the Axon material expanding into a pair of claws. He wasn't going down without a fight.

"Stop!"

The xaxkluth froze as if they had just hit an invisible wall, their tentacles seizing and holding them in the upright position.

A moment later the goliath's massive hand swept around, slamming into the two creatures and holding them tight. Hayden expected the goliath to bring the Relyeh to its mouth to eat them, but instead it clapped its two hands together, smashing both like a pair of annoying insects.

It howled softly, looking down at Hayden and the others. Its mouth spread in a grotesque smile. Then it turned south, in the direction of Sanisco, and started walking away.

Hayden's attention turned to Caleb. The Marine and his Relyeh symbiote had frozen the reapers, and now he had done the same to the xaxkluth.

Or had he?

Caleb had turned to face Sergeant Walt, his look of shock, anger, and fear immediately signaling that he hadn't issued the command.

Sergeant Walt had.

She stared back at him, their eyes locked in an inhuman battle of wills. Nathan noticed it too and began retreating toward Hayden. The dropship landed a short distance away.

Neither Walt or Caleb made a sound, but Hayden could almost sense the pressure between them as if it were a physical thing. Whatever was happening was something he didn't understand.

Whatever was happening, it ended a moment later. At the same instant, both Caleb and Walt stiffened as if they were marionettes. Then they both collapsed as if someone had cut the strings.

What the hell?

"Hayden," Nathan said. "We need to go. Now."

Hayden glanced at his friend. "What is it?"

He asked the question, but he already knew what it was. The answer was in Nathan's voice. It was in Pyro's quick landing. It was even in the goliath's sudden movement south. Hayden turned his head to track the giant, his pulse quickening as he saw the truth he wanted more than anything to deny rising in the distance in pillars of smoke.

Sanisco was under attack.

59

Natalia

"Natalia," Ghost said. "It's been a long time."

Natalia's heart pounded, her entire body shivering with sudden fear. Ghost. The man who had once taken her from Hayden, who had convinced her that her husband was dead and she was alone in the universe. In her despair, in her submission, she had slept with him, hoping that it would ensure his loyalty to her over his father—the warlord, King—the tyrant who had run Sanisco before Hayden killed both father and son.

She had been stupid and naive. It was all a game to Ghost. Everything was a game to him. A challenge. That's what the trife had done to Earth in his mind. Turned it into a competition.

He couldn't be here. He had been dead for over a year. In her heart, she knew this wasn't real. A hallucination. An Axon. But in her mind, she couldn't sense that. She couldn't come to terms with it. In her head, he was real, tangible. Present and therefore—lethal.

Hallia started crying.

"Did you miss me?" Ghost asked, stepping toward the carriage. "Can I see her?"

"No," Natalia replied. "Yes." She opened the cover. Hallia stopped crying.

"What do you want?" Natalia said.

Ghost looked past her to the interlink. "Thousands of years of war can come to a quick end with that device."

"How?"

"Imagine sending a virus through the Collective. Imagine killing every single Relyeh in the universe with one push of a button." Ghost stepped closer to Natalia. "But I don't need to tell you that. You know what it can do."

"It isn't possible. The networks are firewalled."

"There's one that's open to all of them, isn't there?"

Natalia didn't speak the answer, but it floated across her terrified mind. Shub-nigu. The Archiver. The One Who Sees.

"I've missed you, Nat," Ghost said. He reached out for her, putting his hand on her shoulder. He was warm, and as he drew in close his familiar scent slipped into her nose. "Does Hayden know the truth?"

"What do you mean?" Natalia asked softly.

"You know what I mean. About our little one."

"She isn't yours."

"No? Are you sure of that, Natalia?"

Ghost leaned in further, putting his face right in front of hers. His eyes burned into her. Accusing. She was shaking and numb. She had never been sure. Hayden had always accepted Hallia as his, and neither of them ever questioned it.

"You've questioned it," Ghost said. "When you look into her eyes. When you see me there. Look at my face, and then look at hers."

Natalia did, her eyes going from Ghost to Hallia. Hallia smiled back at her, amused by the look on her mother's face because she didn't understand it. The fear. The pain. The guilt.

"Do you mind if I hold her?" Ghost said, backing up beside the carriage.

"You don't touch her," Natalia hissed. "You don't ever touch her."

Ghost smiled. "Come now, Natalia. You don't think I would hurt her, do you?" He reached into the carriage, stroking the side of Hallia's face. Hallia laughed in response.

"You aren't real," Natalia said softly, trying to convince herself of what she already knew.

"No? Then how does she feel my touch? Why is she laughing? Because she knows who her real daddy is."

"No!" Natalia cried.

"Mom?"

Natalia looked up, past Ghost to the small light that appeared ahead of the stairs.

"Ginny," Natalia said.

"Mom, were you waiting here for me?" Ginny started toward her, too far away to see anything clearly. "The power went out, and I heard gunfire in the distance. I think there's trouble. We need to get out of here."

"What?" Natalia whispered.

"I came for the machine," Ghost said.

"You want to use it?" Natalia replied. "To end the Hunger?"

"Mom, who are you talking to?" Ginny said.

"No," Ghost said. "I don't want the Hunger to end. They're the most powerful weapon ever created. Too good to waste. I want them under my control."

"Who are you?"

"I told Hayden to make the right choice. He didn't. This all could have been avoided."

"Is someone there?" Ginny asked, getting closer. Natalia heard the action of a gun being prepared for use.

"Ginny stop," Natalia said.

She did. "What's going on?"

"You're very intelligent for a human. Except when it comes to your baser nature." Ghost put his hand around Hallia's face, squeezing it lightly. "Hayden denied me. And then he challenged me. This was your worst mistake." He let go of Hallia. "That will be his."

"Get the hell away from her," Ginny said, moving closer, the light of her small flashlight joining with Natalia's comm.

Hallia started to cry.

Natalia's breath caught in her throat. There really was someone there. It wasn't all a hallucination.

"No. I don't think I will."

Shots boomed in the darkness, the muzzle flash of the gun revealing Ginny's tense face behind it. The rounds from the revolver hit Ghost in the side, blue flashes causing the projection to drop and the hallucination to fade.

The Axon wasn't like the others she had seen. It was larger and more alien in form, its featureless head a larger, more elongated shape, its hands ending in three fingers instead of four, its limbs longer and leaner. It turned away from her, raising its hand toward Ginny, who kept shooting it until the revolver clicked empty.

"No!" Natalia shouted as a blast of blue energy launched from the Axon and into Ginny's chest.

She didn't even have time to scream before collapsing to the floor.

Natalia lunged at the Axon, raking at its face with her nails. She couldn't damage its Skin. It reached up and grabbed her wrist, bending it until it threatened to break and pushing her to her knees.

The Axon lifted its other hand over her head, a blue light forming in its palm.

A bright flash and everything went black.

Thank you for reading!

Thank you for reading Invasion. I know there are a lot of options for great books out there, and I appreciate that you chose mine.

The next book in the Forgotten Vengeance series is available now! Follow the link and start reading today!

mrforbes.com/isolation

Thank you again!

Cheers,
    Michael.

Forgotten Universe

The Forgotten Universe is still growing! Whether this is your first series in the universe or your fourth, there may be more books featuring your favorite characters - Sheriff Duke, Caleb Card, John Washington, Nathan Stacker, and more that you haven't met yet.

mrforbes.com/forgottenuniverse

Other Books By M.R Forbes

M.R. Forbes on Amazon

mrforbes.com/books

Forgotten (The Forgotten)

mrforbes.com/theforgotten

Some things are better off FORGOTTEN.

Sheriff Hayden Duke was born on the Pilgrim, and he expects to die on the Pilgrim, like his father, and his father before him.

That's the way things are on a generation starship centuries from home. He's never questioned it. Never thought about it. And why bother? Access points to the ship's controls are sealed, the systems that guide her automated and out of reach. It isn't perfect, but he has all he needs to be content.

Until a malfunction forces his Engineer wife to the edge of the habitable zone to inspect the damage.

Until she contacts him, breathless and terrified, to tell

him she found a body, and it doesn't belong to anyone on board.

Until he arrives at the scene and discovers both his wife and the body are gone.

The only clue? A bloody handprint beneath a hatch that hasn't opened in hundreds of years.

Until now.

Deliverance (Forgotten Colony)
mrforbes.com/deliverance

The war is over. Earth is lost. Running is the only option.

It may already be too late.

Caleb is a former Marine Raider and commander of the Vultures, a search and rescue team that's spent the last two years pulling high-value targets out of alien-ravaged cities and shipping them off-world.

When his new orders call for him to join forty-thousand survivors aboard the last starship out, he thinks his days of fighting are over. The Deliverance represents a fresh start and a chance to leave the war behind for good.

Except the war won't be as easy to escape as he thought.

And the colony will need a man like Caleb more than he ever imagined...

Earth Unknown (Forgotten Earth)
mrforbes.com/earthunknown

A desperate escape to the most dangerous planet in the universe... Earth.

Nathan's wife is murdered. The police believe he's the killer, and why wouldn't they? He's a disgraced Centurion

Marine pilot, an ex-con, and an employee of the most powerful crime syndicate on Proxima.

The evidence is damning. The truth, not as clear. If Nathan wants to prove his innocence and avenge his wife, he'll have to complete the most desperate evasive maneuver of his life:

Steal a starship and escape to Earth.

He thinks he'll be safe there. He's wrong.

Very wrong.

Earth isn't what he thinks. Not even close. What he doesn't know isn't only likely to kill him, it's eager to kill him.

If it doesn't?

The Sheriff will.

Starship Eternal (War Eternal)

mrforbes.com/starshipeternal

A lost starship...

A dire warning from futures past...

A desperate search for salvation…

Captain Mitchell "Ares" Williams is a Space Marine and the hero of the Battle for Liberty, whose Shot Heard 'Round the Universe saved the planet from a nearly unstoppable war machine. He's handsome, charismatic, and the perfect poster boy to help the military drive enlistment. Pulled from the war and thrown into the spotlight, he's as efficient at charming the media and bedding beautiful celebrities as he was at shooting down enemy starfighters.

After an assassination attempt leaves Mitchell critically wounded, he begins to suffer from strange hallucinations that carry a chilling and oddly familiar warning:

They are coming. Find the Goliath or humankind will be destroyed.

Convinced that the visions are a side-effect of his injuries, he tries to ignore them, only to learn that he may not be as crazy as he thinks. The enemy is real and closer than he imagined, and they'll do whatever it takes to prevent him from rediscovering the centuries lost starship.

Narrowly escaping capture, out of time and out of air, Mitchell lands at the mercy of the Riggers - a ragtag crew of former commandos who patrol the lawless outer reaches of the galaxy. Guided by a captain with a reputation for cold-blooded murder, they're dangerous, immoral, and possibly insane.

They may also be humanity's last hope for survival in a war that has raged beyond eternity.

(War Eternal is also available in a box set of the first three books here: mrforbes.com/wareternalbox)

Hell's Rejects (Chaos of the Covenant)
mrforbes.com/hellsrejects

The most powerful starships ever constructed are gone. Thousands are dead. A fleet is in ruins. The attackers are unknown. The orders are clear: *Recover the ships. Bury the bastards who stole them.*

Lieutenant Abigail Cage never expected to find herself in Hell. As a Highly Specialized Operational Combatant, she was one of the most respected Marines in the military. Now she's doing hard labor on the most miserable planet in the universe.

Not for long.

The Earth Republic is looking for the most dangerous individuals it can control. The best of the worst, and Abbey happens to be one of them. The deal is simple: *Bring back the starships, earn your freedom. Try to run, you die.* It's a suicide mission, but she has nothing to lose.

The only problem? There's a new threat in the galaxy. One with a power unlike anything anyone has ever seen. One that's been waiting for this moment for a very, very, long time. And they want Abbey, too.

Be careful what you wish for.

They say Hell hath no fury like a woman scorned. They have no idea.

Man of War (Rebellion)

mrforbes.com/manofwar

In the year 2280, an alien fleet attacked the Earth.

Their weapons were unstoppable, their defenses unbreakable.

Our technology was inferior, our militaries overwhelmed.

Only one starship escaped before civilization fell.

Earth was lost.

It was never forgotten.

Fifty-two years have passed.

A message from home has been received.

The time to fight for what is ours has come.

Welcome to the rebellion.

About the Author

M.R. Forbes is the mind behind a growing number of Amazon best-selling science fiction series including Rebellion, War Eternal, Chaos of the Covenant, and the Forgotten Universe novels. He currently resides with his family and friends on the west cost of the United States, including a cat who thinks she's a dog and a dog who thinks she's a cat.

He maintains a true appreciation for his readers and is always happy to hear from them.

To learn more about M.R. Forbes or just say hello:

Visit my website:
mrforbes.com

Send me an e-mail:
michael@mrforbes.com

Check out my Facebook page:
facebook.com/mrforbes.author

Chat with me on Facebook Messenger:
https://m.me/mrforbes.author

Printed in Great Britain
by Amazon

31974381R00212